DANIEL MULHALL was
spent more than forty ye
vice, and is currently Ireland's ambassac
States, having previously served as ambassador in Kuala
Lumpur, Berlin and London. In 1998 he was part of the
Irish Government's delegation at the negotiations that
produced the Good Friday Agreement. Over the years,
he has written and lectured extensively on Irish literature, including the writings of James Joyce. Throughout
his diplomatic career, he has drawn on literature to help
tell Ireland's story internationally, and has worked tire-
lessly to increase the impact and reach of Irish writing
around the world. He is President of the Yeats Society,
Sligo. Married to Greta, they have two children, Tara
and Jason.

PRAISE FOR *ULYSSES*: *A READER'S ODYSSEY*

'*Ulysses* [...] remains in need of chaperones and guides. Mulhall's winningly modest tour of Joyce's Odyssey is certainly one of the better beginner's guides available: highly readable, personable and well researched.'—Kevin Power, *The Times*

'While Mulhall's celebration of *Ulysses* is exuberant, nowhere can his writing be accused of being exhibitionist. He modestly refers to his book as just turning the sod on Joyce's masterpiece, but it is more than that. An informed, enjoyable guide, it homes in on *Ulysses*' emotional core'—Dermot Bolger, *Irish Independent*

'Powerfully, [Mulhall] argues that Joyce and Ireland for him are indissociable and that he retains a burning relevance today because he undertook "such a lavishly forensic portrait of the country".'—Prof. Anne Fogarty, *The Irish Times*

'As soon as Mulhall lays out his shortcutting map [...] you know you're in the hands of someone who takes the whole thing seriously, but not too seriously, which is, if I had to hazard a guess, an approach that Joyce himself would have approved of. That being said, the ambassador wades in, and tackles each chapter as they come up, offering insight and erudition'—*Hot Press*

'Our thanks must go to Dan Mulhall for his enthusiasm for the living document that Joyce has left us, and for making *Ulysses* more accessible to regular readers.'—*Irish Central*

ULYSSES
A READER'S ODYSSEY

NEW ISLAND

U

DANIEL
MULHALL

LYSSES
A READER'S ODYSSEY

ULYSSES: A READER'S ODYSSEY
First published in 2022 by
New Island Books
Glenshesk House
10 Richview Office Park
Clonskeagh
Dublin D14 V8C4
Republic of Ireland
www.newisland.ie

The right of Daniel Mulhall to be identified as the author of this work has been asserted in accordance with the provisions of the Copyright and Related Rights Act, 2000.

Print ISBN: 978-1-84840-829-6
eBook ISBN: 978-1-84840-830-2

British Library Cataloguing in Publication Data. A CIP catalogue record for this book is available from the British Library.

The images featured in this book are reproduced by kind permission of The Rosenbach library of Philadelphia, The University at Buffalo Libraries Special Collection, and The National Library of Ireland, respectively. The map of Dublin featured on the inner cover is a 1900 Ordnance Survey map © Government of Ireland.

Typeset by JVR Creative India
Edited by Neil Burkey neilburkey.com
Cover design by Jack Smyth, jacksmyth.co
Printed by Scandbook, scandbook.com

New Island received financial assitance from The Arts Council (An Chomhairle Ealaíon), Dublin, Ireland.
New Island Books is a member of Publishing Ireland.

10 9 8 7 6 5 4 3 2

To my wonderful grandchildren,
Alice, Jessica, Liam and George

CONTENTS

PROLOGUE

A Diplomatic Odyssey
Representing Ireland with James Joyce as a travelling companion

OMEWHERE

in the east: early morning: set off at dawn. Travel round in front of the sun, steal a day's march on him. Keep it up for ever never grow a day older technically. Walk along a strand, strange land, come to a city gate, sentry there [...] Wander through awned streets. Turbaned faces going by. Dark caves of carpet shops [...] Probably not a bit like it really. Kind of stuff you read: in the track of the sun.

– Leopold Bloom, imaginary world traveller, from *Ulysses*, Episode 4, 'Calypso'

Like Leopold Bloom (in his imagination), I set off at dawn one day (it was 10 March 1980, to be precise) headed for somewhere in the East, New Delhi in my case. While there, I often wandered through the awned streets of Old Delhi and other cities across the subcontinent, saw plenty of turbaned faces and even bought a carpet or two during the years I spent there.

My forty-year journey 'in the track of the sun' means that I have indeed walked along strands in 'strange' lands, for every land is strange to us in its own way, even our native shores. And yes, I have grown much older and not just 'technically', as in Bloom's imaginative reckoning. When I set out on my journey as a diplomat, I had few possessions besides my clothes, vinyl records and a collection of books I had assembled during my student days; works on Irish literature, history and biography for the most part, reflecting my academic interests. The volumes I had shipped to join me in New Delhi included a copy of James Joyce's *Ulysses* and, after the passage of four decades during which that volume has been one of my figurative travelling companions, and from which I have learned a great deal, I decided to write *a book* about *that great book*. As I look in my rear-view mirror, I realise that I have been in dialogue with Irish history and literature ever since my student days. The pages that follow are a product of that dialogue.

I am part of a fortunate generation of Irish people who benefited from sustained and substantial investment in education. As the first member of my family to go to university, I owe much to those in government from the 1960s onwards who chose to prioritise education as a means of enabling Ireland to fulfil its potential. During my lifetime, I have witnessed Ireland's transformation as it progressed from being an outlier in western European terms to a fully developed country at the heart of the European Union. The national transformation that has occurred has not been purely economic. It has also led to a more open and tolerant society in whose present condition, albeit of course not a perfect one (and with no sense of complacency), I take genuine pride. And we have developed a more expansive attitude towards our culture, including a keener appreciation of James Joyce and his work, which is now a focal point for Dublin's Museum of Literature Ireland, MoLI. As we approach the centenary of the publication of *Ulysses*, it is time to have another look at that great Irish, European, and indeed global, novel.

WHY ME?

My justification for undertaking this venture derives from the fact that I have spent four decades travelling the world with Irish literature as part of my diplomatic

[4]

baggage, actual and intellectual. My copy of *Ulysses*, purchased in 1974, and my edition of Yeats's *Collected Poems*, acquired in January 1976, have both criss-crossed the globe with me. I have used those two books, and many others besides, in order to present Ireland to people of different backgrounds whose interest in my country often stems from an affinity with our literature and our history. I wrote this book during my time as Ambassador of Ireland to the United States, where part of my role is to tell the story of modern Ireland to Americans across that vast country. I also strive to connect with Irish America and to promote Ireland's considerable economic interests in the USA. In the course of this assignment, and during earlier ones in Scotland, Malaysia, Germany and Britain, I have sought to use the lure of our literature as a resource for creating vital affinities with Ireland. Many people across the world who have no ancestral connection with us often engage with Ireland, initially at least, through our writers and their works.

James Joyce's writing has been part of my life going back to my student days, and I have returned to it again and again throughout my decades of diplomatic service. His work, and that of other major Irish writers, has helped shape my thinking about the country I have been privileged to represent internationally for more than four decades now.

In writing this book, I have read a lot of academic literature on Joyce and *Ulysses* and, wherever I have come across insights I found helpful, I have made use of those in the chapters that follow. Frankly though, much of the expert analysis I consulted would be of no value to the regular reader, often serving to complicate instead of clarifying, entangling Joyce's text rather than elucidating it. In saying this, I am not being critical of the Joyce industry, for I fully appreciate that scholars and students need to subject works of literature to a deeper level of analysis. My efforts, however, have a different purpose, and my audience is a different one. What follows is not a paragraph-by-paragraph explainer of *Ulysses*, but rather a series of personal reflections on its eighteen episodes.

Ulysses Affect on reader

It so happens that Ireland enjoys the advantage of having a literary tradition that attracts international attention and admiration. The reach of our literature is such that I can recall being at the National Library of Vietnam in Hanoi in 2004 to launch a Vietnamese translation of *A Portrait of the Artist as a Young Man*. In Germany in 2011, the expiry of copyright on *Ulysses* led to two German radio stations producing separate dramatised readings of the novel, which drew positive attention to Ireland at a time when our national reputation was still recovering from the fallout from the economic and financial crisis of 2009/10. During my time in Washington, I have paid repeated visits to Philadelphia's Rosenbach Museum, home to the original manuscript of *Ulysses*, where, through the celebration of Joyce's work, Ireland's literary heritage is cherished and treasured. My diplomatic career has been peppered with such experiences that testify to the profile of Irish literature and its value in boosting international appreciation of our country. 'Soft power' diplomacy is the current buzzword used to describe this phenomenon, which is a very real asset for Ireland.

CULTURAL DIPLOMACY

During my first diplomatic assignment in New Delhi (1980–3) – in the course of which I met and married Greta, who has partnered me in everything I have done since then – I came to know the distinguished Indian novelist and academic Chaman Nahal. At that time he was Professor of English Literature at the University of New Delhi. Nahal was involved in organising the All-India English Teachers Conference and invited me to participate. At that conference in 1982, I delivered two talks, one on 'Yeats and the Idea of a National Literature' and another on 'James Joyce's Ireland'.

My Yeats lecture was delivered in a huge theatre, and to the largest audience I have ever addressed at an indoor venue, for there were 1,500 delegates to the conference. Virtually all delegates seemed to have turned up for the conference's opening session. They had come not to see me, but because the other keynote speaker was Karan Singh, the titular Maharajah of Kashmir, and a wonderful public speaker who could recite by heart large chunks of Yeats's poetry. In my speech, I drew out those elements of Yeats's work that I expected would be of interest to an Indian audience, namely his nationalism, his insistence that Irish literature could be written in the English language, and his interest in Indian philosophy and religion.

In my presentation on Joyce, which was delivered in the year of the centenary of his birth, I cited his determination, expressed in *A Portrait of the Artist as a Young Man*, to fly the 'nets' of 'nationality, language, religion' that he believed sought to hold the soul back from flight in the Ireland of his youth. Those so-called nets were pertinent in India in the 1980s, at least as much as they were in Joyce's Ireland seventy years earlier.

My experience in India taught me an important lesson about the value to Ireland of our literary heritage. There I was, thousands of miles from home, in the world's second most populous country, where our literature was the focus of attention and enthusiasm. What other country of our size could hope to have such a following for its literature? The English language, acquired – or imposed – as a consequence of conquest, had given us visibility in faraway countries where our great writers were read and admired. This gave us a profile in the world that we could never otherwise have expected to achieve.

I doubt that our literature would have been of such interest had it not been allied to our national story, which was seen in the India of the early 1980s as comparable in some respects with their own national struggle. When I arrived in New Delhi, the British Raj, which came to an end in 1947, was still well within living memory. There was considerable awareness of the extent to which Ireland's example had impacted on India's subsequent effort to assert its independence.

Mrs Vijaya Lakshmi Pandit was in her early eighties when I met her through her granddaughter, Gita Sahgal. Pandit's brother, Jawaharlal Nehru, had led the Indian National Congress during the last years of the Raj, and became India's first prime minister in 1947. His sister had a distinguished career of her own as an Indian diplomat and while serving as Indian High Commissioner in London she had also been accredited as Ambassador to Ireland.

I was invited to lunch at her New Delhi home and, when she discovered I was Irish, she immediately launched into word-perfect recitations of 'The Lake Isle of Innisfree' and 'When You Are Old'. Mrs Pandit told me she had memorised those great poems when she was interned with her brother during the country's struggle for freedom. Yeats, she said, had been a favourite, his nationalism giving him a special appeal for her family.

I have never forgotten the lessons I learned in India about the value of our history and literature to Ireland's international standing. I have carried them with me through diplomatic postings in Vienna, Brussels, Edinburgh, Kuala Lumpur, Berlin, London and Washington. Thus, my genuine interest in Irish history and literature has combined quite neatly with my professional responsibility to promote Ireland around the world.

This has encouraged me to prioritise cultural diplomacy and to avail of the opportunities provided by the widespread interest in our literature in order to get a hearing for other aspects of Ireland's story. An example of this was when I arrived in Germany in October 2009 just as the economic clouds were darkening for Ireland. Early in my time in Berlin, the Embassy participated in an open day, when the public were invited to visit diplomatic missions. I was struck by how many of our visitors that day stopped to view a poster of Ireland's major writers that hung on a wall in the Embassy's reception area. I heard a number of our visitors remark to each other how they had not known that Shaw, Swift, Wilde, Yeats and Joyce were Irish. This encouraged me to believe that we could draw on Irish literature so as to help soften

Ireland's image in German eyes at a time when we were viewed primarily in the light of the then ongoing economic and financial crisis.

Armed with a small exhibition on the life and work of W.B. Yeats, we declared 'A Year of Yeats', during which I travelled to German universities to open the exhibition and lecture on Yeats. I would always preface my remarks with a comment to the effect that 'Ireland is in the spotlight at the moment on account of our economic and financial difficulties, but here is how things are with us. Our economy, while undermined by problems in our banking sector, is fundamentally sound, based as it is on competitive, export-oriented businesses. We will recover strongly from our current travails.' Thus, our literature became a door-opener for me, allowing me to spread the message about Ireland's performance and recovery prospects.

ULYSSES AND ME

I arrived in Washington in August 2017. The United States is a marvellous assignment for an Irish Ambassador on account of the warmth of welcome there is for Ireland's representatives across the USA, something that, to the best of my knowledge, does not exist anywhere else in the world. Everywhere I have been, I have encountered individuals and groups who are deeply proud of their Irish heritage, even when the people in question may be several generations removed from Ireland.

One of our calling cards in America is the appeal of our culture, including the work of our great writers. I have lost count of the number of Irish literary treasures

I have seen at American universities and libraries, including many first editions of *Ulysses*. Three places stand out for me – the Burns Library at Boston College, the University at Buffalo's fabulous collection of Joyce material and Philadelphia's Rosenbach Museum. In 2018 and 2019, I read at the Rosenbach's Bloomsday celebration, for which they close the street outside their building and put on a ten-hour feast of readings and songs from *Ulysses*.

In 2018, I began posting blogs on *Ulysses* on our embassy website. This was aimed at elucidating Joyce's great novel for American audiences. It also encouraged me to re-engage with this monumental Irish book, arguably our greatest modern cultural treasure. I did so out of a conviction that you cannot fully come to terms with the origins of modern Ireland without grappling with its most complete depiction in literature. And, as a corollary, it is not possible to understand *Ulysses* without being properly acquainted with the country and the era that produced it.

The blogs I have written on the eighteen episodes of *Ulysses* – which went on to inform the chapters of this book – represent an exercise in what I call public diplomacy, an increasingly important element of what modern diplomats do. The chapters that compose this book – while imbued with decades of engagement with Joyce and his work – are not intended to be scholarly. They are the fruits of considerable research on Joyce in preparation for this book, combined with the knowledge I have accumulated over the decades by dint of reading Joyce and speaking and writing about his work during my various diplomatic assignments.

For the most part, they were written late at night or at weekends, when I could snatch an hour or two from my busy schedule of official engagements and family commitments. They represent a turning of the sod on *Ulysses* rather than a deep academic excavation. I hope that this sod turning will be of value to readers who may be thinking of attempting to scale this modern Mount Parnassus, especially those who wish to read it in connection with the centenary of *Ulysses*'s publication in Paris in 1922.

Upon reflection, I realise that this book is not just about James Joyce and his famous novel. It is about Ireland too. That is because it is the Irishness of Joyce's work and the Ireland he depicts that really tickles my fancy. I approach *Ulysses* with the eyes of a historian, and with the instincts of someone who – even while having lived overseas for much of my adult life – has always operated in an environment supercharged with all things Irish. As a representative of Ireland, I have spent my career thinking about Ireland, talking about Ireland and surrounded by Irish people and Irish concerns. I also recognise that this book is, on one level, an exploration of the things I looked at in my Master's thesis all those years ago: twentieth-century Ireland as seen through the lenses of our leading writers. It has always intrigued me how a country of Ireland's size and population produced such a deep well of literary achievement in the opening decades of the twentieth century, at a time when it was undergoing a profound political transformation.

Harry Levin, an early scholar of Joyce's work, captured the uniqueness of early-twentieth-century Ireland

when he wrote about John Millington Synge's Preface to
The Playboy of the Western World:

> In Irish life and language, he [Synge] indicated,
> writers would find both a vital theme and an
> expressive medium. With the Irish literary move-
> ment – with the achievement of Synge himself in
> the drama, of Yeats in poetry and Joyce fiction –
> these indications have been filled out. It would be
> hard to find a comparable body of writing, with-
> out going all the way back to the Elizabethans, in
> which the qualities of highly imaginative expres-
> sion and closeness to familiar experience are so
> profusely intermingled.[1]

The combination of 'a vital theme and an expressive
medium'. This raises the question, did Irish history
and Irish literature play mutually supportive roles in
the pursuit of artistic and political achievement in the
decades between the fall of Parnell in 1890 and Joyce's
death in 1941? *Ulysses* provides at least part of the
answer to that puzzle.

I have long been intrigued by the fact that the publication of *Ulysses* coincided with the emergence of
the independent Irish State that I have represented
for more than forty years. Joyce wanted his novel to be
published on his fortieth birthday, 2 February 1922.
That date happened to fall just a couple of weeks after
the keys to Dublin Castle were handed over to Michael
Collins, in what was the first symbolic moment in the formal establishment of an independent Irish state. Thus,
perhaps the first great modernist novel was published at

[13]

the same time as the emergence of what I have come to view as the first modern state, one which set a pattern that was followed by the many countries that obtained their independence during the decades following the Second World War.

Our achievement in prising our independence from one of the victors of the First World War, which occurred while Joyce was busy writing *Ulysses,* became an inspiration for many African and Asian nations who had to extract their independence from their initially uncooperative colonial masters. In my experience, our position as a trailblazer has given Ireland a degree of international cachet that we retain to this day.

This book is also about my personal odyssey, a life spent in ten different countries across the globe. Rome-based Joyce expert John McCourt has argued that Trieste, where James Joyce spent so many years of his life, is 'surreptitiously present as a continental perspective in the Irish world and worldview of *Ulysses*'.[2] As someone who has spent many years in multiple countries, I feel that each of them has maintained a continued presence, often surreptitious, in my own life, providing an external perspective on my personal Irish world view, and on my understanding of the wonder that is Ireland.

AMERICA, 2021

On 20 January 2021 – eighty years after the death of James Joyce in January 1941, shortly after he had met with Seán Lester, an Irish diplomat based in Geneva – I attended the inauguration of America's forty-sixth President, Joseph R. Biden Jr. His election in November

2020 had been widely welcomed in Ireland. That was due to the manner in which President Biden has consistently highlighted his Irish heritage. He is the most Irish president of the USA since John F. Kennedy, and has a reputation for frequently quoting Irish poets. President Biden has often said: 'I don't quote Irish poets because I'm Irish. I quote them because they are the best poets.' He released a powerful campaign video of his reading of Seamus Heaney's 'The Cure at Troy', which served further to highlight the president's affinity with Ireland as well as the enduring appeal of our literature. Speaking on arrival in Britain as part of his first overseas trip, President Biden quoted those memorable lines from Yeats's 'Easter 1916':

All changed, changed utterly:
A terrible beauty is born.

When then President-elect Biden left his home in Delaware on 19 January to travel to Washington for his inauguration the following day, he quoted James Joyce's comment to the effect that when he died, Dublin would be written on his heart. President Biden remarked that in his case Delaware, where he had lived for most of his life, would be written on *his* heart. At such an emotional moment in his life, when he was on the verge of entering into the highest office in the land, Joseph Robinette Biden Jr quoted James Augustine Joyce. Enough said!

Daniel Mulhall
Washington DC, July 2021

An Introductory Tour of James Joyce's Ulysses

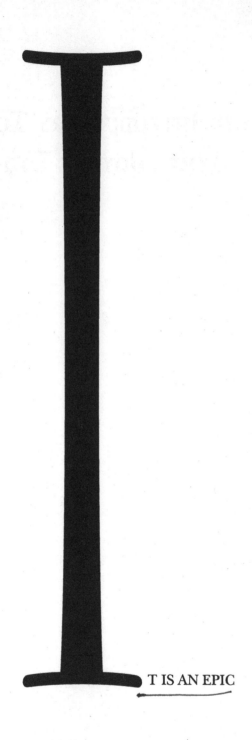

T IS AN EPIC

of two races (Israelite and Irish) and at the same time the cycle of the human body as well as a little story of a day ... It is also a sort of encyclopedia.

– James Joyce on *Ulysses*[3]

James Joyce's encyclopaedic description of *Ulysses* gives us an idea of just how much is going on within its covers. There are many streams running through this hundred-year-old book that can be explored for a fuller understanding of its hidden depths. My aim is to be helpful to readers who are journeying into Joyce's book by providing a commentary on its content and on the manner in which it is written. I will be quoting freely from the novel so that even those who do not make it to the starting line will get a flavour of one of the twentieth century's premier works of literature. This is not a *Ulysses* encyclopaedia, more a personal sketchbook offering what I hope will be a palatable taster rather than a full-scale scholarly banquet. I am, like most explorers of *Ulysses,* a learner and a searcher rather than a master, but, as a reader, I have been learning and searching for quite a store of years. I finished *Ulysses* for the first time many years ago, but have continued to go back for more.

Palm Beach may seem like a strange place in which to begin a journey through James Joyce's *Ulysses,* but you need to start somewhere. Diplomatic journeys have taken me to all kinds of places. During my time in our foreign service, I have been to villages in India, to an Irish development aid project in the mountains of Lesotho, to the 'Bangkok Hilton' to visit prisoners, and to Krabi in Thailand searching for Irish people caught up in the Asian tsunami of 2004.

But diplomacy also brings its practitioners to locations like, in my case, the Habsburg Palace in Vienna for an East-West Conference in the late-1980s, Frankfurt for the annual Book Fair during my time as ambassador in Germany, the City of London, where I was made a Freeman during my assignment in Britain, Silicon Valley in California with a visiting Taoiseach, and Palm Beach in February 2019 for the annual Ireland Funds winter gathering. While there, I came across Raptis Rare Books, an exclusive bookshop full of expensive volumes. Although the books on show in the window were well beyond my reach, I entered the shop to take a peek. Inside the door, in the first locked display case I gazed into, what should I see but a first edition of *Ulysses,* signed by the author, that was on sale for $150,000! I chatted with the shop's owner and agreed that, when I next returned to Palm Beach, I would come to the shop to talk about *Ulysses.* I did so the following year on one of my last journeys outside of Washington before the coronavirus shut everything down.

I wanted to pitch my talk in a way that would connect with my audience, which was made up of well-to-do local residents and some Irish people living in the vicinity. Many were customers of this upmarket bookseller, but I figured they might not necessarily be fully familiar with Joyce or *Ulysses.* I decided that it might be helpful to offer my audience a guided tour, as if they were visitors to an exotic land. In some respects, everyone who sets out to explore *Ulysses* is undertaking a demanding but ultimately, I believe, rewarding journey. My aim at that bookshop in Palm Beach was to be their tour guide and that is my goal with readers of this book. My remarks in Raptis Books, which I structured as a Q&A session much like Joyce's in 'Ithaca' – the penultimate episode of his masterwork – went down very well with that evening's attendance. With that experience in mind, this strikes me as a good way to begin our odyssey through *Ulysses*. Here goes.

WHO IS YOUR TOUR GUIDE?

When you take a tour, the first thing you need to learn is the identity of your tour guide and what their qualifications are for conducting this tour. Full disclosure: I do not have a doctorate on James Joyce or his novel *Ulysses*. I have, however, maintained a lifelong engagement with Irish history and literature, including James Joyce and his writings. This stretches back to my days as a student in the 1970s, when I became interested in the fact that what I call 'the age of Yeats and Joyce' (1880–1940) coincided with an era of political transformation in Ireland marked by the advent of independence in 1922.

I have spent my professional life in Ireland's foreign service and, during four decades of serving Ireland overseas, I have talked a lot about Irish literature, including of course its greatest individual achievement, *Ulysses*. I hope that this experience will qualify me to act as a tour guide for those who are not steeped in the subject, first-time visitors looking for an introduction to the novel, or those returning to its pages in search of a deeper understanding. I hope too that Joyce scholars and students of his work will find something of value in the observations I have to offer.

IS THERE SOMEONE ELSE GUIDING OUR TOUR?

Yes, there certainly is. In fact, the mainstay of this tour is James Augustine Aloysius Joyce. I am his helper and my role is to act as an explainer. Mr Joyce, the author, is a brilliant man, but can – when he puts pen to paper – sometimes get a little carried away. His sparkling contributions may need a bit of elucidation on my part.

James Joyce was born in Dublin on 2 February 1882, the son of John Stanislaus Joyce and Mary Jane 'May' Murray. The family lived at quite a number of Dublin addresses as its financial standing went into steady decline. Joyce attended two Jesuit schools in the Dublin area, Clongowes Wood and Belvedere College, before studying English, French and Italian at University College Dublin. After graduating in 1902, he spent a short time in Paris before being called back to Dublin to be with his dying mother. He left Ireland for good in 1904, accompanied by the Galway-born Nora Barnacle, whom he had, to use the idiom of Joyce's time, first 'stepped out' with on 16 June of that year. He only returned to Ireland three times after 1904. The couple, who had two children, Giorgio and Lucia, spent the rest of their lives in a number of continental cities, Pola, Trieste, Rome, Zurich and Paris. Joyce died in Zurich on 13 January 1941 and is buried in the city's Fluntern Cemetery.

During his lifetime, he published two volumes of poetry, *Chamber Music* (1907) and *Pomes Penyeach*

(1927), a collection of short stories, *Dubliners* (1914), a play, *Exiles* (1918), and three novels, *A Portrait of the Artist as a Young Man* (1916), *Ulysses* (1922) and *Finnegans Wake* (1939). As one source puts it, 'More than any other writer his adult life and his work are inseparable, and he might be said to have lived merely to translate his adolescent impressions of Dublin into literature.' He saw himself as an 'interpreter of Ireland to itself',[4] and that's how I see him also.

WHAT'S THE TOUR ABOUT?

It's about a book, 783 pages long in my American edition (1934), and its characters, real and fictional, its author, and the city in which it is set. The book was published originally in Paris on 2 February 1922, Joyce's fortieth birthday. *Ulysses* is written in a great variety of literary styles, some of them innovative and daring for their time. It is one of the world's most famous books, but certainly not the most widely read. I hope that this tour will encourage new readers to dip into it, or to give this century-old literary warhorse another go. At a minimum I want to provide an insight into what the literary fuss surrounding *Ulysses* is all about.

WHERE IS OUR TOUR'S LOCATION?

That's quite straightforward, or is it? In one sense, we are in Dublin on the 16th of June in the year 1904. But in another sense we are also in the three European cities – Trieste, Zurich and Paris – where this novel was written. Each of them holds its own significance, for *Ulysses* was composed during and after the First World War, at a time of great upheaval across Europe, including as a result of the 1918–19 flu pandemic. It is, therefore, a European novel, albeit one with a forensic focus on early-twentieth-century Dublin. Its 'European' character was highlighted in early reviews of *Ulysses.*

Another location Joyce had in mind when working on *Ulysses* was classical Greece, as he used Homer's *Odyssey* as part of his inspiration when he sat down to write his novel. Some explorers of *Ulysses* may find the classical parallels a bit off-putting, but not to worry. When you visit an art gallery, you can appreciate a painting without knowing all there is to be known about the artist and the background to the painting. The same is true with reading *Ulysses.* Background knowledge about its Homeric parallels is an aid and an advantage to readers, but not a prerequisite to their enjoyment of the novel.

Palestine also plays its part, for Leopold Bloom – the novel's protagonist – is acutely conscious of his Jewish heritage, and is made to feel an outsider by many of his fellow Dubliners. Someone with Bloom's background would have been something of a rarity in turn-of-the-century Dublin, which had fewer than 2,200 Jews in its population of 450,000 in 1901, although the size of the Jewish community had been on the increase in the last decades of the nineteenth century. The idea of investing in a plantation on the shores of Lake Tiberias takes his fancy early in the novel, and recurs a number of times throughout the day.

WHAT KIND OF A TOUR IS THIS?

It's a book tour – and a walking tour. The book is a colossus of modern literature that has fascinated and frustrated readers for more than a century now. It is much like a big city, with lots of nooks and crannies to be explored. The book's main characters spend the day – and the novel's eighteen episodes, as its chapters are usually called – wandering around Dublin, mainly on foot. There are references to the city's many tramlines, which are used occasionally, as when two of the novel's main characters travel from the National Maternity Hospital at Holles Street to the city's nighttown, where the fifteenth and longest episode of the novel takes place. There is also a carriage ride in the 'Hades' episode, which takes us through the streets of Dublin from Sandymount to Glasnevin Cemetery.

Our tour starts in Sandycove on the south side of Dublin Bay, where we meet Stephen Dedalus for the first time in the book's opening episode. It continues in the nearby suburb of Dalkey, where Dedalus is employed as a temporary teacher, and then moves on to Dublin's city centre, where the novel's *dramatis personae* spend most of their day.

It will end at Howth at the north end of Dublin Bay, although none of the book's characters actually go there during the day. Our last tour stop will be in Molly Bloom's bedroom on Eccles Street, from where her thoughts ramble, ultimately to Howth and her first intimate tryst with her future husband, Leopold Bloom.

WHO ARE THE MAIN PERSONALITIES INVOLVED?

Like most cities, early-twentieth-century Dublin had a host of notable characters, many of whom flit in and out of the narrative, but our tour will focus on three main figures.

The first is Leopold Bloom, who inhabits the bulk of the novel's pages. He is a not-especially-successful advertising salesman. A man in his late thirties in 1904, Bloom is the son of a Hungarian Jew, Rudolph Virag. Rudolph moved to Dublin in the 1860s, married a local woman named Ellen Higgins (whose father's original name was Karoly), changed his name to Bloom and converted to Protestantism. Bloom senior died by suicide in a hotel room in County Clare, an event that is alluded to quite a few times in the pages of *Ulysses*.

The second is Stephen Dedalus, who is modelled on James Joyce himself. He is an aspiring writer and a young man of precocious intelligence. He comes from a troubled family. His father, Simon Dedalus, who is based on Joyce's father, John Stanislaus Joyce, is a sharp talker and a man about town, but someone who provides poorly for his family. Stephen has been staying with Malachi 'Buck' Mulligan, a wise-cracking medical student and would-be writer.

The third of our main characters, Marion 'Molly' Bloom, is Leopold's wife, who was born in Gibraltar, and was a talented concert soprano under her maiden name, Marion Tweedy. She is the daughter of a British officer, Major Brian Tweedy, and his Spanish wife, Lunita Laredo, whose 'lovely' name Molly envies. In the novel's fourth chapter, we get a glimpse of the Blooms' relationship. Leopold fusses over Molly, bringing her breakfast in bed, whereas she is impatient with her husband's convoluted personality. When she asks him to define the word 'metempsychosis', his elaborate definition boggles her: 'O rocks! she said. Tell us in plain words.' Molly is planning an amorous rendezvous later the same day with her concert promoter, but more of that a little later.

The Blooms had two children, Milly, their daughter, and Rudy, a son. Rudy's death when he was less than two weeks old weighs heavily on Bloom, and on his relationship with his wife. This brings into play a father-son theme, which runs through the novel, culminating in Bloom fleetingly finding in Dedalus a version of the son he has lost. Milly, fifteen years old, has left the family home and is working at a photographic shop in Mullingar, County Westmeath, where she is evidently enjoying herself and attracting attention from a friend of Buck Mulligan's there.

ARE THERE ANY VILLAINS WHO WILL CROP UP ON OUR TOUR?

Yes, there are two that I want to mention. The first is a fictional character, Hugh 'Blazes' Boylan, a concert promoter and man-about-town, who is having an affair with Molly Bloom that her husband knows about. Boylan is due to visit her that afternoon at four o'clock, supposedly to discuss her concert programme. Bloom is aware of their appointment, and the looming encounter obsesses him all day. Understandably, he regards Boylan as a disreputable character, describing him as the worst man in Dublin. Over the course of the novel, Boylan keeps crossing Bloom's path and cropping up in conversation. Some of those Bloom meets are evidently aware of Molly's secret.

The second character is a more notorious historical figure. After they escape from nighttown in Episode 15, Bloom and Stephen visit a cabman's shelter in central Dublin, run by a man who is reputed to be Skin-the-Goat Fitzharris, although his identity is uncertain. Fitzharris was one of the Irish National Invincibles, a secret Fenian group, which in May 1882 sensationally attacked and killed the Chief Secretary for Ireland, Lord Fredrick Cavendish, and his Under Secretary, Thomas Henry Burke, while they were out walking in the Phoenix Park. Five of the Invincibles were executed but, as one Irish historian has written, 'the workings of the society were never fully uncovered'. They may, he suggests, have been funded by radical elements within the Irish Land League, and with 'the possibility of direct Irish-American involvement'.[5]

Fitzharris's role here is to give voice to an irreconcilable Irish separatist sentiment that had seemed dormant in 1904 but came into its own again in the wake of the Easter Rising of 1916. Joyce was evidently deeply interested in the Invincibles, as other members of the group – Joe Brady, who was executed in 1883, and James Carey, who turned Queen's evidence at the trial of his co-conspirators – are also mentioned in *Ulysses*. In revenge for his actions, Carey was shot and killed while he was on board a ship bound for a new life in South Africa. The Phoenix Park murders are also mentioned in the 'Aeolus' episode, where Ignatius Gallaher's scoop in being the first journalist to report on the murders for the American press is acclaimed by *Evening Telegraph* editor, Myles Crawford.

ANY RECOMMENDATIONS ON PLACES TO EAT AND DRINK?

Yes, this tour of *Ulysses* takes us to three Dublin pubs (and there is mention of a fourth), a hotel and one restaurant. Bloom has his lunch in Davy Byrne's 'moral pub', where he orders a glass of burgundy and a Gorgonzola sandwich. This shows that Bloom was an unusual Dubliner, for most of his fellow citizens in 1904 would almost certainly have favoured pints of Guinness over glasses of French wine, but not Bloom. Davy Byrne's is still on Duke Street and you can order Bloom's repast there.

The second drinking spot is Barney Kiernan's pub, which stood on Little Britain Street (a street perhaps deliberately chosen by Joyce as aptly named for an exploration of early twentieth-century Irish nationalism), where Bloom gets into a heated argument with a character known as 'the citizen' about national identity. This pub no longer exists. For me, the 'Cyclops' episode set in Kiernan's pub is at the heart of the novel. It contains Bloom's and Joyce's plea for tolerance, and for the triumph of love over hate.

A third pub mentioned is Burke's, where the last part of the 'Oxen of the Sun' episode takes place. The various characters from the *Freeman's Journal* offices in the 'Aeolus' episode are seen on their way to Mooney's pub, but we part company with them before they arrive there.

'The Sirens' episode of *Ulysses* takes place in the Ormond Hotel, where Bloom eats a plate of steak and kidney. I often visited the Ormond as a child on family visits to Dublin. It was a place where people 'up from the country' for football matches, etc. often rendezvoused.

The restaurant that features is the Burton (now called the Bailey) across the street from Davy Byrne's, which is still in business today, but with a far better menu than the unappetising fare described by Joyce. Irish cuisine has come on leaps and bounds in recent decades.

WHAT ARE THE MAIN SITES TO BE VISITED?

Ulysses really does take us on a tour of Dublin, starting at the Martello tower in Sandycove, which became an attraction on the back of its starring role in Joyce's novel. It is now a museum dedicated to Joyce, who lived there for a few weeks in 1904.

For those who like visiting cemeteries, *Ulysses* is just the book for you, as it takes us to Ireland's national cemetery at Glasnevin for the funeral of Bloom's acquaintance, Paddy Dignam. While there, we are reminded that it also hosts the graves of the two major Irish figures of the nineteenth century, Daniel O'Connell and Charles Stewart Parnell.

Late in the day we spend time at Ireland's National Library on Kildare Street, which has a beautiful main reading room, one of my favourite spaces in Dublin. We also pay a fleeting visit to the National Museum in the company of Leopold Bloom, who goes there to check on the intimate anatomy of its classical sculptures.

WHAT ABOUT RELIGIOUS BUILDINGS?

Religion features quite a lot in *Ulysses*. Bloom and Stephen are both religious sceptics, while Molly has complicated views on that subject, as she has about many other things. She mocks her husband's atheism, but also mulls over the advantages of having an affair with a clergyman; 'theres no danger with a priest if youre married hes too careful about himself'.

During his wanderings around Dublin, Bloom visits St Andrew's Church on Westland Row and witnesses a religious service, which gives Joyce free rein to flaunt his and Bloom's disregard for the Catholic Church. Joyce was the product of a Jesuit education, at school and university.

The Star of the Sea Church at Sandymount features in the 'Nausicaa' episode. A temperance service is being conducted there while Bloom stands across the street looking onto the strand ogling Gerty MacDowell as she knowingly gives him a glimpse of her undergarments.

DOES POLITICS REAR ITS HEAD?

The Dubliners depicted here were a politically conscious group. There are references to the Boer War, which had just concluded two years before, to the Russo-Japanese War which was raging in 1904, and to Roger Casement's report on atrocities committed in the Belgian Congo. Irish politics is, of course, the prime preoccupation of the characters in the novel, and there is quite an amount of political discussion going on here. Although we might expect Joyce – who left Ireland to escape the nets of 'nationality, language, religion' as he explained in *A Portrait of the Artist as a Young Man* – to have had a lofty disdain for the political world, in fact he appears to have been infused with the politics of the country he left behind. In *Ulysses*, there are references to such political figures as Daniel O'Connell, Charles Stewart Parnell (a Joycean favourite) and Arthur Griffith (founder of Sinn Féin in 1905), as well as a number of Irish MPs.

The 'Cyclops' episode is a full-on exploration of Irish nationalism viewed through an over-the-top portrayal of 'the citizen', a character based on GAA founder Michael Cusack (1847–1906).

In the 'Nestor' episode, school principal, Mr Deasy, expresses the pro-British views of Ireland's substantial unionist community of the early twentieth century.

IS THERE ANY NIGHTLIFE?

There's plenty of nightlife in *Ulysses* as the story continues into the small hours of 17 June 1904. The book's longest chapter gives a surreal account of Bloom and Stephen's visit to Dublin's nighttown after they had spent a couple of hours drinking with medical students and others at a Dublin maternity hospital and then at Burke's pub. The 'red light' district depicted in the novel – based on the actual area in Dublin known as 'the Monto' – was closed down in the 1920s. The cabman's shelter Bloom and Stephen visit in the 'Eumaeus' episode is the equivalent of a late-night café or take-away in today's Dublin.

AND SCANDALS?

Yes, *Ulysses* was immersed in scandal from the outset. It was massively controversial when it first appeared, as its earthy candour shocked many. Virginia Woolf, for example, thought that the novel 'reeked with indecency'.

Joyce's brother, Stanislaus, in his initial reaction shared some of Woolf's misgivings, when he asked 'isn't your art in danger of becoming sanitary science? ... Everything dirty seems to have the same irresistible attraction for you as cow-dung has for flies.'[6]

The Daily Express chirruped in with its condemnation. 'Reading Mr Joyce is like making an excursion into Bolshevist Russia: all standards go by the board.' The prominent Irish writer and aristocrat, Sir Shane Leslie, fumed about the book's 'anti-Christian' nature and described it as 'an Odyssey of the sewer'.

But, there were those who approved of what Joyce had done. T. S. Eliot, though a very conservative man, was deeply impressed by Joyce's achievement, which he reckoned demonstrated the 'futility' of all English literary styles.[7] 'How,' he asked, 'could anyone write again after achieving the immense prodigy of the last chapter.' And F. Scott Fitzgerald, who is said to have worshipped Joyce, observed that *Ulysses* was 'the great novel of the future'.

From the start, the novel was mired in legal challenges. When it was first published serially in an avant-garde American literary magazine, *The Little Review*, between 1918 and 1920, the magazine's publishers were brought to court and found guilty of obscenity. Copies of the first edition of *Ulysses* were seized in Britain and America.

WHAT CAUSED THIS REACTION?

Joyce was unflinching in his portrayal of humanity. In Bloom, he set out to produce the most complete account of any character in literature. We live inside Bloom's head for a good part of the novel. Not only that, we also

accompany him to the toilet and we observe him masturbating while watching a young woman on Sandymount
Strand. Even that unflinching modernist, Ezra Pound,
found some parts of the book unnecessarily explicit.

Then, of course, there is Molly Bloom's sixty-two-page
soliloquy with just a single punctuation mark at the end,
which, although it is brilliantly written, and reaches a wonderful crescendo in the book's closing pages, does not
take any prisoners in its depiction of Molly's sexual experiences and fantasies. This material seems to have mirrored
aspects of Joyce's relationship with Nora Barnacle.

HOW DID IT FINALLY GET PUBLISHED?

In a landmark judgement in 1933, John M. Woolsey, a
New York Federal District Judge, lifted the ban on Joyce's
novel. A strong line-up of American writers, including F.
Scott Fitzgerald and John Dos Passos, rallied to the novel's defence, arguing that it was 'a modern classic in every
sense of the word'.[8] Judge Woolsey described Joyce's work
as 'an amazing *tour de force*', which, on account of its style
and literary ambition, could not be considered obscene.
Ulysses was, he believed, 'a sincere and serious attempt
to devise a new literary method for the observation and
description of mankind'. He concluded that, while the
effect of *Ulysses* was in places 'somewhat emetic, nowhere
does it tend to be an aphrodisiac'.[9]

When Woolsey's judgement was upheld by two
Appeals Court judges, cousins Learned Hand and
Augustus N. Hand, this opened the way for *Ulysses* to
be published in America in 1934. Learned Hand argued
that 'the offending passages are clearly necessary to the

epic of the soul as Joyce conceived it'.[10] Joyce was indeed fortunate to fall into the hands of such 'Learned', literate New York judges.

IS IT A BEACH NOVEL?

As it happens, *Ulysses* was published by Sylvia Beach (1887–1962), an American who ran the Shakespeare and Company bookshop in Paris.

The book can of course be read and enjoyed on a beach in summer, although it may raise some eyebrows among your fellow beachgoers immersed in their books of popular fiction. Others will undoubtedly be impressed, and it may lead to some interesting conversations with neighbouring sun-lovers. Carrying a copy of *Ulysses* with your beach towel might be the equivalent of placing a personal ad in the *New York Review of Books*. 'Mid-50s, passionate about Ancient Greece, Rome, philosophy, entrepreneurship, Venice, the eighteenth century, painting, Chekov, Proust, short stories, wine, food and more.' (How much more can there be? Reading *Ulysses*? Perhaps.)

Mind you, there are beaches that feature in the novel. It opens beside Sandycove Beach, location of the tower where Stephen Dedalus had slept the night before in the company of Buck Mulligan and an English visitor, Haines. This is where you will find the Forty Foot bathing place, once an all-male domain but now open to all, including many year-round swimmers who take to what Joyce called the 'scrotumtightening sea' in all kinds of weather.

In Episode 3 we find Stephen 'walking into eternity along Sandymount Strand'. This is a difficult part of the novel, because it takes place inside Stephen's rather self-consciously artistic mind, which may intimidate the general reader. Bloom also goes to Sandymount Strand that evening in the 'Nausicaa' episode.

So what are the key takeaways from this introductory tour?

Ulysses brings a city to life in all its ragged glory. Dublin in 1904 possessed a hodgepodge of characters, many of whom appear in the pages of Joyce's novel. Most are based on individuals Joyce or his father knew who appear lightly disguised: Simon Dedalus, John Wyse Nolan, and the brash, inimitable Buck Mulligan to name but a few. Others appear under their own names: the poet-mystic George Russell (Æ), Celtic scholar Richard Best and essayist John Eglinton (the real-life penname of William K. Magee). It was a city where gossip and conversation flourished – as we will learn from our acquaintance with Nosey Flynn in the 'Lestrygonians' episode, and from the fizzing exchanges between the drinkers in Barney Kiernan's pub.

Joyce once described the city as a 'centre of paralysis', but there was lots of nationalist energy under the surface that bubbled forth in the decade that followed his departure. Joyce captured Dublin through his microscopic literary lens at a time when Ireland was in a kind of antechamber ahead of an intense period of political change that began a decade later.

For his main characters, Joyce chose outliers: Bloom with his Hungarian-Jewish background which makes him suspect in the eyes of many of his fellow Dubliners; Molly, born in Gibraltar; and Stephen with his 'absurd Greek name' and his innate sense of intellectual superiority.

Bloom is one of the most intriguing characters in modern literature. Because so much of *Ulysses* takes place inside his head, we know far more about him than is usual in more conventional novels. We become aware of all his failures and foibles. He is ponderous and finnicky, but he is also authentic and tolerant at a time when such virtues were at a premium as empires preened themselves and suppressed nationalities awaited their moment.

When, in the 'Cyclops' episode, 'the citizen' (depicted as a one-eyed nationalist) asks Bloom what nation he hails from, he replies, 'Ireland … I was born here. Ireland', thus backing an expansive notion of nationality that was not common in the early twentieth century.

Bloom is an unlikely Odysseus. Instead of sailing home in triumph from the Trojan War, Bloom returns warily (and wearily) from the verbal battlefields of early-twentieth-century Dublin. He has few traditionally heroic qualities, and his life is not, as such, a success. He is a struggling advertising salesman, his wife is unfaithful to him, and he appears to have lots of acquaintances but no close friends. Somehow, his life sums up the hopes, fears and frustrations of humanity. He derives a diffident pleasure from his workaday existence.

Despite all of the vicissitudes he endures, Bloom comes through his day-long odyssey and puts his head to rest in his own little Ithaca on Dublin's Eccles Street, beside his Penelope, the redoubtable Molly Bloom, who gets the last word with her magnificent monologue that is full of sparky, irreverent commentary on life and love.

Take Molly's acerbic observations with you when you finish *Ulysses* and you'll be the better for it. She's what Irish people tend to call 'a character', a term of general, but perhaps not thoroughgoing, approval. You don't have to agree with her or follow her example (I wouldn't), but she is a force of nature whose all-too-human take on a range of things is worth savouring.

DO YOU HAVE A RECOMMENDED READING LIST IF I WANT TO KNOW MORE?

This book plans to tell you most of what you need to know about Joyce and *Ulysses*, but I will make further suggestions later on for those who want to undertake a deeper dive. For now, I will recommend a biography (*James Joyce* by Richard Ellmann, 1959), a guide to the novel (*Ulysses Unbound: A Reader's Companion to James Joyce's Ulysses* by Terence Killeen, 2004) and a collection of literary criticism (*James Joyce in Context*, edited by John McCourt, 2009). I have also found value in Frank Budgen's book, *James Joyce and the Making of Ulysses* (1960). Budgen, an English artist, was a friend of Joyce's, and was also an astute reader of literature. Much of what is in his book clearly comes directly from his own conversations with Joyce, which makes it invaluable.

Do join me now in a run-through of the eighteen episodes of *Ulysses*, one by one. Each of my chapters is both a commentary on and a conversation with an individual episode of the novel.

EPISODE 1, 'TELEMACHUS':
A Stately, Plump Martello Tower

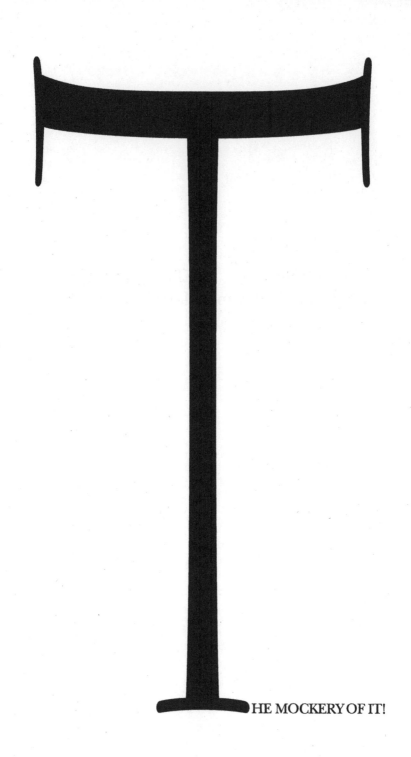

HE MOCKERY OF IT!

he said gaily. Your absurd name, an ancient Greek!

– Buck Mulligan to Stephen Dedalus

Here we are. On the opening page of the first of the novel's eighteen episodes, we get a reminder from a jaunty Buck Mulligan that there is more to *Ulysses* than the comings and goings of an ordinary Dublin day. Who's the 'ancient Greek'? I will come back to this classical dimension, but first to the assessment of someone who is mentioned here and there in the pages of Joyce's novel, Ireland's national bard, W. B. Yeats. I have had a lifelong enthusiasm for the poet's work, and as I am currently Honorary President of the Yeats Society, I am happy to begin this journey by quoting his opinion of *Ulysses:* 'It is a work perhaps of genius'.[11] 'Perhaps' is an interesting word. I would say that it is essentially a work of genius, with an accent on the word 'essentially', but I will get back to that later. Let the show begin.

Wake up! It's eight o'clock on 16 June 1904 and we have a long day ahead of us, roaming through 'the heart of the Hibernian metropolis' with James Augustine Joyce as our guide. As we explore the first page of *Ulysses*, we're in Sandycove on the south side of Dublin Bay, looking out over the 'scrotumtightening sea'. To our left as we gaze across the bay, we can see 'the mailboat clearing the harbour mouth of Kingstown' (whose name was changed to Dún Laoghaire two years before Ireland became independent in 1922, the year in which Joyce's *magnum opus* was published).

The opening chapter of *Ulysses* dwells on the activities of the three residents of the Martello tower at

Sandycove as they rise to face the day. Martello towers were defensive fortifications built across the British Empire throughout the nineteenth century. Around 50 towers were erected in Ireland, mainly during the Napoleonic Wars, with 29 of these located around Dublin.

Stephen Dedalus, a young poet, will be one of the three main characters in *Ulysses*, the other two being Leopold and Molly Bloom. Readers familiar with Joyce's earlier novel, *A Portrait of the Artist as a Young Man*, will recognise Dedalus, that novel's principal character. He is clearly Joyce's alter ego, a budding writer of lofty aesthetic ambition and with an aloof manner.

Malachi 'Buck' Mulligan, one of 'the brood of mockers', is a carousing medical student who, by his own account, is 'tripping and sunny'. An ebullient character ('I remember only ideas and sensations'), Buck Mulligan is based on the writer Oliver St John Gogarty. Mulligan will reappear a number of times in subsequent episodes of *Ulysses*. Joyce depicts Mulligan as a loquacious, cocksure personality. Mulligan makes most of the running in this opening episode, as if he were the novel's main character. Gogarty was furious about what he saw as Joyce's unflattering portrayal of him. He described Joyce as 'Dublin's Dante' who had 'to find a way out of his own Inferno',[12] and dismissed *Ulysses*, in his typically feisty manner, as 'a book you can read on all the lavatory walls of Dublin'.[13] Gogarty, whom Yeats once described as a writer of 'heroic song' and 'one of the great lyric poets of the age',[14] went on to have a successful career as a medical doctor, an Irish senator and a successful writer who spent the last two decades of his life in the United States, dying in New York in 1957.

The third character is Haines, an Englishman, who is an enthusiast for the Irish literary revival and 'a ponderous Saxon'. According to Mulligan, Haines thinks that Stephen is not a gentleman. For his part, Stephen is resentful of Haines, with his 'smile of a Saxon'. Haines is based on Richard Samuel Chenevix Trench (1881–1909), a graduate of Eton and Balliol College, Oxford, who had taught himself to speak Irish. In the novel, Haines had alarmed Stephen by raving in his sleep about a black panther. In reality, Joyce ended his brief stay at the Martello tower in understandable alarm after Trench discharged a gun during the night. Trench ended up committing suicide, shooting himself in the head while described as temporarily insane.[15]

The novel opens with Buck Mulligan strutting around the roof of the tower in a yellow dressing-gown breezily jousting with Stephen who is 'displeased and sleepy' because his night's rest has been disrupted by Haines's nocturnal antics.

We are in early twentieth-century Dublin, but there is a sense in which we are also brushing up against classical Greece. Although *Ulysses* can be enjoyed without any knowledge of its parallels with Homer, an awareness of a few key points can enhance a reader's enjoyment of the novel. It is worth noting that the book's main character, Leopold Bloom, a Dublin advertising salesman of Hungarian-Jewish background, is Joyce's equivalent of Homer's protagonist Odysseus from the *Odyssey* ('the man of many ways, who was driven far journeys, after he had sacked Troy's sacred citadel'[16]). Here, I have used Richmond Lattimore's translation of the *Odyssey* which I bought during my most recent visit to Greece. The best-known translation is by Robert Fagles (the *Odyssey*, Penguin Classics, 1999), in which this passage is rendered more poetically: 'Sing to me of the man, Muse, the man of twists and turns driven time and again off course, once he had plundered the hallowed heights of Troy'. Both translations – 'the man of many ways' and 'the man of twists and turns' – seem to me to capture the intricate character that is Leopold Bloom. Odysseus – or Ulysses, as he is known in the Latin version of that mythic tale – is the main character in Homer's epic, which recounts its hero's lengthy journey home from the Trojan War.

This first episode of Joyce's novel is known as 'Telemachus', named after Odysseus's son in the *Odyssey*. He awaits his father's return home to the island of Ithaca after the Trojan war. In *Ulysses*, Stephen Dedalus is presented by Joyce as akin to Telemachus, while Molly Bloom is our Penelope, wife of the Homeric hero. In this opening salvo of the novel, we are introduced to Stephen, who is the central character in the novel's first three episodes. After that we come into contact with Leopold Bloom, who dominates most of the rest of its pages.

One way of understanding Joyce's novel is to see Bloom's journey home through the streets of Dublin, and his urge to find a substitute for his deceased son, as symbolic of Odysseus's journey home to Ithaca in the *Odyssey*. This is coupled with Stephen Dedalus's more or less unwitting search for a father figure – much like Telemachus's quest to find the absent Odysseus. Those familiar with Joyce's first novel, *A Portrait of the Artist as a Young Man*, in which Stephen is the budding artist at its heart, will recall that Stephen's own father, Simon Dedalus (based on Joyce's father, John Stanislaus Joyce), was an improvident character and a neglectful father. By the time James Joyce entered university, the family's fortunes had declined to the point where he listed his father's occupation as 'entering competitions'. In *A Portrait*, his father is described by Stephen as 'a praiser of his own past'.

Bloom and Stephen finally discover each other in the book's sixteenth and seventeenth episodes, but there are references in these opening pages to the father-son theme. Mulligan refers to Stephen as Japhet (Noah's son) 'in search of a father'. Referring to Stephen's theories about Shakespeare's *Hamlet*, Mulligan jests that 'he proves by algebra that Hamlet's grandson is Shakespeare's grandfather and that he himself is the ghost of his own father'. Haines recalls reading a theological interpretation of *Hamlet*, 'The Father and the Son idea. The Son striving to be atoned with the Father.' In 'Telemachus', however, it is Stephen's recently deceased mother who hauntingly occupies his thoughts.

For a book of such linguistic and conceptual daring, *Ulysses* begins in a fairly conventional vein. Its opening lines – 'Stately, plump Buck Mulligan came from the stairhead, bearing a bowl of lather on which a razor and a mirror lay crossed' – could be drawn from any nineteenth-century novel; its opening pages are a lively, enjoyable read. In all of the Bloomsday readings I have organised over the years across three continents, these pages of the novel have always featured. Together with its closing passage, this must be the best-known part of *Ulysses*.

'Telemachus' contains little enough of the 'stream of consciousness' technique (also known as an 'interior monologue') through which Joyce gives us direct access to the characters' thoughts and impressions of the world around them. This is something the reader needs to get used to as they progress through many of the 750-or-so pages that follow. Here is an example of a sudden shift within a single paragraph from the third person 'he' of the narrator's vantage point to the first person 'I' of Stephen's inner world: 'It lay behind him, a bowl of bitter waters. Fergus's song: I sang it alone in the house, holding down the dark chords.' Warning: it gets more difficult to spot these transitions later on in the book. By the time we get to the closing episode, 'Penelope', the narrative has shifted entirely to 'interior monologue'.

This particular literary device puzzled some of the novel's early readers and gave *Ulysses* a reputation for difficulty and obscurity that it has never managed to shed. My advice to readers who encounter passages they struggle to understand is not to be deterred, but to move on. This is not a novel with a plot in which everything needs to be fully grasped. Most of its 'action' takes place within the minds of its three main characters.

If you're a reader who wants to become acquainted with *Ulysses* but do not feel you have the stamina to read the entire book, you could do worse than to read this episode, together with Episodes 2 ('Nestor'), 4 ('Calypso'), 6 ('Hades'), 8 ('Lestrygonians'), 12 ('Cyclops') and 18 ('Penelope'). Taken together, they will give the reader a flavour of what it has to offer and of the feat of writing it represents. After being exposed to the more accessible and immediately compelling parts of *Ulysses*, readers may be encouraged to tackle its more taxing portions. One of my aims throughout this book is to allow my readers to do some tasty sampling of Joyce's work. The eighteen episodes *of Ulysses* can be read as more or less self-contained short stories or, in the case of the longer episodes, novellas, and in one case a full-length play!

In this opening episode, the writing is descriptive and contains quite a lot of dialogue. There are plenty of examples of Joyce's mastery of prose style. Take for example, 'They halted, looking towards the blunt cape of Bray Head that lay on the water like the snout of a sleeping whale', 'Warm sunshine merrying over the sea' or 'Inshore and farther out the mirror of water whitened, spurned by lightshod hurrying feet. White breast of the dim sea ... Wavewhite wedded words shimmering on the dim tide.'

As the critic Edmund Wilson puts it, the early chapters of *Ulysses* are 'as sober and clear as the morning light of the Irish coast in which they take place'.[17] For W. B. Yeats, the pages set in the Martello tower were 'full of beauty'.[18] He thought that those early episodes he had read in *The Little Review* in 1918 were 'an entirely new thing – neither what the eye sees or the ear hears, but what the rambling mind thinks and imagines from moment to moment. He has certainly surpassed in intensity any novelist of our time.'[19] Even before *Ulysses* was fully published, Yeats was spot on in his understanding of what Joyce was attempting.

Although *Ulysses* concentrates on the private thoughts of its principal characters, it is interesting to see how much of the public life of early-twentieth-century Ireland butts into its pages. Themes of 'nationality, language, religion' that had bothered Stephen Dedalus in *A Portrait of the Artist as a Young Man* all make their way into the 'Telemachus' episode.

The novel opens with Mulligan, described as looking like 'a prelate, patron of the arts in the middle ages', parodying the Latin mass and poking fun at Stephen on account of his Jesuit manner. For Mulligan, Stephen is a 'jejune Jesuit' and full of 'gloomy Jesuit jibes'. He is rightly critical of Stephen's stubborn unwillingness to pray at his dying mother's bedside, telling him 'there is something sinister in you', and that Stephen is 'an impossible person', which, indeed, in these pages he appears to be. Mulligan irreverently recites 'The Ballad of Joking Jesus':

> With Joseph the joiner I cannot agree,
> So here's to disciples and Calvary.
> …
> If anyone thinks that I amn't divine
> He'll get no free drinks when I'm making the wine
> But have to drink water and wish it were plain
> That I make when the wine becomes water again.

But Stephen is troubled by his mother's death, and by her appearance in his dreams wearing her grave clothes, 'giving off an odour of wax and rosewood'. Discussing religion with Haines, he describes himself as 'a horrible example of free thought', and complains to Haines that he is 'the servant of two masters', 'the imperial British State' and 'the holy Roman catholic and apostolic church'. Stephen adds a third master too, 'who wants

me for odd jobs', a reference to the demands of nationalism to which so many of his generation responded
devotedly.

Although Mulligan and Stephen are both dismissive
of the Irish literary revival of the late nineteenth century,
Mulligan quotes some lines from Yeats's poem, 'Who
goes with Fergus?':

And no more turn aside and brood
Upon love's bitter mystery
For Fergus rules the brazen cars.

Joyce's biographer, Richard Ellmann, tells us that this
poem was Joyce's favourite of all of Yeats's lyrics.

For his part, Stephen conjures up an image of Irish
art as 'the cracked lookingglass of a servant'. Joyce considered the Irish literary revival to be backward-looking.
As a student, he had published an intemperate essay,
'The Day of the Rabblement', deriding Yeats and others
for pandering to popular taste. In *A Portrait of the Artist
as a Young Man*, Stephen thought that Yeats 'remembers forgotten beauty', while he himself desired 'to press
in my arms the loveliness which has not yet come into
the world'.

Mulligan and Stephen consider themselves European
modernists, scornful of Irish pieties. Mulligan thinks
that he and Stephen can do something for Ireland: they
can 'Hellenise it'. And in a way that is what Joyce does,
by structuring his novel, very loosely it has to be said,
around Homer's *Odyssey*.

Ireland's two greatest twentieth-century writers, Yeats
and Joyce, had a complicated but generally positive

relationship. Yeats was supportive of the younger writer and helped get Joyce an honorarium from Britain's Royal Literary Fund, which greatly boosted his finances during the First World War. Joyce could be ungrateful to those who helped him, though, and there are some gentle barbs at Yeats in *Ulysses*, for example, in 'Telemachus', where he has Mulligan refer obliquely to Lily and Lolly Yeats as the 'weird sisters'. When Yeats won the Nobel Prize in 1923, Joyce, who certainly deserved this honour but was never awarded it, sent him a message of congratulations. Years later he dispatched a wreath to Yeats's funeral in the south of France, although it did not arrive in time.

In 1904, the Gaelic League, founded in 1893 with the aim of reviving the Irish language, was attracting growing numbers of enthusiastic members among Joyce's contemporaries, many of whom went on to play leading roles in the 1916 Rising and its aftermath. Ireland's ongoing language issue also surfaces in conversation at the Martello tower. Haines, the Hibernophile Englishman, believes people in Ireland should speak Irish, but the old woman who delivers milk to the tower has no knowledge of the language. She has been told that 'it's a grand language by them that knows'. Joyce himself took a few Irish language lessons, with Patrick Pearse – one of the leaders of the 1916 Rising – as his teacher, but he quickly lost interest in the language. He objected to Pearse's habit of denigrating the English language.[20] Joyce's preference was that Ireland should become more European. Like Yeats, Joyce detected a narrowing of national ambition in the early years of the twentieth century, and he resolved to remove himself from its influence by moving to Trieste, seeing broader European culture as an antidote to the Irish preoccupations that were on the rise in the Ireland he left behind. This theme of national identity is explored more fully in Episode 12, 'Cyclops'.

In conversation with Stephen, Haines confesses that he regrets Britain's treatment of Ireland – 'We feel in England that we have treated you rather unfairly' – and concludes that 'history is to blame'. Stephen will return to the theme of history in the novel's second episode, 'Nestor'.

Another of the novel's themes that initially surfaces here is anti-Semitism. Joyce deliberately gave his protagonist Bloom a Jewish heritage, something unusual in the Ireland of the time. Bloom was once described by Gerald Goldberg, former Lord Mayor of Cork, as 'a loyal, lovable, kindly human who bridges the gap between Irish man and Irish Jew'.[21] Joyce would probably not have recognised such a gap, nor would we do so in today's Ireland, where there is a greater acceptance of multifaceted identities. Throughout *Ulysses* there are expressions of anti-Jewish prejudice from the novel's minor characters of which Joyce clearly disapproved. Here Haines reveals his anti-Semitic bias when he says that he identifies as 'a Britisher', and does not want to see his country 'fall into the hands of German jews either. That's our national problem, I'm afraid, just now.'

In Trieste, Joyce made a number of Jewish friends and came to see his own trials as a literary exile as akin to those of Europe's Jews. He regarded anti-Semitism, which had come into focus across Europe on the back of the Dreyfus Affair in turn-of-the-century France, as the touchstone for bigotry.[22] In deciding that Bloom should be Jewish, he may also have been influenced by the fact that the summer of 1904 had witnessed anti-Semitic agitation in Limerick, with a boycott of local Jewish businesses.

Although Leopold and Molly Bloom do not appear until the book's fourth episode, there is an indirect reference to them in 'Telemachus', when Mulligan mentions a letter received from his friend Bannon, who is in Westmeath and has developed an interest in 'a sweet young thing down there. Photo girl he calls her.' Bannon will make an appearance later on in Episode 14, 'Oxen of the Sun'. In Episode 4, we learn that Bloom's daughter, Millie, is working in a photographic studio in Mullingar, County Westmeath. Such is the interconnected web that Joyce weaves!

As we exit the first episode, we follow Stephen as he walks along 'the upwardcurving path', making his way to the adjoining suburb of Dalkey, the setting for the next episode. He vows not to return to the tower: 'I will not sleep here tonight. Home also I cannot go.' Our Telemachus, having lost his mother and absented himself from his father's house, becomes a homeless roamer of Dublin's streets, crisscrossing them throughout the day, just like that other inveterate wanderer, Leopold Bloom.

EPISODE 2, 'NESTOR':
History Men

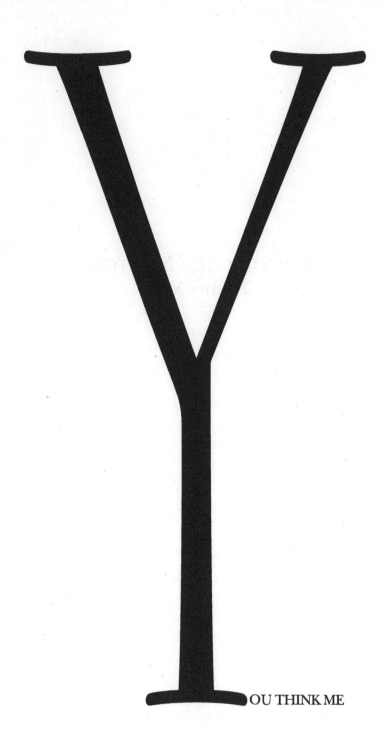
OU THINK ME

an old fogey and an old tory, his thoughtful voice said. I saw three generations since O'Connell's time. I remember the famine in '46. Do you know that the orange lodges agitated for repeal of the union twenty years before O'Connell did or before the prelates of your communion denounced him as a demagogue? You fenians forget some things.

Glorious, pious and immortal memory.

– Mr Garrett Deasy in *Ulysses*, Episode 2

This second episode of *Ulysses*, 'Nestor', illustrates the fact that James Joyce never forgot anything, but turned the Ireland of his youth into a window through which the whole of human life could be examined. 'Nestor' would make an exemplary short story or one-act play. It's a tale about a school, a teacher, his pupils and their headmaster. And, yes, it's also about history and prejudice.

The time has moved on to ten o'clock, and Stephen Dedalus, to whom we were introduced in the 'Telemachus' episode, has made his way from Sandycove to the neighbouring Dublin suburb of Dalkey. Stephen, having been overshadowed by the swaggering, voluble Mulligan in the novel's opening pages, comes into his own in this episode as he jousts with a character of starkly different experience and values.

The setting is a private school where Stephen is employed as a temporary teacher. The fictional school is run by Mr Garrett Deasy, a character based in many ways on Francis Irwin, a real-life headmaster of the Clifton School in Dalkey. Irwin was born in Ulster but moved to Dublin to study at Trinity College, and went on to found this private school. James Joyce taught there for a time in 1904 following his return to Ireland from Paris, where he had dabbled briefly with the study of medicine. He had come back to see his dying mother, whose passing, as we can infer from Stephen's inner monologue in the novel's opening episode, continued to prey on Joyce's mind.

This is the shortest chapter in the book, just fourteen pages long. It is, like its predecessor, a straightforward piece of writing. It does, however, contain a number of passages in which Stephen's innermost thoughts are put before us in all their tangled grandeur. In subsequent chapters of *Ulysses*, Joyce uses this technique to explore in exhaustive detail the innumerable cavities of Leopold Bloom's freewheeling, quirky mind. This can cause hiccups for the uninitiated reader, who has to figure out when Bloom's or Stephen's thoughts are cascading across the page, mimicking the workings of their dissimilar minds.

This episode has some fine examples of Joyce's dense but stylish writing. Here, as he thinks back on being in a library in Paris, Stephen ruminates on the mind and the soul:

Fed and feeding brains about me: under glow-lamps, impaled, with faintly beating feelers: and in my mind's darkness a sloth of the underworld, reluctant, shy of brightness, shifting her dragon scaly folds. Thought is the thought of thought. Tranquil brightness. The soul is in a manner all that is: the soul is the form of forms. Tranquility sudden, vast, candescent: form of forms.

[56]

This second episode of *Ulysses* is known as 'Nestor', although that name appears nowhere in Joyce's text. We know about the book's Homeric parallels because Joyce let some of his friends in on the secret and they informed the rest of us. In a schema Joyce supplied to his Italian translator, Carlo Linati, in September 1920, when he was still immersed in writing *Ulysses*, he also associated with each episode a technique, an organ of the body, an art form and a symbol. I will only alert you to these elements when I think that they can be helpful in understanding what Joyce is trying to say.

In 'Nestor', the art form is history, a theme that runs through Joyce's novel, but is especially evident here. One critic has argued that this episode 'provides essential material for the understanding of Joyce's matured concept of the flow of time interpreted in general human terms'.[23] In 'Nestor', Deasy ineptly seeks to give Stephen a history lesson, framing the past through a set of knee-jerk, political clichés. Deasy is an interesting character, for he is almost the only figure in *Ulysses* who represents the pro-British community in Ireland that wanted to preserve the union with Britain. I have seen him described as 'a happy imperialist' who believes that 'history is already at an end, finding its consummation in the British Empire'.[24] Joyce's depiction of Deasy is, in truth, a bit of a caricature, akin to the parodied nationalist, 'the citizen', who looms in a larger-than-life fashion over the later 'Cyclops' episode. Nationalist Ireland in Joyce's time, and indeed in the decades before and after, could be faulted for having an inadequate understanding of Ulster unionism, the political tradition to which Deasy belongs. Joyce seems to have shared some of that myopia.

The Homerian parallel continues in this episode. In Homer's *Odyssey*, Telemachus visits Nestor, a grandson of Neptune, to seek information about his father, Odysseus, and the Trojan War in which they had both fought. Nestor has little information to offer, just as Deasy has nothing of value to impart to Stephen. Nestor is described by Homer as a 'breaker of horses', just as Deasy might be regarded as a breaker of the spirit of the pupils entrusted to him. Homer sees Nestor as 'the most perfect of all his heroes', who 'distinguished himself among the rest of the Grecian chiefs by eloquence, address, wisdom, justice and an uncommon prudence of mind'.[25] Deasy, as we will see, is nothing of the sort. As presented by Joyce, he is someone who is chockfull of pedestrian prejudices.

In 'Telemachus', Mulligan told Stephen that he had 'the real Oxford manner', but here at the opening of the second chapter, Stephen somewhat surprisingly harks back to the exchanges he has had with Haines and sees himself in competition with the Englishman and Oxford graduate with whom he had shared the Martello tower the night before. Despite the superior pose he assumes, Stephen views himself self-deprecatingly as 'a jester at the court of his master, indulged and disesteemed, winning a clement master's praise'. Stephen, though a natural sceptic about politics and nationality, nevertheless feels some degree of resentment towards Britain, represented in this case by Haines. He imagines himself trying 'deftly amid wild drink and talk, to pierce the polished mail of his mind'. It is telling that when Joyce decided to leave Ireland, he did not, like Wilde, Shaw, Yeats and others, choose the conventional path of literary exile in London, but spent the rest of his life in continental Europe.

In the classroom, Stephen is teaching Milton's 'Lycidas' and classical history, specifically the Battle of Asculum in 279 BC, which was part of the Pyrrhic War. Stephen thinks of that battle as 'fabled by the daughters of memory', a beautiful idea is it not? Amid the ruin of conflict, he thinks of time as 'one livid final flame'. The boys in his class mangle the word 'pyrrhic', confusing it with 'pier', which causes Stephen to comment that a pier is 'a disappointed bridge'. His wit, if that is what you'd call it, is not a big hit with the boys in his classroom. Stephen is clearly right when he describes himself to Deasy as a learner rather than a teacher.

Stephen remembers some major moments from classical history: Pyrrhus's victory against the Romans ('another victory like that and we are done for') and Caesar's death. He mulls over history's might-have-beens: 'Time has branded them and fettered they are lodged in the room of the infinite possibilities they have ousted. But can those have been possible seeing that they never were? Or was that only possible which came to pass? Weave, weaver of the wind.' That is another fine example of Joyce's prose in full flow.

The classroom scene ends with an exchange between Stephen and a struggling pupil, Cyril Sargent, who finds it hard to understand the 'sums' he'd been given to do. Stephen pities Sargent's frailty: 'Yet someone had loved him, borne him in her arms and in her heart. But for her the race of the world would have trampled him under foot, a squashed boneless snail. She had loved his weak watery blood drained from her own. Was that then real? The only true thing in life?'

This prompts Stephen to recall his relationship with his own departed mother, and so he identifies with the misfortunate Sargent: 'Like him was I, these sloping shoulders, this gracelessness. My childhood bends beside me.... Secrets, silent, stony sit in the dark palaces of both our hearts: secrets weary of their tyranny: tyrants willing to be dethroned.'

After their class with Stephen, the boys go to play hockey on 'the scrappy field where sharp voices were in strife'. In his account of their childhood, Joyce's brother Stanislaus maintains that while at school at Clongowes Wood, James 'distinguished himself' at sport, and that when he left the school after four years he had 'a sideboard full of cups' he had won at hurdles and walking. James disliked football but liked cricket, in which he was a promising batsman. He had 'speed and endurance' at running.[26] *Quelle surprise!* James Joyce the sportsman! Who knew?

As the boys play, Stephen goes to Deasy's office to be paid for his week's work. In a nod to Homer's 'Nestor', its walls are adorned with images of 'vanished horses' belonging to members of the British aristocracy, with their 'elfin riders' and 'the shouts of vanished crowds'. Horseracing will assume great significance to our narrative later on, especially in the 'Cyclops' episode, where that day's Ascot Gold Cup is on the minds of many of the characters.

Deasy, who knows Stephen to have connections with the press, asks him to get a letter of his published in one of the Dublin papers. It concerns a reputed remedy for foot and mouth disease, which he claims to have learned about from a cousin of his in Austria, Henry Blackwood Price.

This part of the story highlights Joyce's habit of incorporating elements of his own experience into his fiction. Joyce knew Blackwood Price in Trieste and learned about his veterinary cure. Indeed, he passed a letter from

Price on to William Field, MP, who had it published in Dublin's *Evening Telegraph*. Deasy's fictional letter as summarised in *Ulysses* is based on the one Price wrote. Not only that, but in September 1912, an editorial entitled 'Politics and Cattle Disease' appeared in Dublin's *Freeman's Journal*,[27] which argued that the threat posed by foot and mouth disease was being used by British politicians to exclude Irish beef from the British market. This appears to have been written by Joyce and, if that is the case, it must rank as the strangest thing he ever published. His foray into agricultural journalism means that Joyce might have warranted the label 'bullockbefriending bard' which Stephen imagines the mocking Mulligan applying to him.

I apologise in advance to my many friends in Ireland's Department of Agriculture for quoting Deasy's line from his foot and mouth letter about 'the pluterperfect imperturbability of the department of agriculture', but it's too good to pass up! The Department of Agriculture predates the formation of the Irish State, having been established in 1899 under the direction of Horace Plunkett, an energetic advocate of agricultural cooperation.

Deasy, a staunch Protestant, lectures Stephen on the virtues of parsimony, a quality for which neither Stephen in the novel, nor Joyce in life, had any flair. Deasy believes that 'money is power', while for Stephen, the coins he receives from the headmaster are 'symbols soiled by greed and misery'.

Asked by Deasy about an Englishman's 'proudest word', Stephen presumes it would be the adage 'that on his empire ... the sun never sets'. The headmaster has a more prosaic precept in mind: '*I paid my way*'. He brags that he never borrowed a shilling in his life, which leads Stephen to recall the longish list of people to whom he owes money, including two prominent individuals from the Ireland of Joyce's time: Fred Ryan, journalist and socialist who was owed 'two shillings', and George Russell (Æ), poet, painter, editor and mystic, owed 'one guinea'. Deasy invokes Shakespeare's line 'put but money in thy purse', only to be reminded by Stephen that this is spoken in *Othello* by Iago, one of the least likable characters in all of literature. For Deasy, Shakespeare was 'A poet, yes, but an Englishman too'. This down-to-earth view is a far cry from the grandiose debate about Shakespeare and his writing that we will encounter later in the 'Scylla and Charybdis' episode.

The theme of history comes back into play when Deasy claims to be descended from Sir John Blackwood, who, he says, voted for the Act of Union of 1800. That might be difficult to credit. Blackwood was a neighbour in County Down of the family of one of the act's architects, Lord Castlereagh, but Blackwood died in February 1799, while the decisive vote on the Act of Union took place the following year. Blackwood was a Whig, and that political group tended to oppose the union, although many of its members were induced to support it by dint of financial incentives. Blackwood was also a sharp critic of the 1798 rebellion that prompted the British government to engineer the union. During the rise of the French-inspired United Irishmen, he published 'a violent philippic against treason and the French'.[28] Joyce most likely got his perhaps inaccurate information about

Sir John Blackwood from his descendant, Deasy's supposed cousin, Trieste-based Henry Blackwood Price.

Deasy uses the slogan 'For Ulster will fight and Ulster will be right', which comes out of late-nineteenth-century Ulster unionist resistance to Irish Home Rule. In 1904, Home Rule would have seemed to be a fairly remote prospect, because at that time, the Conservative and Unionist Party ruled Britain, a party that was firmly opposed to self-government for Ireland. *Ulysses* was written mainly in the years after 1916, by which time Irish politics had been transformed in the aftermath of the Easter Rising, and the union with Britain was being dissolved.

Looking back, Deasy revels in Britain's greatness. The British, he insists, 'are a generous people but we must also be just'. To this, Stephen retorts that he fears 'those big words ... which make us so unhappy'. Deasy maintains that 'all history moves towards one great goal, the manifestation of God'. Stephen sees things very differently. At the mention of God, he points out through the office window to the boys playing in the fields. 'That is God,' he says. 'A shout in the street.' Deasy is nonplussed by such views.

In contrast to Deasy's view, in Stephen's eyes 'history is a nightmare from which I am trying to awake'. He thinks of his pupils, for whom 'history was a tale like any other too often heard, their land a pawnshop'. There is a sense in which Joyce's decision to leave Ireland in 1904 was an effort to escape the clutches of Ireland's history and to see his homeland from a distance. *Ulysses* is the result of that arm's-length examination.

The episode ends with some heated displays of prejudice on Deasy's part. First, he targets Helen of Troy for causing the Trojan War and marks Mrs Katherine O'Shea (an unnamed 'woman') as responsible for the fall of Parnell. Katherine O'Shea gets a bad rap in *Ulysses*. In the 'Eumaeus' episode, she will be derided as a 'bitch' and 'an English whore'; no blame for the affair that brought about his downfall is ever attributed by Joyce to Parnell. Deasy blames Dervogilla, 'a faithless wife', who 'first brought the strangers to our shore here, MacMurrough's wife and her leman, O'Rourke, prince of Breffni'. This is a reference to the coming of the Normans to Ireland in the twelfth century. Here Deasy gets his history badly tangled. Dervogilla was Tiernan O'Rourke's wife, who was taken by Dermot MacMurrough from her home on Lough Gill in County Sligo while O'Rourke was away on pilgrimage. It was MacMurrough, King of Leinster, who invited the Normans into Ireland with what turned out to be fateful and very long-lasting consequences.

Showing that he possesses a full suite of prejudices, Deasy believes that 'England is in the hands of the Jews. In all the highest places: her finance, her press. And they are the signs of a nation's decay. Wherever they gather they eat up the nation's vital strength.' Once again Joyce highlights the prevalence in the early twentieth century of anti-Jewish sentiment. He does so just before we encounter his Jewish Everyman, Leopold Bloom, and the redoubtable Molly. It's notable that she is also, in her own way, a faithless wife. Bloom's struggle to come to terms with her infidelity is a major strand running through *Ulysses*.

Stephen's thoughts tell us that he has a very different view of Irish history to Deasy, but he chooses not to confront him on this. He does push back against

Deasy's critique of 'jew merchants', reminding him that a merchant 'is one who buys cheap and sells dear, jew or gentile'. Bloom will later encounter, and eventually challenge, these same anti-Jewish prejudices. As Stephen departs, Deasy shouts after him that Ireland was the only country never to persecute the Jews because 'she never let them in'. This is another inaccuracy. In fact, there was a growing Jewish community in turn-of-the-century Ireland, most of whom had arrived during the 1880s and 1890s. Jewish immigrants continued to arrive from Eastern Europe in the first decade of the twentieth century.[29]

'Nestor' ends with a fine Joycean flourish, in which Stephen departs from the school as Deasy 'stamped on gaitered feet over the gravel of the path.... On his wise shoulders through the checkerwork of leaves the sun flung spangles, dancing coins.' A fitting conclusion to an episode in which coinage, and its symbolism, plays such a part.

On we go now to Sandymount Strand, where many readers sink in the quicksand of the dense and difficult 'Proteus' episode.

EPISODE 3, 'PROTEUS':
Stephen's Beach Walk

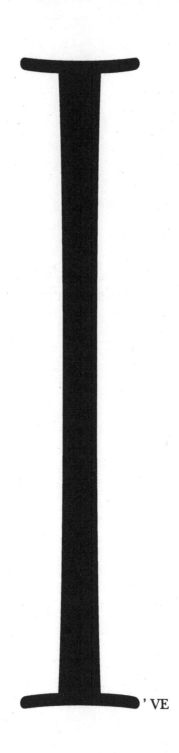

I'VE

put in so many enigmas and puzzles that it will keep the professors busy for centuries arguing over what I meant, and that's the only way of insuring one's immortality.

– James Joyce[30]

The 'Proteus' episode was surely one of those puzzles in *Ulysses* to which Joyce was referring. Frankly, it's a very difficult proposition for the average reader, or even for the more adventurous one. It's as if the writer wanted to test his readers severely at an early stage in the novel, to see if they were up to the task, and to discourage those who were insufficiently committed. It's like a Grand National steeplechase with one of the toughest fences placed towards the beginning of the race so as to thin out the field. In all of the Bloomsdays I have arranged over the years, I have never had anyone volunteer to read a favourite passage from 'Proteus'. This episode wouldn't really lend itself to a light-hearted and accessible celebration of Joyce's novel.

I bought my first copy of *Ulysses* in a bookshop at the University of Missouri-Kansas City (UMKC). It was the summer of 1974 and I was in America on a J-1 visa. During what was my first significant absence from Ireland, I lived at Rockhurst College (now Rockhurst University), a Jesuit institution located near UMKC.

At that time, I had finished my first two years of study at University College Cork, where the literature courses I had taken included the study of Joyce's *A Portrait of the Artist as a Young Man*, but not *Ulysses*. It may be that *Ulysses* was judged to be too daunting for Irish undergraduate students in the early 1970s! I had of course heard of Joyce's most famous novel and, when I saw a copy at the UMKC bookshop, I picked it up. That evening I sat down to read it with a mixture of excitement at the prospect of delving into an acknowledged modernist masterpiece, and apprehension on account of the book's forbidding reputation.

I galloped through the first two chapters, which I enjoyed, even if it was difficult to understand what the book's notoriety was all about. But my first stab at reading *Ulysses* began to go off the rails when I encountered the first sentence of Episode 3: 'Ineluctable modality of the visible: at least that if no more, thought through my eyes. Signatures of all things I am here to read, seaspawn and seawrack, the nearing tide, that rusty boot.'

In what Molly Bloom would call 'plain words', the first part of that sentence probably means something like: we cannot escape from the things we see around us. Yes, the world we live in is constantly changing shape and presenting itself to us in different ways. This was all a bit too taxing for a student's summer reading and, although I persisted with the book for a few more chapters, I eventually put it aside unfinished. But I did not discard it, and I still have that American edition of *Ulysses*, which I had bound in leather during my first diplomatic assignment in New Delhi, 1980–3. I no longer value all of the books I had bound at that time, but *Ulysses* has come to mean more and more to me with the passage of the years. I returned to *Ulysses* some years after my first encounter with it, and read it from cover to cover with admiration and enthusiasm. It has become a mainstay of my lifelong engagement with Irish history and literature.

My American edition of *Ulysses* also contains the text of the court judgement delivered by Judge John M. Woolsey of the United States District Court of the Southern District of New York on 6 December 1933, when he lifted the ban on the book. Morris L. Ernst, the attorney who represented Joyce's would-be publishers, Random House, greeted the judgement by observing that 'the New Deal in law and letters has just arrived'. After the trial, Joyce lauded Ernst as a 'valiant and victorious defender of this book in America'.[31]

I was reminded of that landmark ruling when reading Washington lawyer and literary scholar Joseph M. Hassett's excellent book *The Ulysses Trials: Beauty and Truth Meet the Law*, which tells the story of the legal shenanigans that preceded the book's publication in the United States in 1934. He concluded that Irish-American lawyer John Quinn, who defended the editors of the avant-garde magazine, *The Little Review,* in 1921, had weakened his own hand by declining to argue that the novel's embodiment of truth and beauty justified its publication. A distinguished Washington lawyer and literary scholar who has also written books about W. B. Yeats, Joe and I are kindred spirits, and have become close friends during my time as ambassador in Washington.

I suspect that many readers of *Ulysses* will, like me, have run aground when they encountered this 'Proteus' episode, so called because of the links Joyce sought to make with Book 4 of Homer's *Odyssey*. That part of Homer's narrative features Proteus, 'the ever truthful Old Man of the Sea', who 'knows all the depths of the sea' and resides by the seashore. Homer writes of Proteus:

If somehow you could lie in ambush and catch
hold of him,
he could tell you the way to go, the stages of your
journey,
and tell you how to make your way home on the
sea where the fish swarm.[32]

In Homer, Proteus is also 'difficult to access, and when consulted he refuses to give answers, by immediately assuming different shapes'.[33] With Joyce's tendency to rapidly shift focus and topic in these pages, Proteus, the shape-changing sea deity, strikes me as a suitable presiding spirit!

There is a sense in which the first three episodes of *Ulysses*, with their concentration on the character of Stephen Dedalus, are a kind of prelude to the novel's core, in which we get to know its most endearing (and indeed enduring) character, Leopold Bloom. Despite being based on Joyce himself, Stephen Dedalus is a far less attractive personality than Bloom, or his inimitable wife Molly. From Episode 4 onwards, Stephen will flit in and out of the action, whereas Leopold Bloom will be more or less ever-present.

In the opening episode of *Ulysses*, Stephen is revealed through his relationship with Buck Mulligan and the English Hibernophile, Haines, while in 'Nestor' we viewed him through the prism of his encounters with his pupils and the school principal, Mr Deasy. In 'Proteus', Stephen, who has moved on from Dalkey, travelling along the southern shore of Dublin Bay to Sandymount Strand, is front and centre from start to finish. Here, Stephen is in dialogue with himself. This is Stephen's monologue, which concludes the first section of *Ulysses*. I cannot help comparing and contrasting it with Molly's monologue that comes at the very end of the novel. It would be an interesting experiment to read the two monologues one after the other. Stephen and Molly are very different characters, with deeply divergent thought processes. The content of their respective monologues could scarcely be any less alike.

I do not normally recommend turning to an academic expert on Joyce and *Ulysses*, as I find that such sources tend to complicate rather than clarify. But with an episode as dense and elusive as this one, I did look for expert guidance. A Joycean named J. Mitchell Morse observed, helpfully I think, that the focus of 'Proteus' is on Stephen Dedalus – the embodiment of Joyce's youthful self – becoming the mature James Joyce. He wrote: 'In order for Stephen Dedalus to grow into James Joyce he had to turn and grasp the beast: the concrete, the specific, the consequential, the dog that may very well bite. In "Proteus" we see Stephen sorting out some of the elements that will be involved in a complex decision whose complexity he is only beginning to suspect.'[34]

This has an air of credibility to it. While Joyce clearly sees Stephen as a version of himself, it is hard to imagine that he would have been satisfied with such a self-portrait. Stephen is the apprentice Joyce and not the one who wrote *Ulysses*. Leopold Bloom exhibits some of Joyce's attitudes, but he is clearly no Joyce either. The mature writer who composed *Ulysses* was something of a cross between Stephen and Bloom, and it is reasonable to imagine Joyce trying to grow the character he first introduced in *A Portrait*. This makes it possible to see 'Proteus', for all of its dense evasiveness, as part of Stephen's, and Joyce's, transformation. Joyce once wrote about Stephen that 'he dreaded the sea that would drown his body and the crowd that would drown his soul'.[35]

Although this episode has a narrator, almost everything in these pages happens in Stephen's unnaturally-erudite mind. And it's a chaotic realm, full of strange words, unfinished thoughts, and some fairly obscure literary, philosophical and historical references, coupled with vividly expressed impressions of the world around him. There are echoes of the philosophy of Aristotle running through 'Proteus', but these are not a barrier to understanding this episode. It is enough to know that Stephen grapples with Aristotle's ideas of space and vision. Joyce regarded Aristotle, 'the master of those who knew', as 'the greatest thinker of all times'.[36]

We accompany Stephen as he walks along the strand at around eleven o'clock in the morning of 16 June 1904. There is no dialogue here, except for some snatches in Stephen's memory and imagination. What we get instead is a free flow of Stephen's kaleidoscopic, spur-of-the-moment thoughts. It is sometimes difficult to fathom what is going on inside Stephen's head. It's five fathoms deep like the water in the Irish Sea where, in this episode, a man has been 'Found drowned'.

Not everyone has been intimidated by this intensely literary beach walk however. Margaret Anderson, co-publisher of the *The Little Review*, received this episode from Ezra Pound in February 1918 and was smitten by it. 'This,' she wrote later, 'is the most beautiful thing we'll ever have. We'll print it if it's the last effort of our lives.' And print much of *Ulysses* she did, until prosecution for obscenity stopped the *Review*'s publication of the later episodes of Joyce's novel.

Joyce's English friend, Frank Budgen, spotted how different this episode was from its predecessors in that Stephen, after being 'weary and dispirited' at the school, here is 'free and alone with a vast, bright space around him'. Budgen thought that 'Proteus' was 'exciting' and 'full of light and colour'. He reported that Joyce was pleased with what he had achieved there, and explained that 'change is the theme', 'everything changes – sea, sky, man, animals. The words change too.' Budgen, who is as good a guide to *Ulysses* as I have come across, wondered 'does any other prose writer know and enjoy his own work as Joyce does'.[37] Joyce did, indeed, have a consistently high opinion of his own work, which is hardly surprising considering the intensive seven years he devoted to the composition of *Ulysses*.

This is a part of *Ulysses* which benefits more than most from being read aloud. There is an excellent dramatised reading of *Ulysses* available on the website of the Irish national broadcaster, RTÉ. It was produced for Irish radio in 1982 for the centenary of Joyce's birth, and it is marvellous. I recommend it across the board, but especially for a difficult episode like 'Proteus'.

Those who find this chapter unduly perplexing should feel free to skip it and move on to the following one, which is far more engaging. Although this episode is worth persisting with, nothing actually happens here that is essential to an appreciation of Joyce's masterwork. *Ulysses* is not at all like a regular novel, where the story unfolds step by step and requires that it be read sequentially.

Let me say that I am now far less perplexed by this episode than I was when I first encountered it forty-seven years ago. *The Little Review* co-editor Margaret

Anderson was right. It contains some fine writing, poetic in tone and experimental in nature. Take the following passage, which illustrates Joyce's habit of combining words for greater effect, a technique that will be encountered throughout *Ulysses*: 'Airs romped around him, nipping and eager airs. They are coming, waves. The whitemaned seahorses, champing, brightwindbridled, the steeds of Mananaan.' Here Mananaan refers to the sea god, Manannán mac Lir, an Irish counterpart to Proteus, and the origin of the name of the Isle of Man in the Irish Sea.

Here is another example of Joyce's command of language: 'Paris rawly waking, crude sunlight on her lemon streets. Moist pith of farls of bread, the froggreen wormwood, her matin incense, court the air.' Paris is much on Stephen's mind as he walks along the beach. He remembers the telegram he received there, 'Mother dying come home father', which caused him to return to Dublin to be with his mother on her deathbed.

Stephen also reflects on his encounters with the exiled and embittered Fenian, Kevin Egan, based on Joseph Casey, who had been jailed for his involvement in the rescue of two Fenian prisoners in Manchester in 1867, and was himself the subject of a failed escape from London's Clerkenwell Prison. Here, Stephen recalls Egan speaking 'Of Ireland, the Dalcassians, of hopes, conspiracies, of Arthur Griffith now. To yoke me as his yokefellow, our crimes our common cause', but that is not Stephen's cause. He observes that Egan is 'unsought by any save by me'. Moreover, he is 'loveless, landless, wifeless'. His conclusion is that 'They have forgotten Kevin Egan, not he them'. Joyce seems to be contrasting the frustrations of Egan's political exile with the necessities of his own artistic one. Yeats's beloved Maud Gonne, a 'beautiful woman', also gets a mention here, as does her French lover, Lucien Millevoye.

Not a lot happens on Stephen's stroll along the beach, except in the young writer's fertile mind. He spots two women on the beach and imagines them, for no good reason, to be midwives come down to dispose of an afterbirth. Later, he comes across some cockle pickers, the remains of a dog and a living canine sniffing around the carcass. Joyce was afraid of dogs, as is Stephen in his novel. Stephen relieves himself and writes some lines of verse, using for paper the letter Deasy had given him in Episode 2 for publication in one of Dublin's newspapers.

Early on, Stephen tries walking with his eyes closed and wonders if he is 'walking into eternity along Sandymount strand?' When he opens his eyes he sees, unsurprisingly, that the world was: 'There all the time without you: and ever shall be, world without end.'

He considers visiting his aunt, but does not do so. Here we get a glimpse of Stephen's father's derogatory attitude towards his in-laws ('O weeping God, the things I married into! De boys up in de hayloft. The drunken little costdrawer and his brother, the cornet player.') This reflects the cantankerous mindset of Joyce's father, John Stanislaus Joyce, and his hostility towards his wife's brother, William Murray. In truth, Murray made a better fist of his life than Joyce senior, but that was probably at the root of John Joyce's animosity towards him.

Stephen also imagines the Vikings arriving in Dublin a thousand years before: 'Galleys of the Lochlanns ran here to beach, in quest of prey, their bloodbeaked prows riding low on a molten pewter surf.' And he muses at length about the sea in terms that underline why this episode, for all of its many mysteries, is worth the effort: 'A tide westering, moondrawn, in her wake. Tides, myriadislanded, within her, blood not mine, *oinapa ponton*, a winedark sea. Behold the handmaid of the moon. In sleep the wet sign calls her hour, bids her rise.' You don't have to know exactly what it means to enjoy a passage like that. Think of it more like poetry than conventional prose and savour the dextrous wielding of words.

The poet, John Montague, writing many years after Joyce, made great use of the Homeric 'winedark sea'.

> there is no sea
> except in the tangle
> of our minds
> the wine dark
> sea of history
> on which we all turn
> turn and thresh
> and disappear.

Montague, who taught me English literature in Cork in the mid-1970s, may have been thinking of the 'Proteus' episode of *Ulysses* when he composed his poem. Joyce finishes his sea shanty with the image of a drowned man sunk 'beneath the watery floor' and a boat 'moving through the air high spars of a threemaster, her sails brailed up on the crosstrees, homing, upstream, silently moving, a silent ship'.

Thus ends the book's opening section, which is a kind a prologue, consisting of three chapters devoted

[78]

to Stephen Dedalus, his head full of ideas, snatches of foreign languages, literary and classical allusions, and a sprawl of characters who cross his mind including Arius, the 'Illstarred heresiarch', Aquinas, the scholastic philosopher and George Berkeley, 'the good Bishop of Cloyne'. We now set sail for Eccles Street, home of Leopold and Molly Bloom, a couple with minds of their own, but with far more down-to-earth preoccupations. Our first introduction to them, over breakfast at their home, is the subject of the next chapter.

EPISODE 4, 'CALYPSO':
Cat and Mouse at Eccles Street

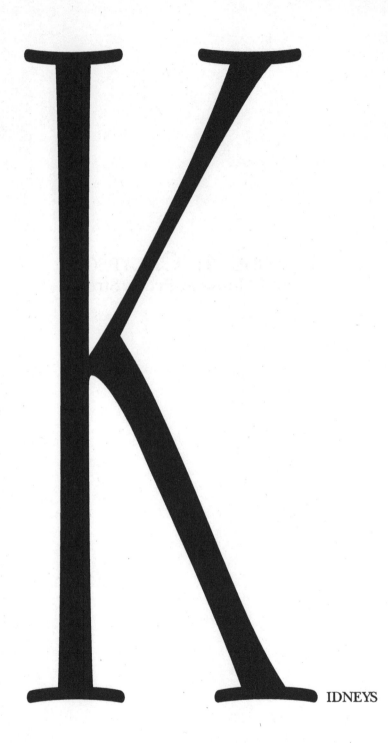
IDNEYS

were in his mind as he moved about the kitchen softly, righting her breakfast things on the humpy tray. Gelid light and air were in the kitchen but out of doors gentle summer morning every-where. Made him feel a bit peckish.

               – Our first glimpse of Leopold Bloom

When Ezra Pound described *Ulysses* as 'an epoch-making report on the state of the human mind in the twentieth century',[38] he was probably thinking about the mind of Leopold Bloom. Here is where we begin our long acquaintance with his fascinating mentality.

As we turn the page from 'Proteus' to 'Calypso', the first thing we notice is the Roman numeral II. This tells us that we have entered into the second section of *Ulysses*, one that contains twelve episodes centred on the wanderings of Leopold Bloom. We are also doing a bit of time travel in that, having left Stephen Dedalus on Sandymount Strand at around noon, it is now eight o'clock again, just as it was when we were introduced to him at Sandycove's Martello tower. We know about the timeframe of the novel from the schema Joyce made available to some of his friends, but one line here may give the game away: 'A cloud began to cover the sun wholly slowly, wholly. Grey. Far.' Sharp-eyed read-ers might recall coming across a very similar line in 'Telemachus': 'A cloud began to cover the sun slowly, wholly, shadowing the bay in deeper green.' Yes, it is the same cloud, seen by Stephen at Sandycove and now by Bloom as he returns home from his jaunt to the local butcher's shop. The cloud alters Bloom's hitherto con-tented mood. Now 'Grey horror seared his flesh'. This is a rarity in Ulysses where Bloom is generally happy enough with his lot. Elsewhere in 'Calypso', he exudes a 'happy warmth' and flashes 'his pleased smile'.

There was a dog on Sandymount Strand that alarmed Stephen in 'Proteus', and later we will meet a fiercer canine in 'the citizen's' poetry-reciting Garryowen. Here it's the family cat that, quite literally, gets the cream. With her 'lithe black form', the cat 'stalked again stiffly round a leg of the table, mewing'. Although we are not told her name, with her knowing ways she could easily qualify for inclusion in T. S. Eliot's *Old Possum's Book of Practical Cats*, or even in Andrew Lloyd Webber's musical based on Eliot's feline poems! 'They understand what we say better than we understand them. She understands all she wants to. Vindictive too. Wonder what I look like to her. Height of a tower? No, she can jump me.'

Here we see the Blooms' practical cat lapping some 'warmbubbled milk'. There was milk on display in the novel's opening episode too: 'rich white milk' brought to the tower by an old woman; here, Bloom's jug was filled by 'Hanlon's milkman'. We are invited to wonder if clipping the cat's bristles means 'they can't mouse after'.

Make no mistake about it, this episode is a bit of a cat and mouse game, with Leopold and Molly Bloom as its contestants. The current object of their game is Hugh 'Blazes' Boylan, whose letter to Molly causes Bloom's 'quick heart' to slow 'at once' when he picks it up in the hallway. Molly reads it when her husband is downstairs preparing breakfast, but stashes it under her pillow when he brings up her tea tray. Molly acknowledges that Boylan is coming to see her that afternoon with the programme for her upcoming concert tour. Bloom is also concealing things from Molly, a slip of paper hidden in his hat pertaining to his surreptitious, flirtatious correspondence with a woman named Martha Clifford. The top cat in this relationship is definitely Molly, snug in her bed being indulged by her husband even though he is aware of her planned infidelity. Bloom comes across as cautious and pernickety, mousey even, although he will do a bit of roaring of his own during this long June day.

Episode 4 of *Ulysses*, known as 'Calypso', is a delightful piece of writing. It is one of the novel's early highlights and begins with one of Joyce's most memorable passages: 'Mr Leopold Bloom ate with relish the inner organs of beasts and fowls. He liked thick giblet soup, nutty gizzards, a stuffed roast heart, liverslices fried with crustcrumbs, fried hencods' roes. Most of all he liked grilled mutton kidneys which gave to his palate a fine tang of faintly scented urine.' Based on the evidence Joyce provides, it is hard to imagine Stephen relishing the kind of pungent repast favoured by Bloom at breakfast time.

Over the years, I have organised Bloomsday celebrations at my various diplomatic postings, beginning in Edinburgh in 1999 and continuing in Kuala Lumpur, Berlin, London and the last four years in Washington. (Incidentally, we have always opted to serve Bloom's lunchtime menu, a glass of burgundy and a gorgonzola sandwich, in preference to his breakfast kidney!) The first few pages of this 'Calypso' episode have invariably featured among the readings. I especially recall the Irish actor, Adrian Dunbar, star of the BBC's excellent crime drama, *Line of Duty*, reading this passage quite beautifully at the embassy in London. Another year it was read by Colin Salmon, who appeared as Charles Robinson in three James Bond films. It's a great piece of writing, which lends itself to the talents of outstanding readers.

In this episode, we enter into the world – and inside the head – of Leopold Bloom, Joyce's twentieth-century Everyman. By the time we finish the novel, we will know Bloom better than any other character in literature. In Bloom's company, we are now a long way from the elaborately stocked, literature-steeped consciousness of Stephen Dedalus that kept us busy during the novel's first three episodes. Here we are 'planted on the solid earth', as Richard Ellmann has noted.[39]

When this episode begins, Bloom is busy preparing breakfast for Molly. It ends with Bloom visiting his out-house, to which the reader accompanies him, a scene that discommoded even Ezra Pound, who was an inveterate champion of Joyce's work, but thought he sometimes took realism a bit too far. Pound fretted about the threat of legal action and suggested amendments to fend off the lawyers, adding with tongue in cheek that: 'Perhaps an unexpurgated text of you can be printed in a greek or bulgarian translation later.'[40] Holding his nose tightly, the novelist H. G. Wells accused Joyce of having 'a cloacal obsession'.[41]

In 'Calypso' we get a first tantalising glimpse of Bloom's relationship with Molly, which will be explored in greater detail throughout the rest of *Ulysses* and especially in the book's concluding episode. Their marriage is at the heart of the novel, even though this is the only time we see them together until the novel's penultimate episode, 'Ithaca'.

In June 1904, Leopold Bloom is thirty-eight years old while his wife, Molly, whose surname at birth was Tweedy, is four years younger. Her late father, Colonel Tweedy, is often alluded to by Bloom, especially in connection with his supposed financial acumen: 'Still he had brains enough to make that corner in stamps. Now that was far-seeing.' Gibraltar-born Molly is a soprano about to embark on a concert tour arranged by Blazes Boylan. The Blooms live at No. 7 Eccles Street, just off Dorset Street. Joyce was clearly trying to make a point when he chose Leopold and Molly as his main characters. Neither has a typical Irish background, and Joyce evidently wanted us to view early twentieth-century Irish society from their oblique angle as atypical Dubliners, somewhat detached observers.

With Molly still asleep upstairs, Bloom goes out to buy a pork kidney. As he walks to Dlugacz's[42] butcher's shop, we get a first taste of the quirkiness of Bloom's mind. Unaccountably, he muses about the exotic east, although we know from other parts of *Ulysses* that he has never ventured outside of Ireland except for one visit to Holyhead in Wales:

> ... set off at dawn. Travel round in front of the sun, steal a day's march on him. Keep it up for ever never grow a day older technically.... Getting on to sundown. The shadows of the mosques along the pillars: priest with a scroll rolled up. A shiver of the trees, signal, the evening wind.... A mother watches from her doorway. She calls her children home in their dark language. High wall: beyond strings twanged. Night sky, moon, violet, colour of Molly's new garters. Strings. Listen. A girl playing one of these instruments what do you call them: dulcimers. I pass.

[87]

But then Bloom's pragmatic cast of mind asserts itself, as he concedes that it is 'probably not a bit like it really. Kind of stuff you read: in the track of the sun.' Quixotically, this prompts him to recall Arthur Griffith's quip about 'a homerule sun rising up in the northwest from the laneway behind the bank of Ireland', which was the location of the eighteenth-century Irish parliament which nineteenth-century nationalists wanted to re-establish. While he may be viewed by fellow Dubliners as a bit of an outsider, Bloom is, like Joyce himself, well versed in the intricacies of early twentieth-century Irish politics.

As he passes Larry O'Rourke's pub, we tap into Bloom's resentful city dweller's wonderment at the success of this import from rural Ireland, this 'Cute old codger'. 'Where do they get the money? Coming up red-headed curates from the county Leitrim, rinsing empties and old man in the cellar. Then, lo and behold, they blossom out as Adam Findlaters or Dan Tallons', both of whom were successful Dublin businessmen. We also get a taste of Bloom's wry humour. 'Good puzzle would be cross Dublin without passing a pub.'

And then we are given a sample of the acidic repartee of Simon Dedalus, father of Stephen. Bloom remembers Dedalus mimicking Larry O'Rourke's strong views on international issues. 'Do you know what? The Russians, they'd only be an eight o'clock breakfast for the Japanese.' This refers to the Russo-Japanese war, which was in full swing in June 1904. The Japanese did indeed put one over on their European adversary, a defeat that paved the way for Russia's political upheavals of 1905 and ultimately for the Russian Revolution of 1917.

In the butcher's shop, we get a good example of Joyce's descriptive powers: 'The ferreteyed porkbutcher folded the sausages he had snipped off with blotchy fingers, sausagepink. Sound meat there: like a stallfed heifer.' Bloom, after resting his eyes on the 'vigorous hips' of a girl buying sausages, sees an advertisement for a Zionist venture in Palestine being organised by a Berlin-based organisation with an address at Bleibtreustrasse 34. On account of his Jewish background, this venture catches Bloom's fancy until he considers the location's downsides – 'A barren land, bare waste.... A dead sea in a dead land, grey and old.'

When I was posted in Berlin, I visited Bleibtreustrasse and wrote about it in *Der Tagesspiegel*, the German newspaper ('James Joyce in Deutschland: ein Meinherr aus Teutschland', 14 June 2013), where I surmised that Joyce liked the meaning of the street's name, 'remain true', and thought it appropriate for a novel with fidelity and infidelity as one of its key themes.

After my piece appeared, a German Joycean, Prof. Wolfgang Wicht, kindly contacted me with further information. It's a long story, but Prof. Wicht concludes that, while Joyce was clearly aware of the plantation at Agendath Netaim and/or 'the model farm at Kinnereth on the lakeshore of Tiberias', he gets some of the details wrong as, for example, the fact that the first building erected at Bleibtreustrasse 34 was not yet in place in 1904! Wicht wisely views this as 'another instance of the novel's playful imaginings'.[43] Its impressive, forensic details are not always 100 per cent accurate. It is, after all, a work of fiction.

This particular street in Berlin is named after a nineteenth-century German painter, Georg Bleibtreu.

The painter's son, Karl Bleibtreu, whom Joyce met in Zurich, developed a theory about the authorship of Shakespeare's plays that captured Joyce's attention and will feature in a later episode of *Ulysses*.

When Bloom returns to Eccles Street from the butcher's, he puts Molly's breakfast on a tray and deposits the kidney on a frying pan. As he enters their bedroom, we discover that, as part of her concert tour, Molly will perform 'Là ci darem la mano' from Mozart's *Don Giovanni*, and 'Love's Old Sweet Song' by the Irish songwriter, James Lynam Molloy. The latter serves as a kind of theme song for this music-infused novel, and I have always made sure to have it sung at Bloomsday festivities I have arranged around the world. The old sweet song of the Blooms' relationship and its somewhat off-key current condition will toll through the rest of the novel. For its part, 'Là ci darem la mano' ('There we will give each other our hands') just about sums up Leopold Bloom's hopes for the future of his marriage.

In 'Calypso', we see the Blooms' relationship from Leopold's angle. He is prudent and solicitous, while Molly is earthy and impatient. He yearns to 'Be near her ample bedwarmed flesh' and delights in the fact that 'The warmth of her couched body rose on the air, mingling with the fragrance of the tea she poured.'

She is more casual about him and, when he offers an elaborate definition of the word 'metempsychosis' she is dismissive. 'O, rocks! she said. Tell us in plain words'. Her reading habits are certainly very different from Stephen Dedalus's, her preferred author being the popular nineteenth-century French novelist Paul de Kock (1793–1871) – 'Nice name he has', as Molly puts it.

When Bloom rushes downstairs to rescue the burning kidney, we leave Molly behind until she resurfaces to tell her own story in the concluding episode of the novel. Her looming infidelity will, however, prey on Bloom's thoughts repeatedly throughout the day, while a number of minor characters will allude to her, usually in unflattering terms.

Back in the kitchen, Bloom enjoys his fried kidney, 'chewing with discernment the toothsome, pliant meat', and reads a letter from his daughter, Milly, who is away working in a photographer's shop in Mullingar, a town in the Irish midlands. Bloom frets about her ripening womanhood. She is, he thinks, 'a wild piece of goods' and a 'pert little piece', which is an odd way for a father to describe his fifteen-year-old daughter, and hints at a complicated relationship between the two. Milly has already been mentioned in the first episode, 'Telemachus', as 'a sweet young thing', the 'photo girl' who had attracted the attention of Buck Mulligan's friend, Bannon.

Milly's letter reveals a bouncy, carefree personality (more like her mother than her father in that respect), enjoying the freedom of living away from home for the first time, attending a concert and going to 'a scrap picnic'. In her letter, Milly mistakenly believes that someone named Boylan had written the song 'Those Lovely Seaside Girls', another of the book's theme songs:

All dimpled cheeks and curls,
Your head it simply swirls.
Those girls, those girls,
Those lovely seaside girls.

Milly adds: 'I was on the pop of writing Blazes Boylan.' Does this unnecessary reference to Boylan suggest that Milly may be quietly aware of her mother's liaison with him?

I know that song well. In Kuala Lumpur in 2004, I formed a makeshift choir that performed it, and other songs from *Ulysses*, on Bloomsday in the atrium of Kuala Lumpur's Petronas Twin Towers during the inaugural Kuala Lumpur International Literary Festival. A memorable experience indeed.

We also learn here about the death of Bloom's son, Rudy, who would have been eleven years old in 1904. Bloom is preoccupied by his lack of a male heir, and we discover that his marriage has not been the same since their son's death. This all contributes to the father-son theme that runs through the novel: Simon and Stephen Dedalus, Leopold and Rudy Bloom, and finally Leopold and Stephen, who eventually, and fleetingly, develop something resembling a father-son bond.

The episode ends with Bloom's visit to the outhouse, where Joyce describes his bowel movements and his reading material, a story called 'Matcham's Masterstroke' in *Titbits*. This gives him the momentary notion of writing a story in this undemanding but lucrative genre, thus echoing Stephen's act of writing a few lines of poetry on Sandymount Strand in Episode 3. There are other parallels between Stephen and Bloom. For instance, we meet them both in their homes: Stephen's a temporary abode to which he will not return, Bloom's a permanent home from which he will be exiled for the rest of the day. Stephen is haunted by the death of his mother, Bloom by that of his son. I could go on, but such cross-referencing, while certainly interesting, is not necessarily germane to understanding the novel, so I will stop there.

Characteristically, Bloom thinks of including Molly in his literary venture by publishing a story as Mr and Mrs L. M. Bloom, and of basing it on one of Molly's sayings. Bloom will probably never write his story, except through the pen of James Joyce in the hundreds of pages that follow this 'Calypso' episode.

The Homeric parallels in this case are less compelling than in the first three episodes. In Homer, the nymph Calypso keeps Odysseus under her control on her island home for seven years. Bloom is clearly under Molly's spell, but does this make Molly Calypso? She also parallels the Homeric hero's wife, Penelope. Is she both wife and goddess? Or does Calypso relate to the picture, the *Bath of the Nymph*, that hangs over their bed and is part of Bloom's fantasy world – 'Naked nymphs: Greece'? This particular nymph will have her say in a later episode.

Bloom cannot escape thoughts of Boylan however. Before he sets out from home for the day, he has a recollection of the first night Molly laid eyes on Boylan, when she asked him 'Is that Boylan well off?' The art ascribed to this episode by Joyce is, after all, economics, and Molly, like her husband, has an eye for the bottom line.

This episode ends as the bells of St George's Church toll for 8.45 a.m. and Bloom leaves his home to begin his wanderings around Dublin, which will take up most of the rest of the book.

EPISODE 5, 'LOTUS EATERS':
Walking into Eternity via Windmill Lane

I AM NOW WRITING

a book based on the wanderings of Ulysses. The *Odyssey*, that is to say, serves me as a ground plan. Only my time is recent time and all my hero's wanderings take no more than eighteen hours.

– James Joyce to his friend
Frank Budgen, in 1918

In 'Proteus', Stephen Dedalus asks himself if he is 'walking into eternity along Sandymount strand'. In the novel's fifth episode, known as 'Lotus Eaters', our down-to-earth walking companion is Leopold Bloom, Joyce's twentieth-century Odysseus (Ulysses, if you recall, is the Latin equivalent of Odysseus). This is where Bloom's Ulyssean wanderings begin in earnest as he takes to the streets of Dublin. If Stephen dazzles (and perplexes) by way of his precocious intelligence, pretentious demeanour, and monumental learning for one so young, Bloom is absorbing on account of his ordinariness. As the literary critic Declan Kiberd has put it, 'By simple actions, such as careful tea-making, thoughtful meat-buying, or sensuous street-strolling, Bloom repossesses on a lazy Edwardian day the lost sacrament of everyday life'.[44] I like that.

Whereas Stephen strolls across the open expanse of a largely empty strand on the shores of Dublin Bay, here we accompany Bloom through the busy streets of Dublin's inner city. In his own unpretentious way, Bloom is also 'walking into eternity', except he's taking the circuitous route, a long and winding road that will occupy him for the remainder of this extended literary day. This must be one of the most sustained and concentrated walks in world literature.

James Joyce once said that 'it had been his hope, when writing *Ulysses* (1922), that it would be possible, in the event of some future cataclysm during which all cities and habitations of men were destroyed, to reconstruct Dublin from the pages of his book'.[45] 'Lotus Eaters' is where we explore for the first time the city Joyce imagined could be reconstructed from those pages. I possess a number of editions of *Ulysses*, including two German translations, but I generally draw on my American edition, first published in 1934, and the Bodley Head edition that first appeared in 1960. This is the text used in the widely available Penguin Classics publication of *Ulysses*. I can especially recommend the Penguin Classics Annotated Student Edition (1992), which includes a fine introduction by Declan Kiberd and 250 pages of helpful notes on the novel's eighteen episodes.

We are able to trace Bloom's journey through Dublin because Joyce gives us plenty of information about his hero's whereabouts, mentioning street names and individual landmarks. This is the first episode of *Ulysses* where it may pay to consult a map of Dublin. For this purpose, I recommend Robert Nicholson's *The Ulysses Guide*, which contains maps charting Bloom's (and Stephen's) movements throughout the day, and has lots of helpful material about the places they visit. Nicholson informs us, for example, that the Blooms' home at Eccles Street, 'the most famous address in world literature', where Joyce's college friend, J. F. Byrne, had once lived, no longer exists. The ground where it stood is now part of Dublin's Mater Hospital.[46]

'Lotus Eaters' is one of the most straightforward of the eighteen episodes of *Ulysses*. It is thoroughly readable, with little here that will befuddle the attentive reader.

Bloom begins his rambles around Dublin as we say in Irish, '*go moch ar maidin*', early in the morning, at 8.45 a.m. to be precise. Why does he leave home so early when his only firm appointment of the day is at 11 a.m.? I use the word 'rambles' advisedly, for there seems to be no overriding purpose to Bloom's day, other than to stay away from home for as long as he can, giving lots of latitude to his unfaithful wife. He drifts around Dublin fairly aimlessly, with only his attendance at Paddy Dignam's funeral and an attempt to place an ad in a Dublin newspaper occupying him purposefully.

By the time we catch up with Bloom at around ten o'clock, he has bought a copy of the *Freeman's Journal* newspaper and has crossed to the south side of the River Liffey. We spy him as 'he walked soberly' along Sir John Rogerson's Quay. Sober is as good a word as any to describe Bloom's demeanour. Not only does he resist the temptations of overindulgence, but his view of the world is characterised by prudence and sobriety, albeit with occasional flights of restrained fancy. We follow him as he strolls past Windmill Lane (now renowned for its recording studio associated with Ireland's premier rock band, U2) and up towards Great Brunswick Street (now Pearse Street) and on to Westland Row.

The unusual warmth of the day, and his perusal of the teas on display in the window of the Belfast and Oriental Tea Company, prompts in Bloom an oriental rhapsody reminiscent of what we got from him in the previous episode as he walked to his local butcher to buy a kidney for his breakfast:

> The far east. Lovely spot it must be: the garden of the world, big lazy leaves to float about on, cactuses, flowery meads, snaky lianas they call them. Wonder is it like that. Those Cinghalese lobbing about in the sun, in *dolce far niente*. Not doing a hand's turn all day. Sleep six months out of twelve. Too hot to quarrel. Influence of the climate. Lethargy. Flowers of idleness.

James Joyce never ventured outside of Europe (unless we go with the nineteenth-century Austrian Chancellor and Foreign Minister Prince Metternich's view that Asia begins at Vienna's Landstrasse, in which case Trieste, where Joyce lived for more than a decade, would qualify), but he certainly imbued Bloom with an intense interest in the East's exotic qualities.

In the *Odyssey*, Odysseus and his ships arrive in the land of the Lotus Eaters, where they are treated kindly and offered lotus leaves to eat. Odysseus's sailors, who ate 'the honey-sweet fruit of lotus ... wanted to stay there with the lotus-eating people, feeding on lotus and forget the way home'. Odysseus had to force his sailors back to their ships and keep them away from the taste of the lotus. Joyce is clearly suggesting that Dublin is a lethargic place from whose effects Bloom will struggle to escape, just as Joyce did when he left Ireland for Trieste in 1904. But there is another way of looking at what Joyce accomplished with regard to Dublin, and this is how I like to view it: 'Those who read *Ulysses* will know that Joyce was recording not merely the Dublin of 16 June 1904, but the quality of Dublin that survives through everchanging forms.'[47]

We accompany Bloom to a post office, where he picks up a letter from Martha Clifford, with whom, under the pen name of Henry Flower (his father's birth name was Virag, 'flower' in Hungarian), he is conducting a clandestine correspondence, thus going some way towards matching Molly's infidelity with Blazes Boylan, something that is never far from Bloom's thoughts. 'Queen was in her bedroom eating bread and. No book. Blackened court cards laid along her thigh by sevens. Dark lady and fair man. Cat furry black ball. Torn strip of envelope'.

Bloom is exceptionally furtive about his correspondence with Martha, and waits to find an out-of-the-way place near the Westland Row railway station where he can quietly savour her letter. Its contents are comparatively innocent – 'Please write me a long letter and tell me more. Remember if you do not I will punish you. So now you know what I will do to you, you naughty boy, if you do not write' – but they clearly titillate Bloom. Martha wants to meet him but he appears to have no intention of doing so for, with his practical streak, he recognises the downsides of a real-life affair. 'Thank you: not having any. Usual love scrimmage. Then running round corners. Bad as a row with Molly.' No matter what the context, Bloom's thoughts invariably come back to Molly.

But he does draw satisfaction from his exchanges with Martha, and resolves to 'Go further next time. Naughty boy: punish: afraid of words, of course. Brutal, why not? Try it anyhow. A bit at a time.' Then, as he examines her letter again, we find him 'murmuring here and there a word. ... Weak joy opened his lips.' Bloom's urges are, it seems, quite easily and inoffensively gratified.

He strays into a church on Westland Row, where we are treated to the novel's first really extended 'interior monologue', as Bloom muses about religion and the Catholic Church. Called All Hallows in the novel, this is actually St Andrew's Church, where two significant Irish writers were baptised, Thomas Moore, famed for his *Irish Melodies*, and the garrulous twentieth-century playwright and novelist, Brendan Behan.

I have walked past this fine building hundreds of times on my way to and from the nearby commuter railway station. I dropped in there during my last visit to Dublin to find that the church's connection with *Ulysses* is highlighted within its nave. This might seem strange given Joyce's religious scepticism and his novel's notoriety, but it reflects the manner in which Joyce and *Ulysses* have come to be seen as a treasured part of Dublin's cultural patrimony. Even those who may never choose to read it are prepared to show respect for Joyce's achievement and his fame.

As he observes the congregation receiving communion, Bloom – who is a baptised Catholic, but evidently an unobservant one – is intrigued: 'Good idea the Latin. Stupefies them first. Hospice for the dying. They don't seem to chew it: only swallow it down. Rum idea: eating bits of a corpse.' With his characteristic regard for economic success, Bloom expresses admiration for the church's institutional ingenuity and its financial acumen: 'Squareheaded chaps those must be in Rome: they work the whole show. And don't they rake in the money too?' He also puzzles about the fact that James Carey (he can't quite remember his first name), a member of the Irish National Invincibles, received daily communion there while plotting the murder of the Chief Secretary. His conclusion is that those 'crawthumpers', as he calls them, are 'shiftylooking'. 'They're not straight men of business either', which for Bloom is akin to the ultimate putdown.

As a not very successful advertising salesman, Bloom often shows a keen interest in money-making, as he does here when he marvels about the earning power of the Guinness family: 'Shows you the money to be made out of porter … A million pounds, wait a moment. Twopence a pint, fourpence a quart, eightpence a gallon of porter, no, one and fourpence a gallon of porter. One and four into twenty: fifteen about. Yes, exactly. Fifteen millions of barrels of porter.' As we all do, Bloom gets his mental arithmetic jumbled, mixing up barrels with gallons, but he does correct himself, as some of us don't!

Bloom's visit to Sweny's pharmacy on Lincoln Place to order a skincare preparation for Molly has left a delightful legacy in today's Dublin. On a recent visit to Dublin, I popped into Sweny's and met the people there who have turned the premises into a shrine to James Joyce. It still has the look and feel of an early twentieth-century pharmacy, but is filled with books and Joyce memorabilia. They host regular readings of Joyce's work, and I was able to buy a bar of the same soap Bloom picked up there fictionally in 1904. The bar of soap that Bloom procures will be mentioned several more times in the episodes that follow. It will even find its voice in the surreal 'Circe' episode.

As he leaves Sweny's pharmacy, Bloom has casual encounters with two typical Dubliners: C. P. McCoy and

Bantam Lyons. His conversations with McCoy and Lyons highlight how out of sync Bloom is with many of those he encounters during his wanderings around Dublin. Usually tolerant in outlook, here Bloom is impatient and irascible, although he exhibits a surface politeness. He has no time for either man. McCoy irritates him when he tries to compare his wife's singing career with Molly's. Bloom is having none of it. Fanny McCoy is a 'Reedy freckled soprano. Cheeseparing nose. Nice enough in its way: for a little ballad. No guts in it.' In his eyes, there's no-one like Molly. Never is. We will discover in the novel's final episode that Molly shares her husband's negative appreciation of Mrs McCoy's singing.

As Bloom engages in an inconsequential exchange with McCoy, his attention is stirred by a woman boarding a carriage across the street: 'Off to the country: Broadstone probably. High brown boots with laces dangling. Wellturned foot.... Sees me looking. Eye out for other fellow always. Good fallback. Two strings to her bow.' In your dreams, Mr Bloom! He is frustrated when his view of her is blocked just as she is about to climb aboard her carriage and, he had hoped, reveal some of her silk-stockinged legs.

Bloom has even less time for Bantam Lyons than for McCoy. 'He sped off towards Conway's corner. God speed scut.' This character, based on Frederick Lyons (1858–1908), would have been remembered by some of his fellow citizens when *Ulysses* was published in 1922. Joyce's habit of inserting recognisable individuals into his work was one of the reasons why his first book, *Dubliners*, took him a decade to have published on account of the sensitivities of local publishers and printers, and their fear of litigation by those in Joyce's stories who could be readily identified. As *Ulysses* was published in Paris, such local sensitivities did not apply, and in any event, there were far more formidable allegations levelled against *Ulysses*.

Bloom's brief conversation with Bantam Lyons turns out to be more consequential than he or we might expect, for it resonates strongly in a later episode. Lyons asks to consult Bloom's newspaper for information about that day's Ascot Gold Cup. This prompts Bloom to reflect disapprovingly on his fellow Dubliners' zeal for betting. 'Regular hotbed of it lately. Messenger boys stealing to put on sixpence.'

When Bloom offers to give Lyons the paper and explains that he was about to throw it away, Lyons takes this to be a cryptic tip for a horse called Throwaway, which went on to win that afternoon's Gold Cup. Most Dubliners seem to have wagered on more fancied horses, whereas Throwaway was a 20/1 outsider. The mistaken notion that Bloom had predicted the winner of the race, but had kept his good fortune quiet, earns him the animosity of those who will gather in Barney Kiernan's pub later in the day as captured in the 'Cyclops' episode.

'Lotus Eaters' concludes with one of Bloom's characteristic raptures, mixing the epicurean with the erotic, this time at the prospect of taking a Turkish bath:

He foresaw his pale body reclined in it at full, naked, in a womb of warmth, oiled by scented melting soap, softly laved. He saw his trunk and

limbs riprippled over and sustained, buoyed lightly
upward, lemonyellow: his navel, bud of flesh: and
saw the dark tangled curls of his bush floating,
floating hair of the stream around the limp father
of thousands, a languid floating flower.

The organ Joyce associated with this episode was 'the
genitals' and, intriguingly, he described the technique
he employed as 'narcissism'. Whose? Considering his
determination to explore every aspect of Bloom's day,
it seems odd that Joyce chooses not to have us eaves-
drop on his sojourn at the Turkish and Warm Baths on
Leinster Street. Instead, we skip forward to Bloom's 11
a.m. engagement attending Paddy Dignam's funeral.

Bloom's character is based in part on a Dubliner,
Alfred Hunter, who in 1904 came to Joyce's aid following an altercation during which Joyce was knocked to
the ground. Joyce never forgot this momentary kind-
ness, and planned to write a short story about Hunter, an
idea that developed into the mammoth that is *Ulysses*.
Hunter inspired him to create the kindly Leopold
Bloom, whom we see in this episode doing everyday
things: collecting mail, talking to acquaintances, visiting
a church and buying soap. We learn about his secretive
nature, his religious scepticism and his aloofness from
the daily life of the city in which he lives. Most of all, we
extend our acquaintance with the richly embroidered
texture of this ordinary man's consciousness, crammed
as it is with a combination of workaday preoccupations,
quirkiness and rich imaginings. Joyce himself summed
up his approach thus: 'In *Ulysses*, I have recorded,

simultaneously, what a man says, sees, thinks, and what such seeing, thinking, saying does, to what you Freudians call the subconscious.'[48] That about sums it up. On we go now to our graveyard chapter, one with an atmosphere that is far from funereal.

EPISODE 6, 'HADES':
All the Living and the Dead

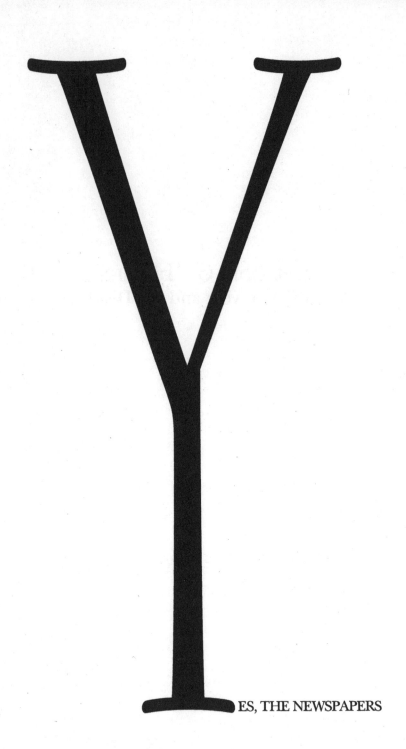

ES, THE NEWSPAPERS

were right: snow was general all over Ireland....
It lay thickly drifted on the crooked crosses and
headstones, on the spears of the little gate, on
the barren thorns. His soul swooned slowly as he
heard the snow falling faintly through the uni-
verse and faintly falling, like the descent of their
last end, upon all the living and the dead.

             – James Joyce, 'The Dead'

While reading Episode 6 of *Ulysses*, known as 'Hades', I find it hard to keep James Joyce's best-known short story, 'The Dead', out of my mind, and especially its closing passage, containing lines that are among the finest in all of modern English literature. That, I suppose, is reason enough for me to want to quote them as I have done above. But there is also a true rationale for doing so at this time, for in this episode we are indeed in the terri-tory of the dead, at Dublin's Glasnevin Cemetery. We are also firmly in the hands of the living, notably those of Leopold Bloom, with his undaunted love of life in all of its imperfect, quotidian splendour.

'Hades', though it is longer than its predecessors, is not an intimidating read. In fact, it's a lively, enter-taining piece of writing, whose style is descriptive and conversational, with a lot of sharp dialogue. This is probably one of the parts of his novel Joyce had in mind when he said about *Ulysses* that: 'They are all there, the great talkers, they and the things they forgot.' The characters in this episode are indeed lively talkers. It also has its fine flourishes, as Bloom's visit to Glasnevin draws from him some homespun ruminations wrapped in graveyard humour.

Throughout this book, I like to quote choice lines from *Ulysses*, and there are plenty of them. I do this as a way of giving my readers, some of whom may never read him, a taste of Joyce's prose. This chapter will have quite a few quotations from *Ulysses*, and that is because the 'Hades' episode is rich in quotable passages.

Joyce's decision to devote an entire chapter of his novel to a funeral was a daring one. It reflects his determination to engage with the world around him in all of its dimensions. In this episode he looks life and death in the face with unflinching candour. Ultimately, life wins out.

'Hades' centres round the burial of Paddy Dignam, who was 'as decent a little man as ever wore a hat'. It sparkles with animated conversation as we accompany Bloom and three fellow mourners – Martin Cunningham, Jack Power and a sharp-tongued Simon Dedalus – on a carriage ride from Sandymount to Glasnevin. Traversing the streets of Dublin, we learn that Dignam's demise, which was a sudden one, 'the best death', in Bloom's estimation, may have been caused by habits of over-indulgence, 'many a good man's fault', according to Simon Dedalus (himself included, no doubt). Displaying his considerate, practical streak, Bloom wonders if Dignam was insured.

On this journey, we hear more about the death in infancy of Bloom's son, Rudy, and how heavily this still weighs on him. Bloom muses about what it would have been like to 'see him grow up. Hear his voice in the house ... My son. Me in his eyes.' He believes that he 'could have helped him on in life. I could. Make him independent. Learn German too.' As a former ambassador to

Germany, I can heartily approve of that ambition. For Bloom, his daughter, Milly, is Molly 'watered down'. She's 'a dear girl. Soon be a woman'. These are the kind of thoughts that every father can probably remember having about a daughter on the verge of womanhood.

This episode could be called 'fathers and sons', for, on top of Bloom's pining after his lost son, we are given an insight into Stephen's relationship with his father, Simon Dedalus, who worries about the 'lowdown crowd' Stephen mixes with, and is especially dubious about Buck Mulligan, whom he sees as a bad influence on his son. By Bloom's reckoning, Dedalus is 'a noisy selfwilled man'. That he is for sure, but he is also one of the outstanding lesser characters in *Ulysses*.

We get a good glimpse of Simon Dedalus's biting repartee. He sees Buck Mulligan as 'a contaminated bloody doubledyed ruffian by all accounts. His name stinks all over Dublin ... I'll tickle his catastrophe believe you me.' Joyce took the latter phrase from Shakespeare's *Henry IV, Part 2*. Dedalus possesses an entertaining turn of phrase, as when he describes the weather as being 'as uncertain as a child's bottom'.

Simon Dedalus is based on Joyce's own father, John Stanislaus Joyce. His biographers describe the elder Joyce as 'a good companion, a relisher and raconteur of life, a font of humour, a blasphemer, a drinker of mythological stature',[49] while his own son saw him, among other things, as 'a praiser of his own past'. Yet, after his father's death, Joyce told Harriet Weaver that: 'I was fond of him always, being a sinner myself and even liked his faults.' Joyce freely admitted that his father had helped shape his work: 'the humour of *Ulysses* is his; its people are his friends; the book is his spittin' image'.[50] As Colm Tóibín puts it, in his study of the fathers of Wilde, Yeats and Joyce, 'In his work, James Joyce sought to recreate his father, reimagine him, fully invoke him, live in his world, while making sure that from the age of twenty-two ... he did not see him much.'[51] Exile had its uses for James Joyce. It removed him from the pull of Ireland, and also from the dubious influence of his errant, potentially overbearing father.

We also get more information during the carriage journey on the suicide of Bloom's father, who ended his life in a hotel in County Clare. He died by poisoning and left his son a farewell letter requesting that he look after the deceased's dog! Here too we are offered a glimpse of how Molly is seen by others; in this instance by solicitor John Henry Menton, a real-life Dubliner who died a decade before Joyce sat down to write *Ulysses*: 'She was a finelooking woman. I danced with her, wait, fifteen seventeen golden years ago, at Mat Dillon's in Roundtown. And a good armful she was.'

Notably, Joyce also reveals to us the manner in which Bloom is resented by some of his fellow Dubliners on account of his aloof manner and his unusual background. Bloom's identity is a complex compound, Dublin-born, with a Hungarian Jewish father who became a Protestant, and an Irish-born mother whose own father was also an immigrant. Bloom became a Catholic when he married Molly, but most of those he meets around Dublin see him as a Jew (as he himself sometimes does). This theme of Bloom's alienation from the city in which he lives is an important one that will recur in subsequent episodes. Menton wonders how Molly ended up marrying someone like Bloom, remembering that 'she had plenty of game in her' when he knew her. Ned Lambert pipes in with the view that she 'has still', which hints that he may know about her liaison with Boylan, who was probably not the sort of man to keep such things to himself.

Bloom's companions are all quick-witted Dubliners, well able to turn out a sharp, idiomatic phrase ('he's dead nuts on that' – Power; 'the devil break the hasp of your back' – Dedalus; and 'Reuben and son were piking it down the quay' – Cunningham). By contrast, Bloom is ponderous and long-winded. He botches a story he tries to tell about a moneylender, Reuben J. Dodd, whose son jumped into the Liffey and had to be fished out by a boatman, for which his father paid him a Florin (two shillings). This was one and eight pence too much, in Dedalus's acerbic opinion! Martin Cunningham steps in to tell the same tale more pithily.

The mourners' passage through Dublin is vividly described: 'The carriage, passing the open drains and mounds of rippedup roadway before the tenement houses, lurched round the corner and, swerving back to the tramtrack, rolled on noisily with chattering wheels.'

And there is the usual Joycean attention to detail as various roads and landmarks are noted. The carriage passes the house 'where Childs was murdered'. This refers to a notorious Dublin murder case from 1899 in which the seventeen-year-old Joyce had taken an active interest, attending all three days of the trial of Samuel Childs for the brutal murder of his brother, Thomas, for which Childs was acquitted. The late Justice Adrian Hardiman, a former member of Ireland's Supreme Court, has written about the Childs case in his book,

Joyce in Court: James Joyce and the Law, in which he makes the point that thirty-two legal cases are featured in *Ulysses*, none more often than the Childs case, which, he calculates, is referred to more than twenty times.

As the uncomfortable carriage ('Corny might have given us a more commodious yoke') makes its way to Glasnevin Cemetery, various people are spotted on the street, including Blazes Boylan, who is out 'airing his quiff'. This naturally makes Bloom uncomfortable knowing that Boylan is destined to cuckold him before the day is out.

Continuing his obsession with his wife's plans for the day, Bloom wonders why Molly is drawn to Boylan: 'Is there anything more in him that they she sees? Fascination. Worst man in Dublin. That keeps him alive. They sometimes feel what a person is. Instinct. But a type like that.'

The conversation runs on in a lively vein when the mourners reach Glasnevin.

How are you, Simon? Ned Lambert said softly, clasping hands. Haven't seen you for a month of Sundays.
— Never better. How are all in Cork's own town?
— I was down there for the Cork park races on Easter Monday, Ned Lambert said. Same old six and eightpence. Stopped with Dick Tivy.
— And how is Dick, the solid man?
— Nothing between himself and heaven, Ned Lambert answered.
— By the holy Paul! Mr Dedalus said in subdued wonder. Dick Tivy bald?

At Glasnevin we are treated to some grimly humorous musings on Bloom's part. As his carriage arrives at the cemetery, this is what runs through his head:

> Coffin now. Got here before us, dead as he is. Horse looking round at it with his plume skeow-ways. Dull eye: collar tight on his neck, pressing on a bloodvessel or something. Do they know what they cart out here every day? Must be twenty or thirty funerals every day. Then Mount Jerome for the protestants. Funerals all over the world everywhere every minute. Shovelling them under by the cartload doublequick. Thousands every hour. Too many in the world.

The sight of the priest receiving the hearse sets Bloom's mind racing. As in the 'Lotus Eaters', he shows a cavalier disdain for the Catholic Church, of which he is nominally a member: 'Father Coffey. I knew his name was like a coffin. *Dominenamine*. Bully about the muzzle he looks. Bosses the show. Muscular christian. Woe betide anyone that looks crooked at him: priest. Thou art Peter. Burst sideways like a sheep in clover Dedalus says he will. With a belly on him like a poisoned pup.' Great stuff! Straight from the lexicon of John Stanislaus Joyce, I imagine.

Bloom has no time for the consoling sentiments expressed at funerals that are designed to touch our hearts: 'Your heart perhaps but what price the fellow in the six feet by two with his toes to the daisies? No touching that. Seat of the affections. Broken heart. A pump after all, pumping thousands of gallons of blood every day. One fine day it gets bunged up: and there you are. Lots of them lying around here: lungs, hearts, livers.'

The cemetery's caretaker, John O'Connell, meets the funeral cortège, and Bloom sympathises with him, wondering 'how he had the gumption to propose to any girl', tempting her to come and live with him in this graveyard! 'Love among the tombstones.' He is impressed when he recalls that O'Connell has eight children.

At this stage, I need to mention one of the great mysteries of *Ulysses*. Who is the 'lankylooking galoot over there in the macintosh?' There are twelve mourners at the funeral, all of whom are named, but then Bloom notices a thirteenth. 'Death's number. Where the deuce did he pop out of?' Bloom would 'give a trifle to know who he is', but we never learn this person's identity. In the newspaper report on the funeral, which we will see later, he is named as McIntosh (maybe that was his name, who knows), while Bloom, to his irritation, is misnamed 'L. Boom'. Why does Joyce dangle this mystery before us? I don't know, and nor does it matter too much, but it's the kind of thing that keeps Joyce enthusiasts on the boil.

After Paddy Dignam is laid to rest, the mourners take note of the graves of two prominent nineteenth-century Irishmen, Daniel O'Connell and Charles Stewart Parnell. For anyone who visits Glasnevin, and it is well worth doing so, O'Connell's resting place is unmissable, for this titan of nineteenth-century Irish politics is entombed inside an Irish round tower. O'Connell, who brought about the first great reform of the British Parliament when he secured Catholic Emancipation in 1829, helped to found the cemetery where he is interred.

While O'Connell does not feature very heavily in Joyce's work, the same cannot be said of Parnell, who is alluded to in *A Portrait of the Artist as a Young Man*, *Dubliners* and in *Ulysses*. John Stanislaus Joyce was a big supporter of Parnell, and he passed this enthusiasm on to his son, who as a nine-year-old had written a poem, 'et tu Healy', taking aim at Parnell's chief detractor within the Irish Party, Tim Healy. Joyce considered that Parnell had been torn to pieces by his erstwhile Irish followers and, with his anti-clerical streak, believed that 'the priests and the priests' pawns broke Parnell's heart and hounded him into his grave'.[52] Parnell also makes repeated appearances in the work of W. B. Yeats.

> The Bishops and the Party
> That tragic story made
> …
> But stories that live longest
> Are sung above the glass,
> And Parnell loved his country
> And Parnell loved his lass.

Parnell's extraordinary political ascent, and the circumstances of his fall from grace, when he was named in a divorce case, clothed him in mystique.

Ulysses is set in 1904, about halfway between the death of Parnell in 1891 and the upheavals of Ireland's revolutionary era in the years after 1916. James Joyce belonged to the generation that engineered Ireland's political transformation, which took place during the years he was busy writing his great novel, 1914–21. Joyce was born just three years after 1916 leader Patrick Pearse

– who tried in vain to teach him Irish – and in the same year as Éamon de Valera, who became the dominant figure in twentieth-century Irish politics. Joyce captured 'the anguished regrets of the bereft Parnellites'[53] as in 1904, when *Ulysses* is set, Parnell's legacy still loomed large. We can see this from Joe Hynes's devotion to him in this 'Hades' episode, and in Joyce's short story, 'Ivy Day at the Committee Room', where Hynes also appears, emotionally reciting a poem in Parnell's memory.

All you need to know about the Homeric parallels in this episode is that Hades is the abode of the dead which Odysseus visits during his journey back to his home in Ithaca. Here Bloom visits Dublin's realm of the dead at Glasnevin. Hades has four rivers, and these are paralleled by the Grand Canal, the Liffey, the Dodder and the Royal Canal, all of which the funeral procession crosses on its way to Glasnevin.

After Bloom's prolonged, often darkly humorous, meditation on death ('Makes them feel more important to be prayed over in Latin'; 'Cremation better. Priests dead against it. Devilling for the other firm'), this episode of *Ulysses* strikes a positive note as he expresses his continued lust for life: 'Back to the world again. Enough of this place. Brings you a bit nearer every time.… Plenty to see and hear and feel yet. Feel live warm beings near you. Let them sleep in their maggoty beds. They are not going to get me this innings. Warm beds: warm fullblooded life.' He never stops thinking of the bed, warmed by Molly, that still belongs to him at home in Eccles Street.

The episode ends on a sour note for Bloom. When he considerately points out to Menton that his hat is a little crushed, Menton responds curtly. Though taken aback by this reaction, Bloom is not dismayed and thinks: 'How grand we are this morning.' Grand (a favourite Irish word), he is indeed, and no amount of funereal philosophising or petty ingratitude will take that away from him.

Yes, despite all the adversities that beset him – his son's death, his father's suicide, his wife's infidelity, his lack of commercial success, the resentment directed at him by his fellow Dubliners – Leopold Bloom is ultimately a life-affirming character, and *Ulysses* a life-affirming novel.

EPISODE *7*, 'AEOLUS':
Blowing in the Winds

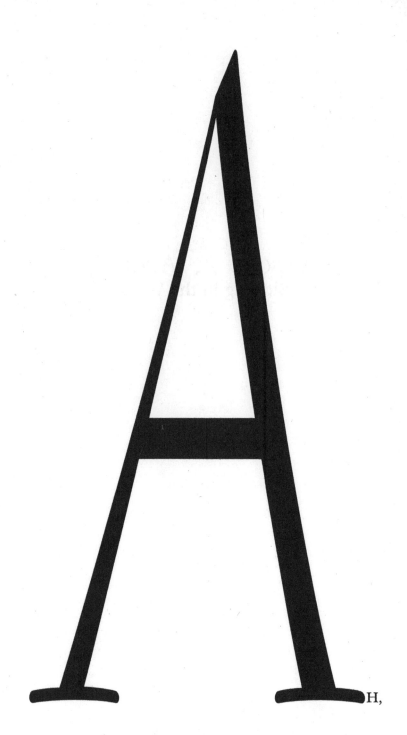

H,

listen to this for God' sake, Ned Lambert pleaded.
Or again if we but climb the serried mountain
peaks ...
— Bombast! the professor broke in testily. Enough
of the inflated windbag!

         – *Ulysses,* 'Aeolus' Episode

Yes, what Joyce enthusiasts and literary scholars refer to as
'Aeolus' is a windy, windbag of an episode, with lots of inflated
language. In this case, the parallel Joyce seeks to draw with
Homer's Odyssey is worth knowing about, because it illumi-
nates the point he was clearly trying to make.

In Greek mythology, Aeolus is the king of storms
and winds, who gave Odysseus an ox-skin bag 'stuffed
full inside with the courses of all the blowing winds'.
This assembly of breezes would help Homer's wanderer
sail safely home to Ithaca. Aeolus's bag of wind worked
wonderfully well until Odysseus's crew, hoping to find
gold inside, opened the bag, at which point 'all the
winds burst out' and 'the storm caught them away and
swept them over the water weeping, away from their own
country'.[54] In this episode of *Ulysses,* the winds are verbal, with Joyce suggesting that many of his characters are
windbags whose pompous rhetoric and aimless repartee
sails Dublin into the doldrums.

As everyone here is blowing in the wind, I could not
help thinking about Bob Dylan's song of that name, an
anthem from my youth. For me, that Bob Dylan song
interacts with the theme of this episode, although the
correspondence is more oblique and, of course, completely unintentional. Leopold Bloom might well ask
how many roads he must walk down before he can

sleep in Molly's warm bed or be accepted as a regular Irishman by his fellow Dubliners. In 'Aeolus' we witness his work as a canvasser for advertisements and see how, despite his innate decency, he is ignored, disregarded or treated shabbily by those he encounters in the course of his day's work.

This episode has been described as 'a forerunner to the book's later stylistic extravagances', and as the place where Joyce's writing 'picks up momentum, complexity and difficulty – along with virtuosity and wonder'.[55] Don't be put off by this. 'Aeolus', for all of its frequently extravagant windiness, is a manageable episode. There are far more daunting challenges to come, but we will get to those in due time.

For the reader, the most striking expression of narrative novelty (or subversion; call it what you will) in these pages is the sprinkling through the text of capitalised, newspaper-style headlines: 'IN THE HEART OF THE HIBERNIAN METROPOLIS', 'HOW A GREAT DAILY ORGAN IS TURNED OUT', 'MEMORABLE BATTLES RECALLED', 'THE CROZIER AND THE PEN', 'LINKS WITH BYGONE DAYS OF YORE', 'ERIN, GREEN GEM OF THE SILVER SEA', 'RAISING THE WIND', etc.

These headlines become more outlandish as the episode progresses – 'DIMINISHED DIGITS PROVE TOO TITILLATING FOR FRISKY FRUMPS. ANNE WIMBLES, FLO WANGLES—YET CAN YOU BLAME THEM?' This feature was inserted by Joyce at a relatively late stage in the composition of *Ulysses*, and the headlines are not essential to understanding this episode. It's as if we are reading a newspaper where, as we know, headlines can be eye-catching and amusing, but the substance is (or ought to be) in the paragraphs that follow. Just as you can choose to ignore headlines, you can also skip over Joyce's CAPITALISED adornments to his text, which serve to break up the episode's dialogue into manageable morsels.

I have a confession to make. Although the 'Aeolus' episode of *Ulysses* was apparently a favourite of James Joyce's, and is beloved of literary critics, it is not one that I like all that much. This may be because, in contrast with the three episodes that precede it, in which Leopold Bloom is omnipresent, here he appears, exits and then returns at the end. The bulk of these pages is populated by Stephen Dedalus, his father Simon and a number of minor characters, Professor MacHugh, J. J. O' Molloy, Ned Lambert, O'Madden Burke and Lenehan et al. For me, that makes this episode less coherent than its predecessors. This, however, is a significant milestone in the novel, for it is where the wanderings of its two main characters, Bloom and Stephen, briefly intersect, although they do not meet until much later in the day.

The action begins at Nelson's Pillar as the Dublin United Tramway Company's timekeeper sets trams on their way to various Dublin suburbs, including Dalkey and Sandymount Tower, two stations between which Stephen must have travelled to get from the school (Episode 2) to Sandymount strand (Episode 3). Nelson's Pillar was Dublin's premier landmark for more than 150 years until it was destroyed by an IRA bomb in March 1966. During my first visits to Dublin with my family as a boy to see the latest Hollywood films, the pillar was always our fallback meeting place, although by then the city's trams had been replaced by double-decker buses.

As ever with Joyce, there is vivid descriptive writing here: 'Grossbooted draymen rolled barrels dullthudding out of Prince's stores and bumped them up on the brewery float.' You can almost feel the thud of the bumping barrels. This episode is also heavy with dialogue, the raciest lines being reserved, as in the 'Hades' episode, for the irrepressible Simon Dedalus: 'Agonising Christ, wouldn't it give you a heartburn on your arse?'

'Aeolus' is set in the offices of the *Freeman's Journal* and the *Evening Telegraph*. Those sister newspapers had been in existence since the 1760s and survived until 1924, by which time dramatic political change in Ireland had rendered their form of Irish nationalism, drawn from the parliamentary struggles of the nineteenth century, somewhat obsolete. In 1904, the *Freeman's Journal*, which had taken Parnell's side in the great parliamentary split of the 1890s, was a supporter of the reunited Irish Party and its leader, John Redmond.

Until now, we have espied Bloom at his home, where we have eavesdropped on his interaction with his wife Molly ('Calypso'). We have accompanied him through the streets of Dublin and into a church ('Lotus Eaters') and have travelled to a funeral in his company ('Hades'). In this case, we get a look at Bloom's professional life as a canvasser for newspaper advertisements, a not especially successful purveyor of 'the gentle art of advertisement'. As the relevant headline puts it, 'WE SEE THE CANVASSER AT WORK', and it's a decidedly unheroic occupation.

Bloom is busy in the newspaper offices trying to place an ad for Alexander Keyes, a wine and spirits merchant, who, as part of the deal, wants his company to get a favourable mention elsewhere in the paper. Aside from those involved with the printing press, no-one in this newspaper office appears to do any work. Talk reigns supreme. Bloom discusses the Keyes ad with the newspaper's real-life foreman, J. P. Nannetti (1851–1915), a man of Italian origin, an Irish nationalist MP at the Westminster parliament, and a future Lord Mayor of Dublin. Bloom muses about him: 'Strange he never saw his real country. Ireland my country.... More Irish than the Irish.' In a sense, Nannetti, with his Italian background, is akin to Bloom, who has Hungarian heritage. Having been elected by the people of Dublin, Nannetti has clearly assimilated more successfully than Bloom, who, whatever he himself thinks, remains something of an outsider in the eyes of his fellow Dubliners.

Bloom's laborious attempt to place the ad and earn his commission (he is essentially a middleman between the advertiser and the newspaper) comes to an unsuccessful end when the *Evening Telegraph*'s editor, Myles Crawford, dismisses Bloom's request, telling him that his client, Alexander Keyes, can 'kiss my royal Irish arse ... Anytime he likes, tell him.' This kind of outburst is foreign to Bloom, who 'stood there weighing the point'. There's not much to weigh there, I would have thought, but Bloom seems undaunted and continues to pursue his unglamorous, uphill chore. When Bloom departs, his walk is mimicked by 'capering newsboys'.

Joyce let it be known that rhetoric is the featured art form in this episode, and that is unmistakably the case. Many of its pages are devoted to a discussion of speeches by some well-known Dublin orators: Dan Dawson (1839–1917), Seymour Bushe (1853–1922), who was the barrister in the Childs' case (which was referred to in the 'Hades' episode) and, most notably, the patriotic orator John F. Taylor (1853–1902). Dawson, who was Lord Mayor of Dublin in the year of Joyce's birth, 1882, is ridiculed for his ludicrously inflated rhetoric: '*As 'twere in the peerless panorama of Ireland's portfolio, unmatched, despite wellpraised prototypes in other vaunted prize regions, for very beauty, of bosky grove and undulating plain and luscious pastureland of vernal green, steeped in the transcendent translucent glow of our mild mysterious Irish twilight ...*' Characteristically, Simon Dedalus is unimpressed with Dawson's bombast, and wonders if he is 'taking anything for it?'

Taylor was, it would seem, an altogether different class of speechmaker. J. J. O'Molloy quotes at length a speech Taylor delivered in October 1901 during a debate on the revival of the Irish language. Taylor's address was notable enough to be published as a pamphlet two years later. Drawing unmistakable parallels with Ireland's political predicament, Taylor recalls the struggles of the ancient Jewish people in the face of the might of imperial Egypt. He quotes an Egyptian high priest who derides the Jewish people: '*You are a tribe of nomad herdsmen: we are a mighty people ... You have but emerged from primitive conditions: we have a literature, a priesthood, an agelong history and a polity.*'

But Taylor turns the tables on those who would dismiss the Jewish and Irish struggles: '*had the youthful Moses listened to and accepted that view of life ... He would never have spoken with the Eternal amid lightnings on Sinai's mountaintop nor ever have come with the light of inspiration shining in his countenance and bearing in his arms the tables of the law, graven in the language of the outlaw.'* Remember that Joyce once described *Ulysses* as an epic of two races, the Irish and the Israelites.

Remarkably, W. B. Yeats, in his *Autobiographies*, also quotes from the same speech of Taylor's. Like Yeats, Taylor was part of the circle of veteran Fenian John O'Leary. They did not always see eye to eye, but Yeats acknowledged that he was no match for Taylor with the spoken word.

Professor MacHugh compares the Irish with the Greeks. He sees Greek as 'the language of the mind'. As for the Irish, 'We are liege subjects of the catholic chivalry of Europe that foundered at Trafalgar and of the empire of the spirit, not an *imperium*, that went under with the Athenian fleets at Aegospotami.' Such are the consolations of a subject people, 'always loyal to lost causes'. Joyce appears to be suggesting that this kind of sentimental tomfoolery will not cut the mustard in the twentieth century.

When Stephen arrives in the newspaper offices, he gets a decidedly warmer welcome than Bloom had received. Stephen had come in to pass on the letter on foot and mouth disease given to him by the headmaster, Garrett Deasy, in Episode 2. As they are written in the margins of Deasy's letter, we finally see the lines of verse that Stephen had jotted down during his walk along Sandymount Strand. They are unexceptional, not far removed from the style of the Celtic revival, of which Joyce and Stephen disapproved:

On swift sail flaming
From storm and south
He comes, pale vampire,
Mouth to my mouth.

Joyce's poetry tended to be far more conventional than his prose, where he set out to stretch the boundaries of the English language.

    Evening Telegraph editor Myles Crawford, a character based on Waterford-born journalist and editor, Patrick Meade (1858–1928),[56] takes the part here of Aeolus, the god of winds, presiding over this feast of rhetoric. Crawford is an experienced journalist who reminisces about the greatest scoop of his time, when Ignatius Gallaher (a fictional character who also appears in Joyce's *Dubliners*) allegedly provided the *New York Post* with the first account of the Phoenix Park murders of 1882 (Crawford, or Joyce, gets the year wrong). References to this notorious historical event run through *Ulysses.* We learn here that Skin-the-Goat Fitzharris, who drove the perpetrators away from the assassination scene, may be running a cabman's shelter in Dublin. Joyce will come back to that nugget of information in Episode 16.

    Crawford agrees to publish Deasy's letter, even though he regards him as an 'old pelters' and his wife, 'The bloodiest old tartar God ever made'. The editor also wants Stephen to write for the paper, 'Something with a bite in it'. Stephen, who has literary ambitions that go well beyond writing for the *Evening Telegraph*, was not likely to be lured into a career in Dublin journalism, of which the 'Aeolus' episode presents an unflattering picture. Joyce inserts a reference to Gabriel Conroy's literary work for the *Dublin Daily Express*. Readers of *Dubliners* will remember Conroy as the main character in Joyce's great short story, 'The Dead'. I have always thought of Conroy as Joyce's image of what he could have become had he remained in Ireland instead of moving to Trieste in 1904.

George Russell (Æ) surfaces in this episode when J. J. O'Molloy poses Stephen a question: 'What do you think really of that hermetic crowd, the opal hush poets: A. E. the mastermystic? That Blavatsky woman started it. She was a nice old bag of tricks.' Æ, a well-known Irish figure in the first third of the twentieth century – poet, painter, newspaper editor – will pop up in person in the next two episodes. Russian philosopher, Helena Blavatsky, was a leading purveyor of theosophy, a late-nineteenth-century movement that attempted a synthesis of science, religion and philosophy. Although Æ tried to be helpful to the young Joyce, in *Ulysses* he is subjected to some gentle ribbing. Æ made his most substantial impact on Ireland not as a painter or a poet-mystic but as a public figure and political commentator.[57] He was unrelenting in his engagement with Irish public life for the first three decades of the twentieth century. It was Æ's somewhat eccentric character and his mystical poetry, rather than his impact on the Ireland of his time, that caught Joyce's (and Stephen's) fancy.

In Homer, the winds provided by Aeolus were intended to steer Odysseus and his crew back home to Ithaca. Joyce's Aeolian winds are of a different stripe. They steer the crew from the *Freeman's Journal* not homewards, but to the nearby Mooney's pub. Heroism is not what it used to be in classical times!

As this exodus passes Nelson's Pillar, Stephen tells a rambling, inconsequential story about two Dublin women buying meat and plums, and eating them at the top of the pillar while tossing the stones down to the pavement below. It is hard to know what to make of this story. It provides a hint that Stephen, for all of his evident intelligence and wealth of scholarship, may not have the storytelling flair of some of his less-gifted contemporaries. Like Bloom, but for different reasons, he is also a bit of an exile from the mores of early-twentieth-century Dublin.

Through 'Aeolus', Joyce evidently wishes to imply that this bastion of journalism and moderate Irish nationalism, the offices of the *Freeman's Journal*, is plagued by the winds of empty rhetoric, endless conversation and ultimately inaction. After being buffeted by a storm of words, it is time for more food for thought in 'Lestrygonians'.

EPISODE 8, 'LESTRYGONIANS':
Food for Thought and a Moral Pub

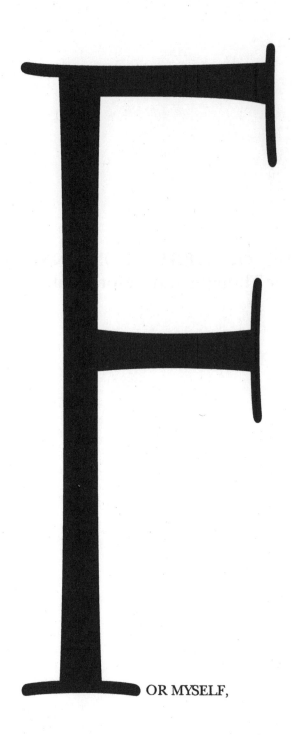

FOR MYSELF,

> I always write about Dublin, because if I can get
> to the heart of Dublin I can get to the heart of all
> the cities of the world.
>
> – James Joyce[58]

James Joyce said he wanted to get to 'the heart of Dublin'. In the eighth episode of *Ulysses*, the streets of Dublin are definitely at the heart of things. This enjoyable chapter is full of fine writing as we follow Leopold Bloom, getting his impressions of the life around him as he walks from what is now O'Connell Street through some of Dublin's best-known streets to the National Museum of Ireland on Kildare Street. 'The voice of each man's inner spirit' is how John Butler Yeats, W. B.'s father, described what Joyce had conjured up when he created Bloom. Yeats senior believed that Joyce wrote with a 'terrible veracity, naked and unashamed', and insisted that 'no place needs him more than Dublin'.[59] In this episode, we again see Bloom doing very ordinary things, such as buying a cake for a penny and using it to feed the gulls on the River Liffey. He muses that you get no thanks for this, 'not even a caw', and casually wonders what swan meat tastes like. After all, 'Robinson Crusoe had to live on them'. Where did that random thought come from? Some inner receptacle of the mind, I suppose. The reason Bloom is such a compelling character is because we recognise bits of ourselves in some of his stray notions.

Although these pages are tame by today's standards, when first published they attracted the attention of the censors. When the 'Lestrygonians' episode of *Ulysses* appeared in *The Little Review* in January 1919, the publication was confiscated by the United States Post Office.

The subsequent edition containing the 'Scylla and Charybdis' episode met the same fate. The publication in July–August 1920 of the 'Cyclops' episode resulted in the publishers of the magazine being brought to trial for obscenity in 1921.[60]

During my assignment in London, I gained an insight into the strict censorship that for a time blocked *Ulysses* from expanding its readership. It was during a visit to the British Postal Museum and Archive in 2014 that I was shown a first edition of *Ulysses* that had been confiscated by the Post Office during the 1920s. This was copy number 895 from the 1,000 copies that were published in Paris in February 1922. With the book, I found a piece of paper with the address 'Jacob Schwartz, Bookseller, 20 Bloomsbury Street' as part of a note stating that 'James Joyce Ulysses 1922' had been sold to the 'Ulysses Bookshop' at a price of £3.0.0.

What made this impounded volume all the more fascinating was a business card I found in the book belonging to David Byrne, 21 Duke Street, Dublin. Yes, that's the very person who features in this episode of *Ulysses:* 'He entered Davy Byrne's. Moral pub. He doesn't chat. Stands a drink now and then.' Could it be that Davy Byrne sold his first edition of *Ulysses* to a London book dealer? It certainly looks that way, but where did Davy Byrne acquire his copy, as the book would have been difficult to come by in Ireland during the 1920s? Did Joyce send it to him? Byrne, whose pub on Duke Street was frequented by such figures as Joyce, Michael Collins, Arthur Griffith, Tom Kettle and painter William Orpen, has been described as 'one of the outstanding characters of his time'.[61]

In Homer, the Lestrygonians were cannibals who devour most of Odysseus's men. There is a lot of devouring going on here, and Joyce even inserts a mention of cannibals eating a white missionary: 'expect the chief consumes the parts of honour'. This random musing is brought on by seeing tinned meat on a shelf. 'What is home without Plumtree's potted meat?' This sight elicits from Bloom a fine pun: 'Ham and his descendants mustered and bred there'. Such is the eccentric drift of Bloom's thoughts.

There are lots of references to food and eating, right from the very start: 'Pineapple rock, lemon platt, butter scotch. A sugarsticky girl shovelling scoopfuls of creams for a christian brother. Some school treat. Bad for their tummies.' As Bloom rambles along with lunchtime looming, he is gnawed by hunger and thinking of food. When he looks into the Burton Restaurant on Duke Street, Joyce goes into overdrive with his description of the dubious eating habits witnessed there:

'Stink gripped his trembling breath: pungent meatjuice, slop of greens. See the animals feed.... A man with an infant's saucestained napkin tucked round him shovelled gurgling soup down his gullet. A man spitting back on his plate: half-masticated gristle: no teeth to chewchewchew it.... Bitten off more than he can chew. Am I like that? See ourselves as others see us. Hungry man is an angry man'.

There is reference to St Patrick converting the king of Ireland to Christianity, but he 'couldn't swallow it all however'. Enough. I've had my fill.

Bloom encounters a diverse group of Dubliners. The first is the misfortunate Mrs Josie Breen, with whom, we will discover later, Bloom has a history. She's what you might call an old flame of his. Now she is worn out looking after her eccentric husband, Denis, whom she describes as 'a caution to rattlesnakes'. He is frantically looking to take legal action against whomever it was that sent him a card with the letters 'U. P.' written on it. He is looking for £10,000 in damages, an outlandish sum in early twentieth-century Ireland. We are never told the significance of those letters, if any, but Bloom is of the view that the card was written 'for a lark' by Alf Bergan or Richie Goulding, two minor characters who will reappear later in the novel. We are also introduced to a noted Dublin eccentric, Cashel Boyle O'Connor Fitzmaurice Tisdall Farrell – one of whose affectations is to walk outside of street lamp posts – and to a blind boy that Bloom courteously helps to cross the street. In their different ways, these individuals have been eaten up by the city in which they live.

As Bloom approaches O'Connell Bridge, he casts a glance down Bachelor's Walk and spots one of Simon Dedalus's daughters outside Dillon's auction rooms, where her father is apparently selling off family furniture in an effort to make ends meet. This prompts Bloom to reflect on the poverty of the Dedalus family and, in tune with his anti-clerical streak, to pour scorn on the church's attitudes towards procreation – and food!:

Fifteen children he had. Birth every year almost.
That's in their theology or the priest won't give
the poor woman the confession, the absolution.

Increase and multiply. Did you ever hear such an idea? Eat you out of house and home. No families themselves to feed. Living on the fat of the land. Their butteries and larders. I'd like to see them do the black fast Yom Kippur. Crossbuns. One meal and a collation for fear he'd collapse on the altar.... All for number one.

Two characters from Irish public life are spied by Bloom during his wanderings: John Howard Parnell and the poet-mystic George Russell (Æ). John Parnell (1843–1923) had a short and undistinguished career in public life as a Westminster MP for five years. In 1904, Parnell was Honorary City Marshal of Dublin. Bloom notices 'the woebegone walk of him. Eaten a bad egg. Poached eyes on ghost.... That's the fascination: the name. All a bit touched.' Joyce's interest in him had to do with his brother, Charles Stewart Parnell, whose importance to Joyce I have already explained in the chapter on 'Hades'.

Early enthusiasts for Joyce's work tended to see him in a European context, with his Irishness as merely an accident of birth, an awkward oddity almost. His French friend Valery Larbaud said that, through *Ulysses*, Ireland was 'making a sensational re-entrance into high European literature'.[62] In those early days of Joyce scholarship, the Irish identity of his work was somewhat played down. As a historian and an Irish diplomat, I tend to play up Joyce's Irish identity. Joyce's first biographer, who was guided by Joyce himself, put his undying attachment to his home place thus: 'As a matter of fact, he had never left Dublin; he carried it about with him wherever he went, in his heart in his brain, in nostalgic returns of the mind; now existing vicariously in it, he could, miraculously enough, stand aside from it and observe it with a calm clinical eye.'[63] I am adamant that *Ulysses* is *both* an Irish and a European novel. Those two identities are intrinsic to Joyce's work, and are interdependent.

Joyce was perceptive in his analysis of Parnell's political achievement. Thus, in a commentary published in 1912 in *Il Piccolo della Sera,* an Italian-language newspaper in Trieste, Joyce accurately observed that Parnell 'united every element of national life behind him and set out on a march along the borders of insurrection'. Parnell's impressive political skills ultimately persuaded Gladstone and his Liberal Party to support Home Rule for Ireland. In his Trieste piece, Joyce caustically observed that the Irish people did not throw Parnell 'to the English wolves: they tore him apart themselves'. Thus, for Joyce, a connoisseur of betrayal, Parnell was the lost leader who had been callously spurned by the Ireland from which Joyce had voluntarily exiled himself.

Æ – George Russell – who has already been mentioned in the 'Aeolus' episode, edited the Irish Agricultural Organisation Society's journal, *The Irish Homestead*, where he published Joyce's first short stories, which later became part of *Dubliners*. In this episode, Joyce persists with his gentle mockery of Russell as Bloom spots him on his bicycle and wonders what Æ stands for. 'Albert Edward, Arthur Edmund, Alphonsus Eb Ed El Esquire'. Then Bloom, plugging into the culinary theme running through this episode, speculates about the origins of Æ's 'Dreamy, cloudy, symbolistic' poetry, and suggests it might have something to do with his vegetarianism. 'I wouldn't be surprised if it was that kind of food you see produces the like waves of the brain the poetical. For example one of those policemen sweating Irish stew into their shirts you couldn't squeeze a line of poetry out of him.'

Although Bloom possesses a detached, sceptical cast of mind, he is fully plugged into the political currents of early twentieth-century Ireland. He conjures up the image of Sinn Féin's founder, Arthur Griffith, as 'a squareheaded fellow but he has no go in him for the mob'. In 1904, Griffith was a dogged polemicist, arguing for Irish abstention from the Westminster parliament and an Austro-Hungarian-style dual monarchy for Britain and Ireland. By the time *Ulysses* was published in February 1922, however, he was President of Dáil Éireann, the parliament of the nascent Irish Free State.

Walking past Trinity College, Bloom passes the statue of nineteenth-century romantic poet Thomas Moore, and thinks how appropriate it is that he has been placed above a public urinal, for Moore, after all, had written 'The Meeting of the Waters'.

Bloom recalls the day he got caught up in a riot after British Government Minister and Home Rule opponent Joseph Chamberlain had been conferred with an honorary degree by Trinity College Dublin. Bloom speculates that some of those 'young cubs yelling their guts out' in support of the Boers would end up as magistrates and civil servants. Irish nationalists were strongly pro-Boer during the turn-of-the-century conflict in South Africa; Chamberlain was a dedicated imperialist.

In this episode, Molly crosses Bloom's mind quite a lot, as she will throughout the rest of the day. He recalls how she can be rude, but witty too, as when she referred to Ben Dollard as 'base barreltone'. He recalls 'people looking after her' during a dinner at Glencree in County Wicklow. The mere sight of a poster advertising pills causes Bloom to worry that Boylan might infect his wife with a venereal disease.

If he ...?
O!
Eh?
No ... No.
No, no. I don't believe it. He wouldn't surely.

Despite her betrayal of him, he spends time examining the window at Brown Thomas's with a mind to buying a present for Molly's birthday. It's almost three months away, 8 September.

In Davy Byrne's 'moral pub', Bloom orders a glass of burgundy and a gorgonzola sandwich, an unusual choice for a Dubliner of that era. He meets Nosey Flynn, a consumer of Guinness and gossip. Flynn mentions Molly's impending concert tour, and with faux innocence asks Bloom 'who's getting it up?' Flynn adds to Bloom's discomfort when he remembers that Blazes Boylan, 'a hairy chap', is involved.

Mellowed by the 'glowing wine' that 'on his palate lingered', Bloom recalls his first amorous encounter with Molly on the hill of Howth years before, a day to which Molly will memorably return in the rapturous closing pages of *Ulysses*:

Touched his sense moistened remembered.
Hidden under wild ferns on Howth. Below us

bay sleeping: sky. No sound. The sky.... Ravished over her I lay, full lips full open, kissed her mouth. Yum. Softly she gave me in my mouth the seedcake warm and chewed. Mawkish pulp her mouth had mumbled sweet and sour with spittle. Joy: I ate it: joy.

Yes, this was the passage that bothered the American censors in 1919!

When Bloom is no longer present, Nosey Flynn remembers seeing him coming out of 'that Irish farm dairy John Wyse Nolan's wife has in Henry Street'. This character is actually John Wyse Power, and the building in question played a notable role in Irish history, for it was in Jennie Wyse Power's shop on Henry Street that the 1916 Proclamation was finalised and signed.[64] Jennie Wyse Power was President of Cumann na mBan in 1916, and later became a member of the Irish Senate, the first woman to attain such a position. I will come back to her family's story when John Wyse Nolan pops up again in later episodes.

Flynn slyly suggests that Bloom is a Freemason, a member of the 'Ancient free and accepted order.... I was told that by a—well, I won't say who.' This is an example of the suspicious attitude towards Bloom shown by many of his fellow Dubliners. There is no indication anywhere in *Ulysses* that Bloom is actually a Freemason. We also hear more in this episode about one of the book's sub-themes, that day's Ascot Gold Cup and the interest it spurs among the novel's minor characters. As Nosey Flynn weighs up the chances of the most favoured horses in the race, Bantam Lyons reveals that Bloom had given him a tip for Throwaway, although we know from the 'Lotus Eaters' episode that this was a misunderstanding on Lyons's part. The 'Throwaway' issue will resurface with a vengeance in the later 'Cyclops' episode.

Bloom's preoccupation with Boylan continues after he leaves Davy Byrne's. Heading for the National Library, he catches a glimpse of him. 'Straw hat in sunlight. Tan shoes. Turnedup trousers. It is. It is.' In a panic to avoid him, Bloom swerves into the National Museum, where he is 'Safe!' – at least until Boylan invades his thoughts again later in the day.

The reader may wonder why Bloom is so obsessed with Molly's looming encounter with Boylan, and yet strangely passive about it. The fact is that Bloom, for all of his frustrations and disappointments, is broadly satisfied with the life he lives, and seems not to have the urge to confront his wife's infidelity. As Davy Byrne, the observant publican, sums him up, 'he's a safe man, I'd say'. For his part, Joyce described Bloom to his friend Frank Budgen as 'a complete man, a good man'. Good and safe – and poised to continue his day's wanderings through the streets of Dublin. Next stop, the National Library, for a very different slice of early-twentieth-century Irish life.

EPISODE 9, 'SCYLLA AND CHARYBDIS':
Shakespeare and All That Jazz

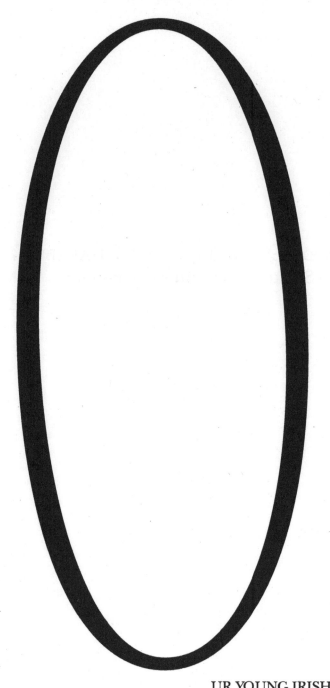

FOUR YOUNG IRISH BARDS

have yet to create a figure which the world will
set beside Saxon Shakespeare's Hamlet.
– 'John Eglinton' at the National Library

Talking about 'young Irish bards', in Episode 9 of
Ulysses, known as 'Scylla and Charybdis', we spend
much time in the company of Dublin's most notable
young bard (at least in his own estimation), Stephen
Dedalus, who unveils for us his singular ideas about
Shakespeare, and Hamlet in particular. We have
already been treated to a jocose send-up of Stephen's
theory courtesy of Malachi 'Buck' Mulligan in the
'Telemachus' episode: 'He proves by algebra that
Hamlet's grandson is Shakespeare's grandfather and
that he himself is the ghost of his own father.'

When the literary critic Harold Bloom described
Ulysses as 'Shakespeare-soaked', I imagine it was this
part of the novel he most had in mind.[65] John McCourt,
a Rome-based Joyce specialist whom I met during my
time at the Irish Embassy in London, has reminded us
that Joyce habitually referred to 'Scylla and Charybdis'
as the 'Hamlet chapter'. Joyce's wife, Nora, once said
about her husband: 'Ah, there's only one man he has
to get the better of now, and that's that Shakespeare.'[66]
Stephen's ideas about Shakespeare appear to be drawn
from a dozen well-attended lectures Joyce gave to the
Società di Minerva in Trieste in the winter of 1912–13.

Comparisons with Shakespeare are always unwise, but
let's just say that Joyce, like Shakespeare, lived through a
golden age for his country, artistically and politically, an
age he helped to make shine. Looked at that way, early-
twentieth-century Ireland stands alongside Elizabethan

England; Shakespeare's England and Ireland in the age of Yeats and Joyce. Two eras of conspicuous literary and political achievement.

John McCourt, who is always worth reading when he writes about Joyce,[67] also points out that this is the novel's ninth episode, the halfway mark in *Ulysses*. McCourt attests to 'the centrality of the Hamlet elements in *Ulysses* as a whole'. He goes on to explain that 'the force of *Hamlet* is felt in how Joyce explores the father-son relationship, themes of paternity and usurpation (literary and real), the subject of betrayal, the connections between a writer's biography and his written texts, and the question of belonging for a great "national" writer'.[68] And yes, Joyce was, and is, a great national writer, who belongs to serious readers everywhere.

There's a lot to unpack in what McCourt writes, but it's all very relevant to a fuller understanding of this complicated episode set in the National Library of Ireland on Dublin's Kildare Street, for all of those themes crop up here. It is also worth pointing out that the organ Joyce associated with this episode is the brain, and that the art form he cites is literature. All of this suggests that 'Scylla and Charybdis' is, in the eyes of its author, a key part of his book.

These pages are very different in tone and content from their predecessors. Whereas Leopold Bloom dominates the 'Lestrygonians' episode, here he appears ephemerally when he comes to the library to track down a copy of an advertisement from the *Kilkenny People* newspaper that he wants to have published in the *Freeman's Journal*. This is the ad about which he was rebuffed by *Evening Telegraph* editor

Myles Crawford, in the 'Aeolus' episode. When Bloom appears, Buck Mulligan, Stephen's loquacious associate from the book's opening chapter, refers to him as 'Ikey Moses' with 'pale Galilean eyes'. He will, it seems, forever be seen as an exotic presence in the city of his birth. Bloom's predicament reminds me of the frustration Philip Roth expressed in 2014 at being called an American Jewish writer when he pointed out that his family had been in America for 120 years, and fumed, 'If I don't measure up as an American writer, at least leave me to my delusion.'[69]

The tone of these pages is elaborately, even showily intellectual, with numerous references to literature and the classical world of Plato and Aristotle. Indeed, Joyce once explained this episode's Homeric title with reference to the two Greek greats. 'The Aristotelian and Platonic philosophies are the monsters that lie in wait in the narrows for the thinker'[70] but that need not bother Joyce's readers unless they want an incentive to delve into classical philosophy. There are allusions in this episode to (among many others) W. B. Yeats, John Millington Synge, Goethe, John Milton, Oscar Wilde, George Bernard Shaw and, above all, Shakespeare ('After God Shakespeare has created most'), the presiding spirit floating across these pages.

Here the main roles are played by Stephen Dedalus and four real-life characters: librarian Thomas William Lyster (1855–1922), a Dublin Quaker and noted German scholar; 'John Eglinton', pseudonym of William Kirkpatrick Magee (1868–1961), who was a talented essayist; the poet-mystic George Russell, Æ (1867–1935), whom we've already encountered; and the Celtic scholar

Richard Best (1872–1959), with whose name Joyce has some fun: 'Mr. Secondbest Best' and 'Bestabed'.

This episode takes the form of an extended dialogue between these six Dublin intellectuals. The Dubliners who dominate this part of the novel are very different from those we have come across in Bloom's company on the streets of Dublin. The sophisticated conversation aired at the library is leagues apart from the chatter of the streets and pubs of Dublin. The denizens of the National Library display no interest at all in the Ascot Gold Cup, which appears to be the commanding topic of the day for many of their fellow citizens.

Mulligan makes some typically irreverent interjections, including when he takes a shot at Stephen for ingratitude because Dedalus had published a negative review of Lady Gregory's *Poets and Dreamers: Studies and Translations from the Irish* (1903), something Joyce himself had done. He accuses Stephen of slating 'her drivel to Jaysus', even though she had secured him this position as a book reviewer.[71] Mulligan asks why Stephen hadn't done 'the Yeats touch', a reference to the logrolling of each other's work that Yeats and his circle often indulged in, during the 1890s especially. In Mulligan's view, what Stephen ought to have written, *à la* Yeats, is: 'The most beautiful book that has come out of our country in my time. One thinks of Homer.'

Joyce described the literary technique used in this instance as 'dialectic'. Such was the intimacy of the Dublin in which he grew up that Joyce personally knew all of those with whom Stephen jousts here. Eglinton ('littlejohn Eglinton') had offended Joyce by declining to publish an essay of his in *Dana*, a Dublin literary magazine. *Dana* evidently missed out on a winner, as Joyce's piece was an early version of what eventually became *A Portrait of the Artist as a Young Man.*

There is an edge to the elaborate, intensely literary exchanges that take place here. Eglinton and Æ are unimpressed with Stephen's literary theories, while Mulligan, with his rambunctious personality, threatens to overshadow the milder-mannered Stephen. We learn that Stephen, despite his precocious literary intelligence, has not been invited to an evening soirée at the home of the leading Irish novelist George Moore (1852–1933), but that the showy Mulligan (and the English Hibernophile, Haines) will be there. There is speculation that Moore might be the one to write 'our national epic' (but that was to be Joyce's fate). Nor is Stephen's work to be included in a forthcoming collection of poems, written by younger Irish writers, which Æ is editing.

The episode begins with Lyster, 'the quaker librarian', purring about Goethe's take on Shakespeare ('a great poet on a great brother poet') in his novel *Wilhelm Meister.* According to Lyster, Goethe sees Hamlet as 'The beautiful ineffectual dreamer who comes to grief against hard facts'. Goethe's own view as expressed in *Wilhelm Meister* was that, in *Hamlet,* Shakespeare had written about 'a great deed imposed upon a soul that was not adequate to it'.[72]

In the late nineteenth century, it was fashionable to see Hamlet as a literary incarnation of Shakespeare himself, but Stephen would have none of that. No, in Stephen's view Shakespeare was the ghost of Hamlet's father, a role Shakespeare the actor played when *Hamlet* was performed in London. This is not a theory that will find many adherents these days; better not to ventilate it in an undergraduate essay.

Stephen dwells on the fact that Shakespeare had a son, Hamnet, who died in Stratford-upon-Avon in 1596 at the age of eleven just a few years before *Hamlet* was written. This equation of Shakespeare with Hamlet's father allows Stephen to draw parallels between Hamlet's mother, the faithless Gertrude, and Shakespeare's wife, Anne Hathaway, whom he charges with infidelity, claiming she had an affair with one (or maybe both) of Shakespeare's brothers, Richard and Edmund. There is, of course, no hard evidence to support Stephen's theories, as the Bard of Stratford's private life has always been a bit of a black hole, one that has prompted endless speculation, most notably about the authorship of the plays attributed to him.

I am inclined to go along with Æ's dismissal of Stephen's intense focus on how Shakespeare's life had shaped his writing:

All these questions are purely academic, Russell oracled out of his shadow. I mean, whether Hamlet is Shakespeare or James I or Essex. Clergymen's discussions of the historicity of Jesus. Art has to reveal to us ideas, formless spiritual essences.... The deepest poetry of Shelley, the words of Hamlet bring our mind into contact with the eternal wisdom, Plato's world of ideas. All the rest is the speculation of schoolboys for schoolboys.

Stephen retorts 'superpolitely' that 'The schoolmen were schoolboys first', and adds that 'Aristotle was once Plato's schoolboy.'

[154]

There is, of course, no doubt that a writer's imagination is always influenced by the things that happen to them and in the world around them. Indeed, there are few writers more heavily influenced by their own experience than Joyce himself, who mined his memories of Dublin comprehensively, even exhaustively, as the building blocks for his literary works. His writing was more autobiographical than most. But, the precise inferences Stephen draws from what is known, or suspected, about Shakespeare's life are largely fanciful. Stephen himself admits that he does not believe his own theories. What appealed to Joyce about *Hamlet* is its tale of a son deprived of his father (Simon Dedalus is alive in 1904, but fecklessly semi-detached from his family) and betrayed by a mother unfaithful to the father, as Molly is to Leopold.

I suspect that the earnest, hard-working Russell may have seen Joyce in those early days as a bit of a dilettantish schoolboy. We should recall that Bloom had spotted Æ cycling along the street in the preceding episode, when he poked fun at his mysticism and vegetarianism. Here Russell is given a significant speaking role. While Joyce's literary pose was very different from Æ's, he was clearly familiar with Russell's thinking, which he reflects accurately in this episode:

> People do not know how dangerous love songs can be, the auric egg of Russell warned occultly. The movements which work revolutions in the world are born out of the dreams and visions in a peasant's heart on the hillside. For them the earth is not an exploitable ground but the living mother.

Although they had their differences, Joyce was indebted to Æ, who had published, and paid him for, two of his stories in the *Irish Homestead*, 'the pigs' paper' as Stephen disparagingly refers to it here. We discover that Stephen also owed a financial debt to Æ, a pound he had borrowed from him five months earlier. Stephen muses that he might not need to repay the loan. 'Wait. Five months. Molecules all change. I am other I now. Other I got pound.' But, he resignedly concludes, 'A. E. I. O. U.'

There is a density to this episode that is more formidable than its predecessors. It is replete with literary allusions. Take this passage: 'Gaptoothed Kathleen, her four beautiful green fields, the stranger in her house.... the Tinahely twelve. In the shadow of the glen he cooees for them.'

Here we have a reference to W. B. Yeats's *Cathleen ni Houlihan* (the play was co-written with Lady Gregory), an overtly nationalist play first produced in 1902 and set during the United Irishmen's rebellion of 1798. The village of Tinahely in County Wicklow was one of the sites of that rebellion, while *In the Shadow of the Glen* is a play by Synge set in the same county. Don't be put off by this. It is not necessary to understand all of these references. There are, of course, plenty of detailed guides to *Ulysses* should you wish to dive down deeper into the novel. My aim in this book is to give you what I think will help clarify and assist enjoyment of Joyce's work.

Stephen comes across here as a confident and exquisitely intelligent young man. His observations, for someone who was twenty-two years old at the time and a very recent graduate, come across as a combination of profundity and pretentiousness. Thus: 'Hold to the now, the here, through which all future plunges to the past', and 'So in the future, the sister of the past, I may see myself as I sit here now but by reflection from that which then I shall be', and 'A man of genius makes no mistakes. His errors are volitional and are the portals of discovery.'

After this, in a typical flourish, Joyce plays with Stephen's words: 'Portals of discovery opened to let in the quaker librarian, softcreakfooted, bald, eared and assiduous.' While Stephen is politely and studiously self-assured, Buck Mulligan makes a very different impression. When asked about Shakespeare, he jokingly responds:

—Shakespeare? he said. I seem to know the name.
A flying sunny smile rayed in his loose features.
—To be sure, he said, remembering brightly. The chap that writes like Synge.

This is an undeniably difficult portion of *Ulysses*, one with which many readers are likely to struggle. It is not easy to figure out what Joyce was up to. The Homeric parallels are not much help in this case. Scylla (a rock monster) and Charybdis (a dangerous whirlpool reputedly in the Straits of Messina between Italy and Sicily) is the classical equivalent of a rock and a hard place, but that doesn't help the general reader much in deciphering this episode. If we want to assign Joycean parallels to Scylla and Charybdis, there are many possible candidates – Stephen and Mulligan, Stephen and Æ, Stratford and London, or 'corrupt Paris and virgin Dublin' perhaps.

So why did Joyce toss this complicated, elusive episode into his novel? It seems to me that it is designed to complete his portrait of Stephen before he comes into contact with Bloom during the evening of this early twentieth-century Dublin day. Joyce's friend from his time in Zurich, the artist Frank Budgen, records the writer's reaction when asked why Leopold Bloom was absent from this episode. Joyce said that 'Bloom's justness and reasonableness should grow in interest. As the day wears on Bloom should overshadow them all ... Bloom is like a battery that is being recharged,' said Joyce. 'He will act with all the more vigour when he reappears.'[73] And so he does. The book's remaining chapters, until its last, are dominated by Bloom and the emergence of his adopted father-son relationship with Stephen. 'Scylla and Charybdis' allows Joyce to explore the paternity motif through Shakespearean literature before he does so in life.

We get a forewarning of the coming Bloom-Stephen nexus at the very end of this episode when, as Stephen and Mulligan exit the library, Bloom passes between them: '—The wandering jew, Buck Mulligan whispered with clown's awe. Did you see his eye? He looked upon you to lust after you. I fear thee, ancient mariner. O, Kinch, thou art in peril.'

Bloom will actually turn out to be Stephen's saviour, but that act of salvation will have to wait. Meanwhile, having spent this intellectual hour at the National Library, we return to the streets of Dublin, to the sprawling cornucopia that is 'Wandering Rocks'.

The building at 7 Eccles Street, above, no longer exists. It is perhaps the most famous address in world literature, home in 1904 to
Leopold and Molly Bloom. (The Rosenbach, Philadelphia)

The Martello Tower at Sandycove, where Joyce lived briefly in 1904.
It is the setting for the opening episode of *Ulysses*. (The Rosenbach,
Philadelphia)

The title page of the original manuscript of *Ulysses*. (The Rosenbach, Philadelphia)

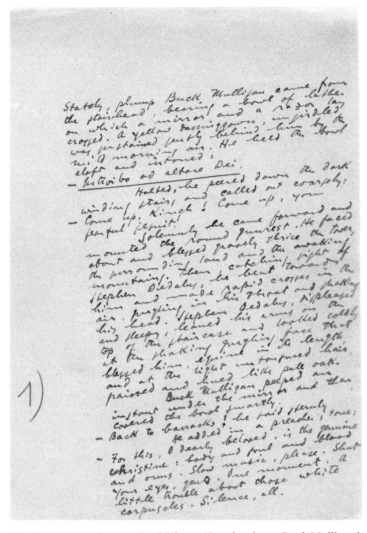

The famous opening words of *Ulysses*, 'Stately, plump Buck Mulligan', from the original manuscript. (The Rosenbach, Philadelphia)

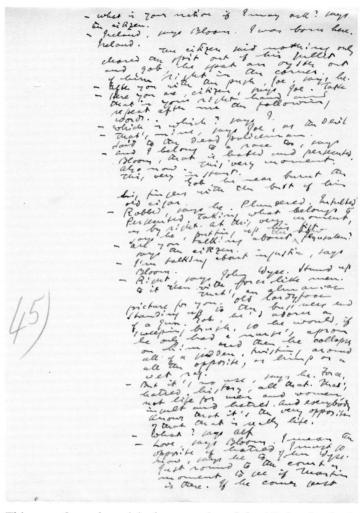

This page from the original manuscript of the 'Cyclops' episode contains a key passage in which Bloom defines his nationality: 'What is your nation if I may ask? says the citizen. Ireland, says Bloom. I was born here. Ireland.' (The Rosenbach, Philadelphia)

Forty-year-old James Joyce in a photograph taken by the artist Man Ray in 1922, the year in which *Ulysses* was published.
(The Rosenbach, Philadelphia)

Mystical poet and journalist George Russell, aka Æ (1867–1935),
features prominently in the 'Scylla and Charybdis' episode,
where Stephen recalls that he owes him money, hence 'A.E.I.O.U.'
(The National Library of Ireland)

In 1904, Dublin had an extensive network of tramways, which are mentioned in the 'Aeolus' episode, 'Before Nelson's Pillar trams slowed, shunted, changed trolley, started for Blackrock ...' (The National Library of Ireland)

Irish political titan Charles Stewart Parnell (1846–1891) features strongly throughout James Joyce's work, including in *Ulysses*, notably in the 'Hades' and 'Eumaeus' episodes. (The National Library of Ireland)

Nora Barnacle Joyce. James Joyce's friend, the artist Frank Budgen, was struck by Nora's 'absolute independence', and wrote that she had 'a scale of values entirely personal, unimitated, unmodified'. (Photographer unknown. The Poetry Collection of the University Libraries, University at Buffalo, The State University of New York.)

James Joyce with Sylvia Beach (1887–1962), the American owner of the Shakespeare and Company bookshop in Paris, which published the first edition of Ulysses on 2 February 1922. Photo taken 1921. (Photographer unknown. The Poetry Collection of the University Libraries, University at Buffalo, The State University of New York.)

EPISODE 10, 'WANDERING ROCKS':
Dublin in the Rare Old Times

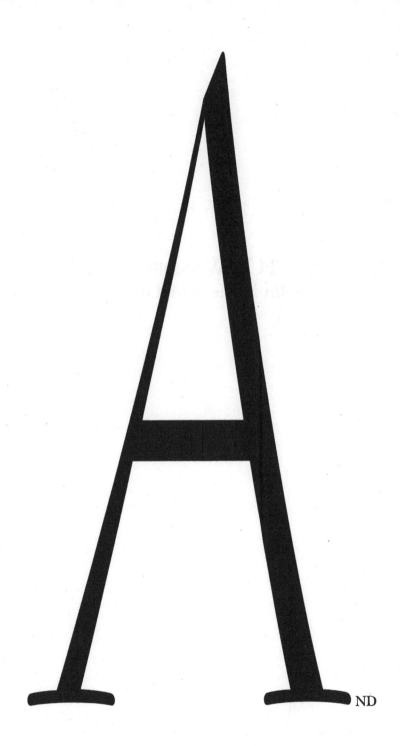

ND

as, in a sense, the theme of 'Ulysses' is the whole
of life, there is no end to the variety of material
that went into its building.

– Frank Budgen, James Joyce and the
Making of Ulysses

Yes, there is indeed a great variety of material in this
'Wandering Rocks' episode. Even if it does not exactly
contain the whole of life, we do acquaint ourselves with
some variegated slices of the life of early twentieth-century Dublin. This is the busiest, most crowded episode in
the novel. There is more action in it than in any other
episode; that is if we define action as things happening,
albeit things that are not at all dramatic or even particularly consequential. 'Incident' would perhaps be a better
word than 'action' in this instance. This is, by the stan-
dard set in *Ulysses*, an incident-packed episode.

It is also a very straightforward part of the novel.
There are no obvious mysteries here. Everything happens
in plain sight. This episode offers us nineteen glimpses
of Dublin life, ingeniously woven together to provide a
potpourri of images and snatches of dialogue. One critic
has called it 'a small-scale labyrinth within which most of
the characters of *Ulysses* appear' and 'a miniature of the
whole' of the novel.[74] This is the episode where the date
on which the novel is set is confirmed, when Miss Dunne
from Blazes Boylan's office types onto 'a sheet of gaudy
notepaper' – 16 June 1904.

Ulysses is a unique novel, which accounts for its fame
and its formidable, frequently off-putting, reputation. It
is unique in many different ways, one of which is Joyce's
employment of such a wide range of writing styles and

approaches within a single work. If the novel has typical chapters, those might include 'Lotus Eaters' (5), 'Hades' (6) and 'Lestrygonians' (8). There, the focus is on Leopold Bloom, as we familiarise ourselves with his well-worn, casually arranged mental furniture as he wanders the streets of Dublin doing largely unexceptional things.

But, we have just finished a chapter, 'Scylla and Charybdis', in which Bloom barely features, and where the conversation is elevated well beyond the level at which Bloom operates. Now in 'Wandering Rocks', Bloom makes just one brief appearance, although he is referred to a few more times. While 'Scylla and Charybdis' is a static episode, set within the walls of the National Library, 'Wandering Rocks' is full of movement. It's a part of the book where a map of Dublin comes in handy if you want to follow the 'action'.[75] Indeed, Joyce is said to have written this episode with a map of Dublin in front of him, on which he could plot the movements of his characters.

The whole of Dublin seems to be out and about, taking advantage of this pleasant June day. In the National Library, there were just six characters, all with substantial roles, whereas in this episode, by my rough calculation, more than sixty named individuals make an appearance. Many have been seen in earlier episodes, such as McCoy, Nosey Flynn, Lenehan, J. J. O'Molloy and the ubiquitous Simon Dedalus, who shows his deeply unpleasant side in his treatment of his daughter when she tries to extract a modicum of housekeeping money from him. Others, such as Father Cowley and Miss Douce and Miss Kennedy, barmaids at the Ormond Hotel, appear here for the first time, and will feature again in the next episode, 'Sirens'. Gerty MacDowell, who merits a brief mention here, will return to play a far more central role in the 'Nausicaa' episode. Others who are namechecked, including 'Mr Dudley White B.L., M.A.', the nine 'quartermile flat handicappers' all listed individually and 'Mr E. M. Solomons in the window of the Austro-Hungarian viceconsulate', disappear from the novel, but isn't that the way life is. In an ordinary day you come across good friends, acquaintances, those you meet once and may never meet again and those you get a glimpse of but will never even meet.

Only Father John Conmee at the start and William Humble, Earl of Dudley, at the end occupy significant space. In the latter case, we see what the Earl sees but have no idea what he makes of it all as he travels through the streets of Dublin in what strikes me as a kind of potted, quickfire version of Bloom's day-long Dublin odyssey.

This episode of *Ulysses* is unusual in another way, in that it is the only one without a direct parallel in Homer's *Odyssey*. The rocks are alluded to in the *Odyssey*, when the enchantress, Circe, warns Odysseus that 'No ship of men has ever approached and slipped past – always some disaster – big timbers and sailors' corpses whirled away by the waves and lethal blasts of fire'.

'Only Jason and the Argonauts had ever made it through.

Joyce added the 'Wandering Rocks' episode at a late stage. He saw it as an *entr'acte,* a gentle distraction before the novel roars towards its conclusion through eight quite challenging episodes. Joyce evidently wished to focus on the life of Dublin rather than on deepening our knowledge of his main characters. We get a rest from Bloom and Stephen, and get to know a little about some of the novel's minor personalities.

We begin in the company of Father John Conmee S.J., whose progress from the city centre to the suburb of Artane on the north side of the city we follow for eight or so leisurely pages. He is on his way to Artane to help secure a place at the residential school there for young Patrick Dignam, whose father was buried in the 'Hades' episode. On a newspaper placard he sees news of the sinking of the *General Slocum*, which caught fire in New York harbour the previous day with the loss of more than 1,000 passengers and crew.

Fr Conmee interacts with a number of his fellow Dubliners, most notably Mrs Sheehy, wife of the Irish Party MP, David Sheehy (1844–1932). The vacuous exchanges between her and Fr Conmee do not do justice to this formidable real-life Irishwoman. She was Bessie Sheehy, a commanding figure within her influential family, who brought up four daughters, all of whom became strongly feminist. One daughter, Mary, 'secretly admired' by Joyce it would seem,[76] married Tom Kettle, a contemporary of Joyce's at school and university who later became an MP and died on the Western Front in 1916.[77] Another daughter, Hanna, married another of Joyce's college friends, Francis Skeffington, the pacifist, who appears as McCann in *A Portrait*, and who was murdered by a deranged British officer during Easter week 1916. As Hanna Sheehy-Skeffington, she was a radical voice in Irish politics into the 1940s. A third Sheehy daughter, Kathleen, was the mother of the Irish diplomat, academic, journalist and political controversialist Conor Cruise O'Brien. During his student days, James Joyce was a frequent visitor to the Sheehy home at Belvedere Place, and it has been said of Bessie Sheehy that Joyce was 'one of her projects', and that she was 'educating him socially'.[78]

Fr Conmee (1847–1910) is taken from real life; he was Rector at Clongowes Wood College during Joyce's time there. In these pages, he is presented sympathetically, as an easy-going, tolerant if self-satisfied Catholic clergyman with a head full of commonplace ideas. Joyce described him to his friend Herbert Gorman as 'a bland and courtly humanist'. In *A Portrait of the Artist as a Young Man*, where Conmee also features, Joyce implies that he had a difficult time at Clongowes, but his biographer, Richard Ellmann, observes that he 'distinguished himself' there, even being a surprisingly good athlete, with a keen interest in cricket.

The second section is very short, but it does give us a glimpse of 'a generous white arm from a window in Eccles street' throwing a coin down to a one-legged beggar on the footpath below. This arm belongs to Molly Bloom. In the third section, we see the man who received Molly's coin swinging past Katey and Boody Dedalus, two of Stephen's sisters. In the fourth section, we get a fuller insight into the dysfunctional nature of the Dedalus family on account of the fecklessness of their father. A third sister, Maggie, has returned empty-handed from the pawnshop, while a fourth, Dilly, is out trying to waylay their father for money to keep their home intact – 'Our father who art not in heaven.' Meanwhile, the Dedalus girls have to make do with bread and pea soup.

In section five, we encounter Molly's paramour, Blazes Boylan, buying a fruit hamper to be sent to her as he flirts with the blond girl in the shop. In other sections we see Ned Lambert, a drinking companion of

Simon Dedalus, showing a Church of Ireland clergyman around St Mary's Abbey, renowned in Irish history as the place where the rebellion of Silken Thomas against the Tudors began in 1534. Later, we come across the spot where the patriot, Robert Emmet, was executed in 1803. We also see John Howard Parnell, brother of the late, lamented Irish political leader, Charles Stewart Parnell, playing chess in a Dublin coffee house. Ireland's contested history is never far from the surface of life in early twentieth-century Dublin, or from the pages of *Ulysses*.

We see Leopold Bloom buying a titillating novel for Molly, *Sweets of Sin*, which is meant to replace the one she finished in Episode 4, *Ruby: The Pride of the Ring*. We get another take on how Bloom is viewed by his fellow Dubliners, this time quite positively, when Lenehan observes that Bloom is 'a cultured allroundman' and that 'He's not one of your common or garden ... you know ... There's a touch of the artist about old Bloom', who, by the way, was thirty-eight years of age in 1904, but, given his personality, he was probably seen as old before his time.

Molly also comes into the picture when Lenehan recalls an annual dinner at Glencree in the Wicklow mountains. On a carriage ride back to Dublin at 'blue o'clock the morning after the night before' on 'a gorgeous winter's night', Lenehan squeezed in beside Molly as Leopold sat opposite examining the starry night sky. Lenehan retains eager memories of the journey. 'She was well primed with a good load of Delahunt's port under her bellyband. Every jolt the bloody car gave I had her bumping up against me ... She's a gamey mare and no mistake.... I was lost, so to speak, in the milky way.'

Whatever else may be said about Molly, she is certainly well able to command the attention of Dublin's menfolk.

Stephen appears in two separate sections, including when he meets his penniless sister, Dilly, and, although he has money from his teaching job and has been drinking at Mooney's pub with pals from the *Freeman's Journal*, he does not offer any support to his financially beleaguered sisters.

Stephen's literary aspirations are also discussed by Buck Mulligan and Haines, the visiting Englishman from the 'Telemachus' episode. Mulligan dismisses Stephen: 'He will never capture the Attic note. The note of Swinburne, of all poets, the white death and the ruddy birth. That is his tragedy. He can never be a poet.' Mulligan also describes Stephen as 'Wandering Ængus', an allusion to Yeats's well-known poem, with its memorable closing lines:

> And pluck till time and times are done,
> The silver apples of the moon,
> The golden apples of the sun.

Ulysses could easily be described as 'the song of wandering Leopold'.

Joyce adds an amusing aside when Mulligan says that Stephen had promised to write something in ten years. A decade after Bloomsday 1904, Joyce announced himself to the world with the publication of *Dubliners* and the appearance of a serialised version of *A Portrait of the Artist as a Young Man*. By his own account, Joyce also started writing *Ulysses* in 1914. Did Stephen's ten-year plan bear fruit through the pen of his alter ego, James Joyce?

We also eavesdrop on a conversation between Stephen and his Italian singing teacher, Almidano Artifoni, named after the owner of the Berlitz language school in Trieste, where Joyce worked for many years. The magpie in Joyce assiduously dug into his own experience for names and characters with which to populate his novel.

There is a poignant scene during which we check in with young Patrick Dignam dawdling on Wicklow Street as he starts to come to terms with his father's demise. At first he seems excited to be missing school and at the prospect of seeing his name appear in the paper as part of his father's death notice, but then the reality dawns. 'Never see him again. Death, that is. Pa is dead.'

Readers may notice that Joyce's prose changes tenor, becomes more poetic, whenever Stephen is around. Here is what he sees in a jeweller's window: 'Dust darkened the toiling fingers with their vulture nails. Dust slept on dull coils of bronze and silver, lozenges of cinnabar, on rubies, leprous and winedark stones.'

The final pages of 'Wandering Rocks' are devoted to the Lord Lieutenant of Ireland, William Humble Ward, 2nd Earl of Dudley, as he travels by horse-drawn carriage from the Vice-Regal Lodge in the Phoenix Park (now the residence of the President of Ireland, Áras an Uachtaráin) to preside over the opening of a local bazaar. This journey is an obvious counterpoint to Father Conmee's stroll, with which this episode begins. Readers may recall the opening episode, 'Telemachus, where Stephen complains that he is 'the servant of two masters' ... 'the British imperial state' and 'the holy Roman catholic and apostolic church'. Here we find

Stephen's two 'masters', Church and State, bookending this chapter.

The Lord Lieutenant was the ceremonial head of the British Administration, the representative of the crown in Ireland. The Earl of Dudley served in Dublin from 1902 to 1906. That was an eventful time politically with the passage of the Wyndham Land Act of 1903 which transformed land ownership in rural Ireland and was akin to a social revolution as former tenants acquired their own land. There was also a failed attempt to deliver a modest version of Home Rule for Ireland, which caused political uproar and resulted in the resignation in 1905 of Dudley's Chief Secretary, George Wyndham.

Irish attitudes towards the Lord Lieutenant and his administration ranged from devotion through indifference to outright hostility. In the course of his carriage ride, the Earl of Dudley comes across many of the characters who have appeared earlier in this episode. He is saluted by 'obsequious policemen', 'watched and admired', made 'obeisance' to, and stared at from 'winebig oyster eyes'. Meanwhile, the Poddle river 'hung out in fealty a tongue of liquid sewage'. A cocky Blazes Boylan dressed in 'a skyblue tie, a widebrimmed straw hat at a rakish angle and a suit of indigo serge' forgot to salute the Earl but offered the three accompanying ladies 'the bold admiration of his eyes and the red flower between his lips'.

At one point on his journey, 'John Wyse Nolan smiled with unseen coldness towards the lord lieutenantgeneral and general governor of Ireland.' Nolan's coldness is hardly surprising, for this character, who will appear again later in the novel, is based on the prominent journalist John Wyse Power. He was something of an archetypal advanced nationalist at a time of nascent political change,[79] a supporter of the Land League, a Fenian, a founder member of the Gaelic Athletic Association and an enthusiast for the revival of the Irish language. His wife Jennie's dairy, where the 1916 Proclamation was signed, has already been mentioned in the 'Lestrygonians' episode. By the time *Ulysses* was published, the Wyse Powers' daughter, Nancy, was in Berlin as a representative of the nascent Irish Free State, setting up a diplomatic mission that I led as Ambassador from 2009 to 2013.

I really like the sparkling manner in which this episode ends:

> On Northumberland and Lansdowne roads His Excellency acknowledged punctually salutes from rare male walkers, the salute of two small schoolboys at the garden gate of the house said to have been admired by the late queen when visiting the Irish capital with her husband, the prince consort, in 1849, and the salute of Almidano Artifoni's sturdy trousers swallowed by a closing door.

On we go now to meet the 'Sirens' at the Ormond Hotel on the north bank of the River Liffey, where we check back in with Leopold Bloom, whose 'adventures' continue, this time in the presence of his nemesis, Blazes Boylan.

Episode 11, 'Sirens':
Music, Music Everywhere

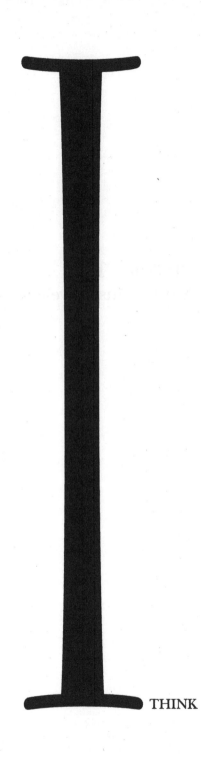

THINK

I can see that your writing has been affected to some extent by your worries.

– Harriet Shaw Weaver, on Receiving a Copy of The 'Sirens' Episode From James Joyce[80]

Joyce's loyal and devoted patron, Harriet Shaw Weaver (1876–1961), who later became his literary executor, had a point when she worried about the 'Sirens' episode, as it is a very different proposition from its predecessors. It took Joyce five months to write 'Sirens', and it could take five months to come to terms with it if you tried to tune in to every note that is sounded in this richly musical episode. It is best to just read the words and hear their music. Then move on. Don't expect to understand everything you read in 'Sirens'.

When revealing the schema he used for *Ulysses*, Joyce let it be known that the art form of this episode is music, and the featured organ, the ear. He told a friend that he 'wrote this chapter with the technical resources of music. It is a fugue with all musical notations, *piano, forte, rallentando.*'[81] Joyce was a fine singer, and had a lifelong enthusiasm for music. *Ulysses* is full of musical references, but 'Sirens' is a veritable symphony of music and song.

Lemprière's Classical Dictionary describes the Sirens as 'sea nymphs who charmed so much with their melodious voice, that all forgot their employments to listen with more attention, and at last died for want of food'. Odysseus makes his way past the Sirens by plugging the ears of his sailors with wax and having himself tied to the mast of his ship.

In this episode we see Bloom tied up at the Ormond Hotel, tucking into a meal of liver and potatoes, and being distracted by singers in an adjacent room, while Blazes Boylan journeys towards Ithaca (Bloom's home at No. 7 Eccles Street) for his amorous rendezvous with Molly. I almost subtitled this chapter 'song and dance men', for Bloom is moored in a place of sentimental song while Boylan almost dances his way jauntily towards his encounter with Molly.

Make no mistake about it, this is a difficult part of *Ulysses*, and many readers will struggle with it. The style of writing makes heavy demands on us. Here's how it begins:

Bronze by gold heard the hoofirons, steelyrining.
Imperthnthn thnthnthn.

Its first few pages are especially testing, for they contain made-up words that try to imitate musical sounds – 'tschink', 'tschunk, pfrwritt' – as well as lines that stop mid-sentence: 'Have you the?' and 'Blue Bloom is on the.' Throughout this episode, there are sentences evidently written for their musicality: 'Jingle jingle jaunted jingling', 'Tiny, her tremulous fernfoils of maidenhair'.

Its opening pages should be viewed as some sort of overture to what follows. Many of the words and phrases that appear at the start crop up again later. Helpfully, the 'overture' ends with the words: 'Done. Begin!', so that we know where we are.

The 'hoofirons' mentioned in the first sentence provide a link with the Earl of Dudley's procession through Dublin that featured in 'Wandering Rocks'. We are told that 'the viceregal hoofs go by, ringing steel', which is an echo of the episode's opening sentence. Let me be clear. The reader does not need to hear these echoes, just as you don't need to hear the sound of every individual instrument in an orchestra. It's the ensemble that counts.

If you find these pages hard going, you are not alone. Critic Hugh Kenner has written that *Ulysses* the naturalistic novel ends with 'Wandering Rocks', and that 'Sirens' marks 'the advent of engulfing stylistic idiosyncrasies'. He saw Leopold Bloom's day as divided in two, before and after four o'clock, when Molly was set to have her tryst with Blazes Boylan. The 'Sirens' episode takes place at that key time in the novel's narrative. After that point, Kenner sees Bloom as being 'in freefall, routine and cuckoldry equally behind him, occupied chiefly with staying away from the house as long as he can'.[82]

Even the modernist poet Ezra Pound, an ardent champion of Joyce's work, who had helped him get it published, did not approve of what he was doing in this part of *Ulysses*. Pound put his point across candidly when he asked Joyce if he had 'got knocked on the head or bit by a wild dog and gone dotty'.[83] Pound thought that 'a new style per chapter not required'. Joyce was stubbornly independent-minded, and would not allow himself to be deterred by Pound's assessment. He thought Pound's disapproval was 'due chiefly to the varied interests of his admirable and energetic artistic life'.[84] In other words, Pound was too distracted to be able to appreciate the persuasive power of Joyce's art.

Nor was he prepared to bow to the views of his wealthy and generous patron, Harriet Shaw Weaver, who had serialised *A Portrait of the Artist as a Young Man* in her magazine, *The Egoist*. In addition to the reservations of hers I have already referenced, she felt that 'Sirens' did not quite reach 'your usual pitch of intensity'. Writing to her, Joyce understood how she might regard 'the various styles of the episodes with dismay, and prefer the initial style'. He went on to explain that 'to compress all these wanderings and clothe them in the form of this day is for me only possible with such variation which, I beg you to believe, is not capricious'.[85] I don't know about that. I think I can detect a bit of caprice at work here.

The role of the sea nymphs is taken here by Miss Lydia Douce (also referred to as 'bronze') and Miss Mina Kennedy ('gold'), two barmaids at the Ormond Hotel. They have already been spied in the 'Wandering Rocks' episode as the Lord Lieutenant's cavalcade passed the Ormond Hotel: 'Above the crossblind of the Ormond Hotel, gold by bronze, Miss Kennedy's head by Miss Douce's head watched and admired.' These words are partially repeated here, but with the order reversed, 'Bronze by gold, Miss Douce's head by Miss Kennedy's head', because this time we are viewing them from inside the hotel instead of from the street looking in. Miss Douce has just returned from a holiday at Rostrevor in County Down, 'Lying out on the strand all day', where she has been sunburnt and 'Tempting poor simple males', as Simon Dedalus sees it.

'Gold' and 'bronze' are not singers like Homer's Sirens, but they do offer their customers some minor aural titillation, as when Miss Douce 'set free sudden in rebound her nipped elastic garter smackwarm against her smackable woman's warmhosed thigh'. For their part, these 'Sirens' have little time for their male customers. 'Aren't men frightful idiots.'

Although there is much coming and going, singing and gossiping at the Ormond Hotel, at the heart of this episode are Bloom and Boylan. Bloom dreams of pocketing five guineas for placing the Keyes ad, and thinks of using some of it to buy Molly 'violet silk petticoats'. Even as Molly is preparing to be unfaithful, Bloom is thinking of ways to please her, and has already bought her a titillating novel, *Sweets of Sin.* He again shows his astonishing naivete about Catholic beliefs when, seeing an image of the Virgin Mary, he thinks 'God they believe she is: or goddess.' No, they don't.

Until now, Bloom has tried to avoid Boylan. At the end of 'Lestrygonians', he ducked into the National Museum in a bid to avoid coming face to face with his nemesis. Now, seeing Boylan for the third time that day, Bloom changes tack. 'Follow. Risk it. Go quick. At four. Near now.' You can almost hear Bloom's heart beating with anguish as he enters the Ormond realising that the fateful rendezvous between Boylan and Molly is set to happen soon. Joyce shows us Boylan drinking with Lenehan, flirting with the barmaid, then wending his way towards Eccles Street. As Bloom obsesses about his wife's infidelity, we find him indulging in his own version of infidelity by surreptitiously writing an amorous note to his pen-paramour, Martha Clifford.

After the Blooms and Stephen, Boylan is one of the most significant characters in the novel, in that he is mentioned in the first episode in which we encounter the Blooms ('Calypso') and also features in Molly's soliloquy that closes the novel. Molly's betrayal of Bloom with Boylan halfway through the novel is probably its central event, even though it is not directly recounted in real time. We only have Molly's retrospective depiction of it to go on, and that, of course, is rendered in Molly's peerless manner.

When Boylan arrives at the hotel, he joins Lenehan, a character who first appeared in Joyce's short story 'Two Gallants', and who is mentioned in nine of the eighteen episodes of *Ulysses*. Like Boylan, he is a bit of a man about town, a gossip and a stirrer. Here we see him teasing Simon Dedalus about Stephen, 'the youthful bard', and poking fun at two of his companions from the 'Aeolus' episode, 'the ponderous pundit' MacHugh and 'that minstrel boy of the wild wet west who is known by the euphonious appellation of the O'Madden Burke'. Lenehan greets Boylan with the words 'See the conquering hero comes', another hint that his 'conquest' of Molly is known about.

Bloom, the 'unconquered hero', arrives just after Boylan. He doesn't allow himself to be conquered by the adversities that confront him. At the Ormond, he keeps Boylan at a safe distance and takes refuge in the company of Richie Goulding, brother-in-law of Simon Dedalus, and Stephen's uncle.

An extraordinarily passive Bloom watches Boylan and almost appears to fret that 'the conquering hero' may miss his four o'clock appointment with Molly. 'Has he forgotten? Perhaps a trick. Not come: whet appetite.' After Boylan leaves – 'Bloom heard a jing, a little sound. He's off. Light sob of breath Bloom sighed on the silent bluehued flowers. Jingling. He's gone. Jingle. Hear.' The word 'jingle' and its derivatives attach themselves readily to Boylan. You could not imagine Bloom being described as jingling. Cogitating perhaps.

We follow Boylan's progress towards Eccles Street while Bloom munches on his early dinner and listens to Simon Dedalus, Ben Dollard, a talented bass (yes, the one Molly described as a 'base barreltone'), and Fr Cowley sing and play piano in an adjoining room. Simon Dedalus sings 'M'appari' from Frederick von Flotow's *Martha*, namesake of Bloom's pen pal. 'M'appari', with its theme of loss and longing, could stand alongside 'Love's Old Sweet Song' as a *Ulysses* theme song:

> Martha, Martha, you have left me
> And my heart with yours has vanished.
> Peace and quiet now gone forever,
> I will surely die of pain.

Boylan is on the move with what sounds like the rhythm of a dance. 'By Bachelor's walk jogjaunty jingled Blazes Boylan, bachelor, in sun in heat, mare's glossy rump atrot, with flick of whip, on bounding tyres: sprawled, warmseated, Boylan impatience, ardentbold' until he reaches his destination at No. 7 Eccles Street: 'One rapped on a door, one tapped with a knock, did he knock Paul de Kock with a loud proud knocker, with a cock carracarracarra cock. Cockcock.'

Joyce abandons Boylan's jaunt at that point. The 'Sirens' episode does not take us inside the door of the Blooms' home. We are not invited to witness Molly's infidelity first-hand, though we will continue to perceive it through Bloom's tortured imaginings. *Ulysses* will take us back to No. 7 Eccles Street for the novel's two concluding episodes in the company of Bloom and Stephen, with Boylan long gone.

Back at the Ormond Hotel, Simon Dedalus and his fellow drinkers size up Molly, 'a buxom lassy'. There is a scurrilous innuendo about Molly, that 'she was doing the other business'. They recall going to her house to borrow a costume for a concert and finding that 'she had some luxurious operacloaks and things there.... Any God's quantity of cocked hats and boleros and trunkhose.' One of the company, Lidwell, remarks that Molly 'has a fine voice. Or had.' Dedalus ungenerously remarks that 'Mrs Marion Bloom has left off clothes of all descriptions'. This is just the latest example of Molly being ogled over. In the 'Hades' episode, John Henry Menton describes her as 'a good armful', while in 'Wandering Rocks' a lecherous Lenehan describes her as 'a gamey mare and no mistake'. Fear not. Molly will have her say before this epic day ends!

We also hear Bloom's assessment of Simon Dedalus. 'Glorious tone he has still. Cork air softer also their brogue. Silly man! Could have made oceans of money. Singing wrong words. Wore out his wife: now sings.... Drink. Nerves overstrung. Must be abstemious to sing.' The supremely sober Bloom disapproves of Dedalus's drinking, and suggests culpability in the death of Stephen's mother. Stephen certainly feels guilt about her death, but we can't be sure of his self-centred father's response to the loss of his wife, as Joyce never permits us to peer into Simon Dedalus's inner world.

The finale of this musical episode revolves around the singing of a patriotic ballad, 'The Croppy Boy'. This song refers to the rebellion of 1798, the aim of which, inspired by developments in the United States and France, was to secure Irish independence.

The version of 'The Croppy Boy' that features in 'Sirens' was written in the 1840s, at the time of the Young Ireland movement, romantic revolutionaries who harked back to the events of 1798. Fittingly, in a book like *Ulysses,* which has marital betrayal at its heart, 'The Croppy Boy' tells of the betrayal of a young revolutionary who, on his way to fight, drops into a church and gives his confession to a priest, who turns out to be a British soldier in disguise.

> At the siege of Ross did my father fall,
> And at Gorey my loving brothers all.
> I alone am left of my name and race;
> I will go to Wexford and take their place.
> ...
> I bear no hate against a living thing,
> But I love my country above the king.

He is arrested and subsequently executed.

Bloom, although sceptical about the sentimental nationalism of Simon Dedalus and his circle, makes a connection with the song's hero, who, having lost his father and brothers in the fighting, is 'last of his name and race'. Bloom thinks: 'I too. Last my race', a reference to the death of his son, Rudy. As he does elsewhere in the novel, Bloom agonises about his son's death. 'Well, my fault perhaps. No son. Rudy. Too late now. Or if not? If not? If still?' There may be life in the old dog yet!

Bloom leaves the hotel before Dollard completes the 'most trenchant rendition of that ballad'. He walks past an antique shop window, where he examines a portrait of the early nineteenth-century Irish patriot, Robert Emmet (1778–1803), emblazoned with the last words of his famous Speech from the Dock, which Abraham Lincoln knew by heart.[86] 'When my country takes her place among the nations of the earth, then, and not till then, let my epitaph be written. I have done.' His perusal of Robert Emmet's speech is accompanied by some unmusical bodily sounds. '*Let my epitaph be.* Kraaaaaaa. *Written. I have.* Pprrpffrrppffff. *Done.*'

Bloom has 'done' and we have made our way past the 'Sirens' and now on to 'Cyclops', my favourite part of *Ulysses*, where Joyce will, through Leopold Bloom, riotously interrogate what he saw as the one-eyed nationalism of the early twentieth century.

Episode 12, 'Cyclops':
Argy-Bargy on Little Britain Street

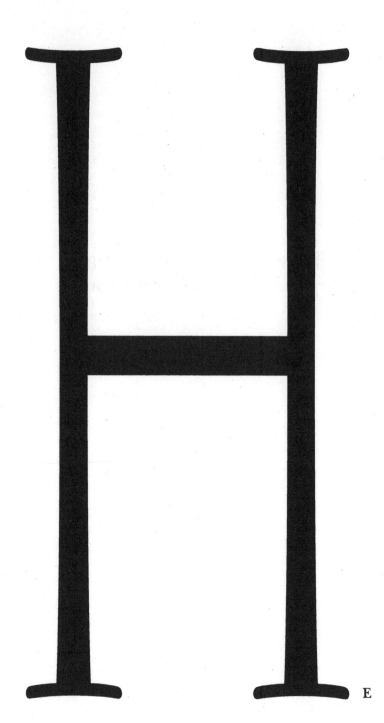

E

> unburdens his soul about the Saxe-Angles in the best Fenian style with colossal vituperativeness.
>
> – James Joyce on 'the Citizen' in
> The 'Cyclops' Episode[87]

I hate to challenge James Joyce on a point of history, but as it happens, 'the citizen', based on Michael Cusack (1847–1906), who was instrumental in the founding of the Gaelic Athletic Association (GAA) in 1884, was probably not a Fenian in the strict sense of that word, as he was not actually a member of the oath-bound Irish Republican Brotherhood (IRB). Given his personality, he was probably not ideally suited to the ways of such a clandestine network. Indeed, Cusack, although he had some associates who were Fenians, ran an academy to train those aspiring to join the British civil service, and had been an enthusiast for cricket and rugby, but was put off by what he saw as the social elitism that enveloped those sports. He was fundamentally a cultural national-ist, a very colourful figure, who was an easy target for Joyce's inflated caricature.

There was, of course, behind-the-scenes IRB (Fenian) involvement in the GAA from the outset, but its influ-ence developed mainly after Cusack was ousted from the organisation after just two years at its helm. It was the over-size, domineering personality Joyce depicts in *Ulysses* that told against him. Aside from the independent Irish State, the GAA is probably the most durable Irish achievement of the late nineteenth and early twentieth centuries, in that it remains to this day the country's premier sporting body. As the historian F. S. L. Lyons once put it, the GAA 'not only revived the Irishman's local pride in his county, but his national pride in his country'.[88] It remains a deep source of pride, excitement and enjoyment to this day. Indeed, as I write this, I am keeping half an eye on the progress of an inter-county hurling match.

Probably because I have come to Joyce through a passion for Irish history, the 'Cyclops' episode is definitely my favourite part of *Ulysses*, no question about it. I relish its over-the-top linguistic flurries and the wild imagination Joyce brought to these pages. Joyce has described the literary style of this episode as 'gigantism'! The dialogue is punchy and often funny. It's a great read, the only difficulty being the inclusion of frequent parodies written in a range of grandiose styles. These are there to be enjoyed for their manifold verbal virtuosity. Perish the thought, there is even a parody of parliamentary questions tabled at Westminster. Here's a small sample of Joycean gigantism.

> In the mild breezes of the west and of the east the lofty trees wave in different directions their first-class foliage, the wafty sycamore, the Lebanonian cedar, the exalted planetree, the eugenic eucalyptus and other ornaments of the arboreal world with which that region is thoroughly well supplied. Lovely maidens sit in close proximity to the roots of the lovely trees singing the most lovely songs while they play with all kinds of lovely objects as for example golden ingots, silvery fishes, crans of herrings, drafts of eels, codlings, creels of fingerlings, purple seagems and playful insects.

I could go on, but I'll stop there, and just add that there is happily a lot more of this kind of virtuoso writing sprinkled across the pages of 'Cyclops'. Enjoy. There's a lot going on in this episode's seventy-plus pages, and it would make an excellent novella. Among other highlights, 'Cyclops' includes a superb description of the brewing of 'Dublin's foamous beer' as Joyce calls it in *Finnegans Wake*:

> ... a crystal cup full of the foaming ebon ale which the noble twin brothers Bungiveagh and Bungardilaun brew ever in their divine alevats, cunning as the sons of deathless Leda. For they garner the succulent berries of the hop and mass and sift and bruise and brew them and they mix therewith sour juices and bring the must to the sacred fire and cease not night or day from their toil, those cunning brothers, lords of the vat.

Hold me back! Guinness advertising department, take note. Lords Iveagh and Ardilaun were the Guinness brothers who owned the famous brewery. Moving from the profane to the sacred, Joyce tosses in a parody of the Creed and British naval discipline: 'They believe in rod, the scourger, creator of hell upon earth ...'

At the heart of this episode is an extended set-to between Bloom and his antagonist, 'the citizen'. The Homeric parallel here is straightforward. It recalls Odysseus's confrontation in a cave with a one-eyed monster, Polyphemus.

Aside from its enjoyable readability, 'Cyclops' also seems to me to be crucial in identifying Leopold Bloom as an apostle of tolerance and moderation in a world trending towards extremes. Bloom defines a nation pragmatically as 'the same people living in the same place', and when asked by 'the citizen', 'what is your nation', he responds defiantly, 'Ireland ... I was born here, Ireland.' Many of Joyce's contemporaries tended to view national identity as a compound of cultural, ethnic and religious homogeneities. In 'Cyclops', Joyce has Bloom stand up against those strictures.

At Bloomsday celebrations over the years in Edinburgh, Kuala Lumpur, Berlin, London and Washington, I have invariably read from these pages, my chosen piece being the passage that lists 'many Irish heroes and heroines of antiquity', an outrageous litany containing some classic figures from Irish history and mythology (Cuchulin,[89] Niall of the Nine Hostages, Patrick Sarsfield, Theobald Wolfe Tone), some unlikely Irish heroes (Charlemagne, Julius Caesar, Christopher Columbus) and quite a number of obscure characters (Boss Croker, Peg Woffington, Valentine Greatrakes).

Irish-born Richard 'Boss' Croker became rich in New York politics as head of Tammany Hall before returning to Ireland, where he owned race horses and occupied the house in Dublin that is now the residence of the British ambassador there. A horse he owned, Orby, won the Epsom Derby in 1907. When *Ulysses* was published, Croker may have been the sole living figure in Joyce's heroic litany. He died a couple of months after the book's appearance. Peg Woffington was an eighteenth-century Irish actress who had a successful career on the London stage, while Valentine Greatrakes was a seventeenth-century Irish faith healer. It is unclear to me why these particular characters came into Joyce's head when he was compiling this list. The bulk of the names were added at a late stage, as the Rosenbach manuscript of *Ulysses* contains just twelve names, all genuine Irish heroic figures, while the published version lists some ninety. Joyce's parody does, however, have a serious purpose, for it highlights the tendency of nationalism (and not just the Irish variant) to overstate its native claims and achievements.

This episode is full of lists: of priests who were present at a debate about the revival of ancient Gaelic sports; of the guests at the nuptials of Jean Wyse de Neaulan, 'grand high chief ranger' of the Irish National Foresters (this patriotic organisation did exist, and was devoted to Ireland's reforestation) with Miss Fir Conifer of the Pine Valley, all of whom bear the names of trees (the happy couple spent their honeymoon in the Black Forest, of course); and a list of those present for the execution of a patriotic Irish martyr (based on Robert Emmet). This latter list contains some outrageous made-up names, including 'Hiram Y. Bomboost', 'Hi Hung Chang' and, believe it or not, 'Mynheer Trik van Trumps'!

The execution scene is wrapped in some of Joyce's finest prose: 'The last farewell was affecting in the extreme. From the belfries far and near the funereal deathbell tolled unceasingly while all around the gloomy precincts rolled the ominous warning of a hundred muffled drums punctuated by the hollow booming of pieces of ordnance.' And so it continues through several pages of sumptuous prose.

'Cyclops' begins with a chance meeting between the episode's unnamed narrator, a 'Collector of bad and doubtful debts', and Joe Hynes, a journalist who has already appeared in the 'Hades' and 'Aeolus' episodes.

In conversations with friends, Joyce referred to this first-person narrator as 'Noman'. In truth, he is what might be called an unpleasant piece of work, who holds vituperative opinions about those around him, but deploys a particular animus towards Bloom on account of his Jewish background. 'Noman' also has it in for Molly, 'a nice old phenomenon with a back on her like a ballalley'. He has, however, an impressive arsenal of one-liners, for example 'I've a thirst on me I wouldn't sell for half a crown', and is undoubtedly the right kind of narrator for this flamboyant chapter. Some have suggested the anonymous narrator could be Simon Dedalus, or be based on Joyce's father. The narrator's sharp turn of phrase is certainly on a par with what we have heard from Dedalus senior. If he is not the unnamed narrator, it is surprising that Simon Dedalus is not to be found carousing among so many of his cronies.

'Noman' and Hynes decide to repair to Barney Kiernan's pub in Little Britain Street to 'see the citizen'. Little Britain Street is an ironic address for an episode that has Irish nationalism at its heart. Bloom, referred to by Joe Hynes as 'the prudent member', comes and goes during this episode. The narrator has seen him 'sloping around', 'with his cod's eye counting up all the guts of the fish'. In fact, Bloom is humanely seeking to help the family of the late Paddy Dignam by sorting out the insurance policy on his dead friend, but that does not spare him from being the butt of rising resentment on the part of the pub's customers.

The immediate cause of this animus is the mistaken belief that Bloom had won money on the Ascot Gold Cup but was too stingy to share his good fortune by buying a round of drinks. Whereas the central event of the novel is Molly's unfaithful encounter with Blazes Boylan, many of the book's minor characters are chiefly concerned with the result of the Gold Cup, an event in which Bloom has no interest. Most Dubliners seem to have wagered on the favoured horses, Sceptre and Zinfandel, but the race was won by a 20/1 chance named Throwaway.

Much of the colour in this episode is provided by 'the citizen', who is accompanied by his dog, Garryowen, said to have the gift of being able to recite poetry. Here's the over-the-top way in which 'the citizen' is described when we first encounter him:

> The figure seated on a large boulder at the foot of a round tower was that of a broadshouldered deepchested stronglimbed frankeyed redhaired freelyfreckled shaggybearded widemouthed largenosed longheaded deepvoiced barekneed brawnyhanded hairylegged ruddyfaced sinewy-armed hero.

We are afforded extended exposure to 'the citizen's' vigorous opinions. He is appalled at the content of '*The Irish Independent*, if you please, founded by Parnell to be the workingman's friend … the *Irish all for Ireland Independent*.' He attributes blame for this decline to the influence of its owner, 'Martin Murphy, the Bantry jobber'. William Martin Murphy (1844–1919) was a leading Irish businessman, owner of the Dublin United Tramways Company, Clerys department store and the Imperial Hotel.[90] In Irish history, he is best known as the leader of the Dublin employers during the 1913 Lockout when he locked horns with trade union leader Jim Larkin. According to one source, 'Murphy was typical of the affluent, conservative nationalists who dominated the Nationalist party.'[91] In Joyce's eyes, Murphy would have been damned on account of his close association with Tim Healy, a leading contributor to Parnell's downfall.

Mr Reasonable, Leopold Bloom, who has joined the company in the pub, gets nowhere in his exchanges with the adamantine 'citizen', who wields his soundbites well: 'The memory of the dead … *Sinn Fein amhain!* The friends we love by our side and the foes we hate before us.' Yes, it is usually easier to mount a rabid attack than to prevail with a measured, reasoned defence.

'The citizen' directs some choice invective at 'the bloody brutal Sassenachs' (an anglicisation of the Irish word for Englishmen). This livewire passage is well worth reading, but diplomatic discretion prevents me from dipping deeper into that prejudicial dish, except to quote some French from Lenehan: '*Conspuez les Anglais! Perfide Albion!*' King Edward VII ('there's a bloody sight more pox than pax about that boyo') is a prime target as the exchanges in the bar become more and more uninhibited. When a complaint is made about the bishops of Maynooth decorating the visiting king's room with his majesty's racing colours, Alf Bergan asks why they didn't put up images of his women, but, quick as a flash, J. J. O'Molloy retorts that 'considerations of space influenced their lordships' decision.' Here is how the vituperation starts: 'And our eyes are on Europe, says the citizen. We had our trade with Spain and the French and with the Flemings before those mongrels were pupped, Spanish ale in Galway, the winebark on the winedark waterway.'

Joyce's portrait of Cusack is, of course, an unfair lampoon, in which 'the citizen' is used to represent a brand of nationalism that flourished in the early twentieth century, best described I think as a preference for an 'Irish Ireland', promoted vigorously by the journalist D. P. Moran in *The Leader.* He might well have been a target for Joyce's barbs, but Moran was alive and potentially litigious in 1922, whereas Michael Cusack was safely in his grave.

While Joyce would not have shared the noisy attitudes of 'the citizen', he was at heart an Irishman of his generation. Articles he wrote for newspapers in Trieste contain a fairly conventional set of Irish nationalist opinions from that time. If I were to hazard a guess, I would say that Joyce's political outlook lies somewhere between the assertive parliamentarianism of Parnell and the more advanced but non-violent nationalism of Arthur Griffith's Sinn Féin. Joyce saw Griffith's *United Irishman* as 'the only newspaper of any pretensions in Ireland'.[92] In an implicit rebuke of the British Empire, during his years in Trieste he came to admire the Austro-Hungarian Empire on account of its diversity: 'They called it a ramshackle Empire', he once said, but 'I wish to God there were more such Empires.'[93]

The type of nationalism Joyce satirises in these pages was not confined to Ireland. Indeed, the rival imperialisms of the late nineteenth and early twentieth centuries that culminated in the First World War were in essence aggressive brands of nationalism. Joyce wrote *Ulysses* in three European cities in the years during and after that cataclysmic war.[94]

The dialogue in this episode explores many of the themes prevalent in the politics of nationalist Ireland in the early twentieth century, the revival of Gaelic Games and of the Irish language (the Gaelic League had been founded in 1893 and was growing rapidly around 1904) and the views of Arthur Griffith, who went on to found Sinn Féin the following year. In 1904, Griffith had published a book called *The Resurrection of Hungary: A Parallel for Ireland*, in which he saw Hungary's success in securing a measure of independence within the Austro-Hungarian dual monarchy as a model for Ireland's political advancement. Joyce plays games in this episode by having John Wyse Nolan and Martin Cunningham credit Bloom with inspiring Griffith's Hungarian ideas. By the time *Ulysses* was published in February 1922, Griffith was one of the leaders of the fledgling Irish Free State.

In his fiery manner, 'the citizen' recalls the full slate of Irish nationalist grievances against British rule – the curtailment of Ireland's economy, reducing the country's population through emigration, even deforestation – and exaggerates Ireland's past glories.

As the episode wears on, 'the citizen' becomes increasingly intolerant of Bloom, and more openly anti-Semitic. I don't know if Michael Cusack was personally guilty of anti-Semitism, but there was a lot of it around in early twentieth-century Europe. 'The citizen's' baiting of Bloom eventually produces a reaction. Bloom puts his cards on the table:

> But it's no use, says he. Force, hatred, history, all that. That's not life for men and women, insult and hatred. And everybody knows that it's the very opposite of that that is really life.
> — What? says Alf.
> — Love, says Bloom. I mean the opposite of hatred.

I see this appeal to transcend force, history and hatred as a key statement of Bloom's and Joyce's credo.

The episode ends in a flourish with a heated argument between Bloom and 'the citizen' in which Bloom defends his Jewish heritage. When Bloom tells 'the citizen' that 'the Saviour was a jew and his father was a jew' (theology was definitely not Bloom's strong suit), 'the citizen' threatens to 'brain' Bloom 'for using the holy name. By Jesus, I'll crucify him so I will'. 'The citizen' then retaliates by throwing a biscuit tin at Bloom as he departs. This parallels Polyphemus throwing a boulder after the departing Odysseus in the *Odyssey*.

In keeping with the many parodies that decorate these pages, 'Cyclops' ends in fine style, with some grandiose biblical language to mark Bloom's exit:

> And they beheld Him in the chariot, clothed upon in the glory of the brightness, having raiment as of the sun, fair as the moon and terrible that for awe they durst not look upon Him. And there came a voice out of heaven, calling: *Elijah! Elijah!* And he answered with a main cry: *Abba! Adonai!* And they beheld Him even Him, ben Bloom Elijah, amid clouds of angels ascend to the glory of the brightness at an angle of fortyfive degrees over Donohoe's in Little Green Street like a shot off a shovel.

Thus Bloom escapes from his altercation with 'the citizen'. We next meet him in a calmer mood, back on Sandymount Strand, for an episode written in a completely different style, and with a very different theme, from the rambunctious 'Cyclops'.

EPISODE 13, 'NAUSICAA':
Those Girls, Those Girls, Those Lovely
Seaside Girls

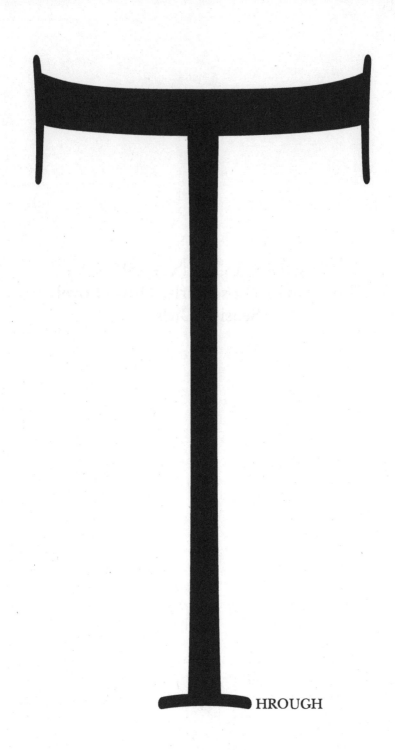
HROUGH

the open window of the church the fragrant incense was wafted and with it the fragrant names of her who was conceived without stain of original sin, spiritual vessel, pray for us, honourable vessel, pray for us, vessel of singular devotion, pray for us, mystical rose. And careworn hearts were there and toilers for their daily bread and many who had erred and wandered, their eyes wet with contrition but for all that bright with hope for the reverend father Father Hughes had told them what the great saint Bernard said in his famous prayer of Mary, the most pious Virgin's intercessory power that it was not recorded in any age that those who implored her powerful protection were ever abandoned by her.

– *Ulysses*, 'Nausicaa'

We know from earlier episodes that Leopold Bloom was pretty clueless about the doctrines and practices of the Roman Catholic Church, to which he nominally belonged. The passage quoted above proves that James Joyce, while certainly a religious agnostic, had, from his upbringing and education in Dublin, a powerful grasp of the traditions of Irish Catholicism, and could write convincingly about piety and devotion.

It is easy to see how the 'Nausicaa' episode got Joyce's publishers into trouble with the censors and the censorious, for it focuses on two virgins, one sacred and the other profane. While the Virgin Mary is being spiritually venerated within the walls of the church, on the beach it is the virginal Gerty MacDowell who is the object of Bloom's carnal yearnings. While earlier episodes of *Ulysses* attracted

[199]

the attention of the US customs and postal authorities, 'Nausicaa' was the straw that broke the camel's back, and landed its US publishers in court in 1921.

The late-Victorian music hall song 'Those Lovely Seaside Girls' is, alongside Mozart's 'Là ci darem la mano' and James Lynam Molloy's 'Love's Old Sweet Song', one of the theme songs of *Ulysses*. It surfaces time and again throughout the novel.

> All dimples, smiles and curls, your head it simply swirls.
> …
> Lace and grace and lots of face – those pretty little seaside girls.

In the 'Nausicaa' episode, we come into contact with Joyce's ultimate seaside girl, Gerty MacDowell. We briefly glimpsed her in the 'Wandering Rocks' episode, but here we see a lot more of her, and are allowed to view the world from her particular angle.

In Homer's *Odyssey*, Nausicaa is a Phaeacian princess who discovers a shipwrecked Odysseus sleeping on a beach, rouses him and enables him to continue his voyage back to his home in Ithaca. In this part of *Ulysses*, Bloom finds himself, after a troubling day, marooned on a Dublin beach, where he is aroused by a princess-like figure in the form of our seaside girl, Gerty MacDowell.

As we turn the page from the 'Cyclops' episode to 'Nausicaa', the atmosphere changes dramatically. 'Cyclops' concludes at a frantic pace, with Bloom fleeing from an assault by 'the citizen' at the end of a tumultuous visit to Barney Kiernan's pub. Bloom's exit is described in hyperbolic terms typical of the language which characterises that super-charged episode of *Ulysses*. As the 'Nausicaa' episode unfolds, we discover that the tone and language are radically different from what has gone before. Its beautifully written opening paragraph illustrates this, and warrants being quoted in full:

> The summer evening had begun to fold the world in its mysterious embrace. Far away in the west the sun was setting and the last glow of all too fleeting day lingered lovingly on sea and strand, on the proud promontory of dear old Howth guarding as ever the waters of the bay, on the weedgrown rocks along Sandymount shore and, last but not least, on the quiet church whence there streamed forth at times upon the stillness the voice of prayer to her who is in her pure radiance a beacon ever to the stormtossed heart of man, Mary, star of the sea.

Here we are submerged in the language of a romantic novel. Joyce said that this episode was written in a 'new fizzing style'. It was, he wrote, 'a namby-pamby jammy marmalady drawersy style'.[95] To prepare himself for writing 'Nausicaa', he asked an aunt in Dublin to send him some popular novelettes. Had he not harboured loftier literary ambitions, Joyce could clearly have turned his pen to the production of superior-class romances! Many readers will, I think, enjoy the easy-on-the-ear manner in which at least the first part of this episode is written.

Evening is about to set in as this long June day draws to a close. Seeking respite after his fraught experience with 'the citizen', Bloom has come to the quiet surrounds of Sandymount Strand. These days it would be a lot busier on such a summer's evening. This was the site of the 'Proteus' episode, the place where that morning Stephen Dedalus imagined himself 'walking into eternity'. It is about eight o'clock in the evening now, and Bloom has just visited the home of his deceased friend, Paddy Dignam. This visit to the bereaved Dignam household at nearby Newbridge Avenue to advise the widow about her husband's life insurance policy, a typically considerate gesture on Bloom's part, represents a rare portion of Bloom's day of which Joyce gives us no direct account.

As Bloom looks across Dublin Bay, he sees three girls, Cissy Caffrey (who is looking after her younger brothers, Tommy and Jacky), Edy Boardman (who is taking care of baby Boardman) and Gerty MacDowell. The three friends had come to 'that favourite nook to have a cosy chat beside the sparkling waves and discuss matters feminine'.

As the episode progresses, Bloom becomes aroused as he observes Gerty behaving with a mild flirtatiousness (novelist Edna O'Brien has described 'Nausicaa' as the novel's 'most seductive chapter', and Gerty as someone in the grip of 'romantic longings'[96]). At the Star of the Sea Church, a temperance service is in progress, and in an adjoining Dublin suburb a bazaar is taking place and fireworks are about to be set off. In the 'Wandering Rocks' episode, we witnessed the Lord Lieutenant making his way through Dublin to be there for the opening ceremony of that very bazaar. Joyce weaves both the sounds emanating from the church and from the fireworks display into his fevered account of a distant, transient, but intense liaison between Leopold Bloom and Gerty MacDowell.

In a case brought to a court in New York in 1921 by John Sumner, Secretary of the New York Society for the Suppression of Vice, the 'Nausicaa' episode resulted in Joyce's American publishers, the proprietors of *The Little Review*, Margaret Anderson and Jane Heap, being convicted of obscenity, for which they were fined $50 each. They escaped imprisonment when their lawyer, John Quinn, assured the judges that 'Nausicaa' was in terms of obscenity the worst episode in the book, although readers of Molly Bloom's soliloquy (which, however, was not published until the following year) would probably beg to differ.

Having read 'Nausicaa', one of the presiding judges described it as 'the ravings of a disordered mind'. The judges were offended by Gerty MacDowell's display of her lingerie in an effort, a successful one, to stir Bloom's interest in her. The court judgement put an end to *The Little Review*'s serialisation of *Ulysses*, and made it more difficult for Joyce to find a publisher for his novel. *Ulysses* was eventually published in Paris in 1922, but an American edition didn't appear until 1934.

It may have been fortunate for Anderson and Heap that the judges did not focus unduly on the fact that 'Nausicaa' depicts Bloom masturbating. Even when looked at today, there is something tawdry and unsettling about Bloom's behaviour which presents him in a different, more ignoble light from the sensible, serious man we have become accustomed to in the novel's earlier episodes. What was Joyce up to? Was this just an effort to shock, to show that he would recognise no taboos? Virginia Woolf, who thought that *Ulysses* was 'underbred ... the book of a self-taught working man', believed that Joyce indulged in 'the conscious and calculated indecency of a desperate man who feels that in order to breathe he must break the windows'.[97] This assessment probably reveals at least as much about Woolf as it does about Joyce and his work. It's hard to fathom how she could have imagined Joyce to be 'a self-taught working man'.

It may be that Joyce was dead set on outraging conventional mores, but it seems to me that there is a serious purpose at work in this strange encounter between Leopold and Gerty. While there are those who dismiss Gerty as a one-dimensional devotee of a gushily romantic view of life, it seems to me that she serves an important function in the novel. Like his exchange of letters with Martha Clifford, his behaviour towards Gerty serves as a kind of rejoinder to Molly's betrayal of him. I also see Gerty as something of a counterpart to Molly in the way that Stephen is a foil for Leopold Bloom. With Gerty, we come to grips with a young, essentially immature, Irish woman, and get an insight into her dreams and aspirations. I tend to agree with the critic Harry Blamires, who wrote that the idiom of the romantic novelette Joyce employed here 'becomes peculiarly touching by virtue of its sheer aptness to her adolescent self-dramatisation. Joyce's linguistic virtuosity and psychological sensitivity together present the two-eyed reader with a feast of blended satire and pathos.'[98] Yes, there is far more going on here than a parody of romantic fiction. With Molly, in the novel's closing chapter, we meet a mature woman with a view of the world at least as authentic as that of her wandering husband.

[204]

The 'Nausicaa' episode is broken into two parts, the first devoted to Gerty and the latter part given over to another display of Bloom's 'stream of consciousness'. The episode starts with a description of Cissy Caffrey, 'a past mistress in the art of smoothing over life's tiny troubles', and just when you might think that she is to be the main object of interest here, the question crops up, 'But who was Gerty?' Now *Ulysses* is not a novel in which the characters are comprehensively described, even if it does famously start with some descriptive words, 'Stately, plump Buck Mulligan …' Joyce, for example, gives little information about what Bloom looked like. But here he provides a two-page description of Gerty, a character who may be based in part on Martha Fleischmann, a Swiss woman Joyce had a brief affair with in Zurich in 1918.[99] Could that be where Joyce got the name for Bloom's pen pal, Martha Clifford? The depiction of Gerty is a glowing one, written in exquisite prose, albeit of a romantic stripe. She was 'pronounced beautiful by all who knew her', and was 'as fair a specimen of winsome Irish girlhood as one could wish to see…. The waxen pallor of her face was almost spiritual in its ivorylike purity though her rosebud mouth was a genuine Cupid's bow, Greekly perfect.' Greece again. Joyce can't seem to put it out of his head.

There is an extended account of how Gerty was dressed, down to her underwear (described in arguably excessive, voyeuristic detail), 'simply but with the instinctive taste of a votary of Dame Fashion', which reminds me of the outlandish description of 'the citizen's' garb in 'Cyclops', except that this one is laced with a glancing admiration as opposed to a blinding satire.

We are given an opportunity to access Gerty's thoughts and desires, for even though this is written in the third person, it is clear that Gerty's feelings and anxieties are being aired here, and that she is, in effect, her own narrator. Joyce's treatment of Gerty is a rarity in *Ulysses*. The book's characters, other than the Blooms and Stephen, are generally seen and heard, but the reader is not invited into their interior worlds. In terms of the attention Joyce devotes to her, Gerty is the fourth most important character in *Ulysses*.

She fantasises about marrying Reggie Wylie, a student at Trinity College Dublin, and has set ideas about what she wants in her man:

> No prince charming is her beau ideal to lay a rare and wondrous love at her feet but rather a manly man with a strong quiet face ... who would understand, take her in his sheltering arms, strain her to him in all the strength of his deep passionate nature and comfort her with a long long kiss.

This relationship, if there ever was one, seems destined to peter out, as Reggie is very young and his father has intervened to keep him at home to attend to his studies.

Gerty and her friends notice Bloom when one of the Caffrey boys kicks a ball in his direction and Bloom returns it. The ball rolls down the beach and lands at Gerty's side. In response, Gerty 'lifted her skirt a little but just enough', deliberately exposing her underwear. She felt 'the warm flush ... surging and flaming into her cheeks'. This was likely because she had started to transfer her amorous attentions from Reggie Wylie to Bloom, whose face, 'wan and strangely drawn, seemed to her the saddest face she had ever seen'. Gerty knows that Bloom is looking at her, and that 'there was meaning in his look'. She senses that 'his eyes burned into her' and 'read her very soul'. Seeing his dark eyes, Gerty concludes that he is a foreigner with a 'pale intellectual face', one that had 'a haunting sorrow' written on it. This is a unique moment in *Ulysses*, as Bloom is, on account of his foreignness, viewed with interest and favour in contrast with the suspicion and irritated hostility habitually shown towards him in earlier episodes.

Gerty imagines Bloom as 'her dreamhusband, because she knew on the instant it was him'. She is impressed by Bloom's obvious interest in her. 'He was eyeing her as a snake eyes its prey.' Her woman's instinct told her that she had raised the devil in him. As the religious service at the Star of the Sea draws to a close and the fireworks display reaches its crescendo, the arms-length tryst between Bloom and Gerty also comes to a head. 'Whitehot passion was in that face, passion silent as the grave, and it had made her his.' And as a Roman candle bursts in the sky above the bazaar, Bloom's excitement reaches its peak: 'O! in raptures and it gushed out of it a stream of rain gold hair threads and they shed and ah! They were all greeny dewy stars falling with golden, O so lovely! O so soft, sweet, soft!'

As Gerty leaves the beach, 'Their souls met in a last lingering glance and the eyes that reached her heart, full of a strange shining, hung enraptured on her sweet flowerlike face.' Bloom notices that Gerty is lame. He responds to this revelation in an ungenerous fashion.

'Poor girl! That's why she's left on the shelf and the others did a sprint. Thought something was wrong by the cut of her jib. Jilted beauty. A defect is ten times worse in a woman. But makes them polite. Glad I didn't know it when she was on show. Hot little devil all the same.'

Why is Bloom so sourly misogynistic? As the episode draws to a close, we can sense the reason for his discomfiture. He continues to brood about Molly's infidelity. He realises that his watch has stopped at 4.30 p.m., around the time when Molly was entertaining Boylan – 'Was that just when he, she?' He wonders if there was any magnetic influence at work in stopping his watch 'because that was about the time he'. A disconsolate Bloom reflects that Boylan 'gets the plums and I the plumstones'.

As dusk falls, Bloom looks across Dublin Bay at the hill of Howth and remembers being there in the rhododendrons with Molly many years before and thinks of 'all that old hill has seen'. As Bloom writes 'I AM A' on the sand, a cuckoo clock sounds from the nearby priest's house, reminding him of his fate.

Cuckoo
Cuckoo
Cuckoo.

Cuckold.

In 'Nausicaa', Bloom plays out with Gerty a diluted version of Molly's infidelity, just as he was doing in his furtive correspondence with Martha Clifford, although, of course, nothing Bloom gets up to matches Molly's doings, but Bloom's reticence mirrors his intrinsic prudence. After their brief and distanced interchange,

Gerty disappears from Bloom's world while his obsession with Molly persists. There is a sense in which *Ulysses* is a great if atypical love story (although not one that Gerty might relish). Bloom accepts his fate as a cuckold and refuses to reject or even confront his unfaithful wife. Nonetheless, after their respective wanderings and infidelities, Leopold and Molly will end up together at their own Ithaca on Dublin's Eccles Street.

Adieu to Sandymount Strand and on to a maternity hospital. Farewell to our lovely seaside girls and hello to some overserved (as Americans say) medical students. From princess 'Nausicaa' to the 'Oxen of the Sun', a beast of an episode!

Episode 14, 'Oxen of the Sun':
'In Woman's Womb Word is Made Flesh'

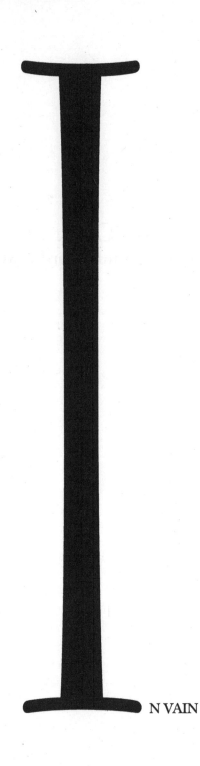

N VAIN

the voice of Mr Canvasser Bloom was heard
endeavouring to urge, to mollify, to restrain.
– *Ulysses*, 'Oxen of the Sun'

There is not much restraint in the pages of this episode,
either in language or in subject matter. The language is
exuberant, exhibitionist. Its author is manifestly intent
on displaying his wares, showing off his writing skills. Mr
Canvasser Bloom is about the only one trying to mollify or show restraint, but he is swimming against a tide
of ribaldry among the medical students with whom he
keeps company in these pages.

When the poet, Ezra Pound, commented that 'the
excuse for parts of *Ulysses* is the whole of *Ulysses*', he
may have been thinking, among other things, about the
part of *Ulysses* called 'Oxen of the Sun'. He probably
considered that this episode was in need of an excuse. If
not an excuse, this episode certainly needs a lot of interpretation, and I will do my best.

Let me be honest with you, 'Oxen of the Sun' is a
forbidding challenge, and not everyone will manage it.
Here's what a leading Joyce scholar, Terence Killeen,
has said about it. '"Oxen of the Sun" is by general agreement the most difficult episode of *Ulysses*. For many
readers, the episode's extraordinary technique is just
too much.'[100] Yes, this episode is a bit of a literary lump,
decidedly difficult to digest. Joyce acknowledged that it
was his book's most testing segment, 'both to interpret
and to execute'.[101] He reckoned that it had taken him
1,000 hours to write. The episode was conceived (an
apt word for something set in a maternity hospital) as
having nine segments corresponding to the months of

a pregnancy, but those internal divisions are neither evident nor particularly pertinent.

Readers should not be surprised, or intimidated, if they find 'Oxen of the Sun' hard work. And allow me to whisper it: if the going gets too tough, don't be afraid to hit the skip button or skim through these pages and move on to the remainder of the novel, which confronts the reader with somewhat less formidable, if still considerable, obstacles.

The Homeric parallel is not all that helpful in this instance. In Homer, Odysseus and his crew visit the island of Thrinacia, where his crew members slaughter the sacred oxen of Helios, god of the sun. In retribution their ship is struck by a thunderbolt, a catastrophe that only Odysseus survives. It is difficult to figure out what has been slaughtered in Joyce's episode – the English language perhaps? There are, however, plenty of cows on display.

The difficulty with this part of the novel stems from the fact that it is written in a succession of English prose styles that mimic the history of English literature from the Anglo-Saxon era to the late nineteenth century. This is an ingenious compositional ploy, but it's not for the faint-hearted reader. That said, the episode can be read with pleasure even though its content is wrapped in a linguistic fog that is often supremely difficult to see through. Allow yourself to be entertained by the frequent changes in writing style even if you need not wrack your brain too much to figure out what is being said in this deliberately opaque prose. Furthermore, you can't be expected to identify the provenance of each featured style, and nor do you need to do so. For those who are interested, Terence Killeen in his book, *Ulysses Unbound*, has helpfully identified thirty-one writers being parodied, including Daniel Defoe, Jonathan Swift, Oliver Goldsmith, Richard Brinsley Sheridan, Edward Gibbon and Charles Dickens.[102] You can have fun tracing the literary lineage of Joyce's mimicry. This is an episode that could have done with an editor, as some of the parodies can go on a bit too long, and are too contrived and contorted.

I want to quote one passage to exemplify the nature of the writing found here and the challenges it poses for the reader:

> But this was only to dye his desperation as cowed he crouched in Horne's hall. He drank indeed at one draught to pluck up a heart of any grace for it thundered long rumblingly over all the heavens so that Master Madden, being godly certain whiles, knocked him on his ribs upon that crack of doom and Master Bloom, at the braggart's side, spoke to him calming words to slumber his great fear, advertising how it was no other thing but a hubbub noise that he heard, the discharge of fluid from the thunderhead, look you, having taken place, and all of the order of a natural phenomenon.

What's going on here? It's like a puzzle isn't it? Fun to disentangle. It's all about Stephen's (and Joyce's) fear of thunder, and the efforts of Bloom to calm him by means of a scientific explanation of what was going on in the heavens. The reference in 'cowed he crouched in

Horne's hall' is to Sir Andrew Horne (1856–1924), the hospital's Master in 1904. Another bovine allusion too!

'Oxen of the Sun' is set in Dublin's National Maternity Hospital at Holles Street. After his visit to Sandymount, Bloom, who is not yet ready to return to Molly, goes there at ten o'clock to enquire about the condition of one Mrs Mina Purefoy, who has been enduring a difficult, three-day labour. Purefoy's name is based on Richard Dancer Purefoy (1847–1919), who was Master of another Dublin maternity hospital, the Rotunda.[103] At the hospital he meets a group of medical students who are carousing there. Bloom disapproves and marvels at the fact that once they graduate these revellers will become ever so respectable and prudishly critical of the excesses of youth.

This episode features the three characters from 'Telemachus', the novel's opening episode: Stephen Dedalus, Buck Mulligan and the Englishman Haines (who makes an appearance, it would seem, as an apparition). Bizarrely, Haines confesses to the murder of Thomas Childs, the sensational turn-of-the-century Dublin murder we have heard about earlier in the text, for which Childs's brother, Samuel, was accused but acquitted.

Writing to his friend Frank Budgen, Joyce explained the gynaecological parallels: 'Bloom is the spermatozoon, the hospital the womb, the nurse the ovum, Stephen the embryo'.[104] The organ featured in this episode is the womb, while the technique employed is, of course, embryonic. The evolution of the English language mapped in this episode equates broadly with the development of the foetus in the womb.

The episode begins with some Latin, followed by a snatch of Anglo-Saxon idiom: 'Send us, bright one, light one, Horhorn, quickening and wombfruit.' By the time we reach its conclusion, we're in the realms of early twentieth-century American English, and what one critic has termed 'hot-gospeller' commercialese: 'The Deity ain't no nickel dime bumshow. I put it to you that he's on the square and a corking fine business proposition. He's the grandest thing yet and don't forget it.'

There are two sentences at the beginning, each a half-page in length, from which I have failed to extract any screed of meaning, although I am led to believe that this passage may concern fertility – as hinted at by the presence there of the words 'reiteratedly pro-creating function' – a subject certainly not out of place at Holles Street hospital. Bloom's arrival there is recounted in medieval English with reference to his Jewish background and his daylong wanderings around Dublin: 'Some man that wayfaring was stood by housedoor at night's oncoming. Of Israel's folk was that man that on earth wandering far had fared.' When he enquires about an old medical acquaintance who had worked at the hospital, he is told that he is deceased, 'O'Hare Doctor in heaven was'. The good doctor had died of 'bellycrab'.

Bloom joins the company of the revellers. We eaves-drop on an increasingly inebriated conversation between medical students Dixon (who had previously treated Bloom for a bee sting), Madden, Lynch, Punch Costello, Crotthers (a Scottish medical student), and Lenehan, a bit of a hanger-on whom we've encountered in earlier episodes. And then there is Stephen Dedalus, 'who was of a wild manner when he was drunken', and by this time he is definitely the worse for wear after a day's drinking.

Especially in those pages in which medieval English is being parodied, it can require much effort and imagination to figure out what's going on. Hence 'a vat of silver that was moved by craft to open in the which lay strange fishes withouten heads' refers to – a tin of sardines! And what is this? 'And there were vessels that are wrought by magic of Mahound out of seasand and the air by a warlock with his breath that he blases into them like to bubbles.' Glasses for drinking from, of course. I could go on, but you get the idea.

Having seen Bloom in the previous episode on Sandymount Strand in a somewhat acerbic mood, here he is back to being the essence of reasonableness and possessed of a somewhat ponderous intelligence and plenty of good sense. Here he is 'Mr Cautious Calmer'. He joins the revellers, but hardly drinks. Bloom, 'sir Leopold', is described in a pastiche of medieval English as 'the goodliest guest that ever sat in scholars' hall and … the very truest knight in the world'.

Although a sober Bloom is out of place in this raucous company, he remains with them out of a concern for Stephen's welfare or, as Joyce puts it, in a medieval idiom, because 'he bore fast friendship to sir Simon and to this his son young Stephen', although as it happens Bloom has only limited respect for the elder Dedalus. While the student drinkers indulge themselves loudly, Bloom is full of characteristic concern for those giving birth upstairs in the hospital.

We are exposed to a discussion of the ethics of childbirth, especially the rights of the mother as against those of the child in the womb. In cases where a choice needed to be made between the life of the mother and the child, 'all cried with one acclaim nay, by our Virgin Mother, the wife should live and the babe to die'. Only Stephen, although a religious sceptic, dissents from this view, arguing that 'those Godpossibled souls we nightly impossibilise' represent a 'sin against the Holy Ghost, Very God, Lords and Giver of Life'. Reflecting Catholic doctrine, he maintains that 'at the end of the second month a human soul was infused'. Stephen is, of course, showing off his skill as an intellectual contrarian, confident of his ability to win any argument. Asked for his opinion, Bloom characteristically sits on the fence, 'dissembling as his wont was'. In keeping with his anti-clerical bent, he observes that the Church benefits financially from both birth and death.

This discussion causes Bloom to brood on the birth of his son, Rudy, and his death eleven days later, whom 'no man of art could save so dark is destiny'. The loss of his son troubles Bloom throughout the day. He is described here as someone who 'had of his body no manchild for an heir' and 'shut up in sorrow for his forepassed happiness'. This vacuum in his life causes Bloom to develop a paternalistic attitude towards Stephen – 'so grieved he also ... for young Stephen for that he had lived riotously with those wastrels and murdered his goods with whores.' Bloom's burgeoning interaction with Stephen becomes one of the key themes of the novel's closing episodes.

An impressively articulate Stephen, considering the inebriated condition he's in, observes that 'time's ruins build eternity's mansions'. Then comes a key sentence in this episode, when Stephen, at his imperious best, pronounces that: 'In woman's womb word is made flesh but in the spirit of the maker all flesh that passes becomes the word that shall not pass away.' Here Joyce turns Catholic theology on its head by asserting the eternal veracity of the word in the hands of a great writer. Artistic creativity becomes the ultimate purpose of procreation.

Discussion of a foot and mouth outbreak, which is referred to in Episode 2, 'Nestor', when Mr Deasy hands Stephen a letter on the subject for publication in one of Dublin's newspapers, gives rise to an extended, humorous discussion about bulls. Its main focus is the Papal Bull, *Laudabiliter*, issued by Pope Adrian IV in 1155, which was used by King Henry II to justify the Norman invasion of Ireland. Pope Adrian, born Nicholas Breakspear, was the only Englishman ever to ascend to the Papacy. Thus in 'Oxen of the Sun', we read about 'farmer Nicholas, the bravest cattle breeder of them all'. Ireland's contested past is never far from the minds of the characters in *Ulysses*.

The company is enlivened by the arrival of Buck Mulligan, whose larger-than-life presence will be recalled from the opening episode of the novel, and from a number of subsequent appearances. Mulligan is accompanied by his friend Alec Bannon, who speaks of a young woman he had met in Mullingar, 'a skittish heifer, big of her age and beef to the heel'. This ungenerous reference is to Bloom's daughter, Milly, who we have learned in earlier episodes is working in Mullingar.

The rakish Buck Mulligan jokes that he planned to set himself up as a '*Fertiliser and Incubator*', thus devoting 'himself to the noblest task for which our bodily organism has been framed.' With an egalitarian flourish, he pledged that 'the poorest kitchenwench no less than the opulent lady of fashion ... would find in him their man'.

There is also, in this episode, a description of Bloom's character that helps us understand the kind of Everyman he is:

It was now for more than the middle span of our allotted years that he had passed through the thousand vicissitudes of existence and, being of a wary ascendancy and self a man of a rare forecast, he had enjoined his heart to repress all motions of a rising choler and, by intercepting them with the readiest precaution, foster within his breast that plenitude of sufferance which base minds jeer at, rash judgers scorn and all find tolerable and but tolerable.

In plainer language, Bloom is seen as a wary individual who avoids the temptation to be angry, and cultivates a tolerant outlook. This passage, by the way, is said to be written in the style of the eighteenth-century Irish political philosopher and politician Edmund Burke.

Eventually, word arrives that Mrs Purefoy has at last given birth. This happy news gives rise to ribald speculation about the identity of the father, the medical students doubting that her elderly husband, 'old Glory Allelujurum', was up to the task. The birth also ushers in some fine writing, including a parody of Carlyle: 'The air without is impregnated with raindew moisture, life essence celestial, glistening on Dublin stone there under starshiny *coelum*.' In these gynaecological surroundings,

Bloom remembers his first sexual experience, with a local prostitute, Bridie Kelly.

When Stephen calls on his companions to move to a nearby pub, Burke's, the language becomes more like that which Joyce would employ in *Finnegans Wake*, erratic and difficult to make sense of. This is just the kind of patter you might expect to hear from late-night drinkers in a busy pub. A reference to 'two Ardilauns' only means something if you know that Lord Ardilaun was one of the owners of Dublin's Guinness brewery.

The chapter ends with Stephen heading for Dublin's nighttown, 'to seek the kips where shady Mary is', with a sober Bloom ('the johnny in the black duds'; Bloom is still wearing the clothes he wore to attend Paddy Dignam's funeral) on his trail, determined to play a paternal role by watching over Stephen.

And thus we come to the end of this challenging section, but what purpose does it serve aside from its display of Joyce's literary virtuosity? It allows us in that place of birth to examine the embryo of a new relationship between Bloom and Stephen; a man without a son of his own meets a young man in need of a father figure.

We now move on to by far the longest episode in *Ulysses*, 'Circe', written in the form of a play. The variety and literary diversity of *Ulysses* is ocean deep, but after the rigours of 'Oxen of the Sun', we're still swimming above water.

EPISODE 1 5, 'CIRCE':
All the World's a Stage

R

Bloom! You down here in the haunts of sin! I
caught you nicely. Scamp!
> – Mrs Breen to Leopold Bloom

Having been exposed to the revivalist preacher
Alexander J. Christ Dowie at the end of 'Oxen of the
Sun' – he 'that's yanked to glory most half this planet
from Frisco beach to Vladivostok' – in this 'Circe' episode we do indeed plunge headlong into the haunts of
sin (aka nighttown), and there's a lot of sin around the
place, even if most of it inhabits some ambiguous, amor-
phous psychic realm.

Until it was shut down in 1923, Dublin's nighttown
– or the Monto, as it was known – was located in the
north inner city around Montgomery Street. When I was
ambassador in Malaysia in 2003, I came across a story in
the *New Straits Times*, a publication to which I contributed frequently during my time there, about one of the
brothels that flourished in that area of Dublin around
the turn of the century. This was such an unlikely place
for a story of this kind to appear that I cut it from the
paper and came across the clipping recently in one of
my copies of *Ulysses*. The establishment in question
was run by Madam Oblong, and was said to have been
frequented by King Edward VII (who features in the
'Cyclops' episode of the novel – 'There's a bloody sight
more pox than pax about that boyo').

According to the *New Straits Times* piece, that
Dublin brothel was so famous that it merited a mention
in *Encyclopaedia Britannica*! Joyce knew the area well.
Mary and Padraic Colum, who were both acquainted
with him during their student days, testify that Joyce

enjoyed a huge reputation on account of his immense knowledge of literature and his imperious manner, but it was also known by his contemporaries that he 'went in for evil frequentations of all kinds'.[105] This is polite code for Joyce having reputedly had a dissolute lifestyle and been a periodic visitor to the notorious nighttown.

An exploration of Dublin's long-gone red-light district might seem like an entertaining proposition, but be warned, this is an onerous journey for the reader. Even the most eminent Joyce scholars have found the 'Circe' episode a tall order. In the view of Richard Ellmann, Joyce's peerless biographer, this part of the novel 'awakened some of Joyce's most extreme methods, not less extreme for being couched in terms of music hall or vaudeville'.[106] For Hugh Kenner, who was part of the first generation of academic critics bewitched by Joyce's work, the whole episode is 'phantasmagoric'.[107] He also makes the very good point that, in contrast with the preceding two episodes, where little happens, there is a good deal of activity in 'Circe', even if much of it is the product of hallucinations. The Irish Joycean Declan Kiberd has written that 'In "Circe", the book itself becomes drunk and teases the reader by lifting its skirts to reveal many secrets.'[108] 'Drunk', 'phantasmagoric' and using 'extreme methods'. What a chapter! No short summary can do it justice. My advice is to dip into it, but not to let its convolutions get you down.

The leading literary critic Harold Bloom once wrote that 'James Joyce was the master agonist, daring to contend even against Dante and Shakespeare for the foremost place.'[109] He was right to highlight Joyce's competitive literary pugnacity, his persistent daring, fuelled by an unshakable belief that he had a mission to fulfil, and an ability to deliver on it equal to the best in literary history. The 'Circe' episode is a perfect illustration of those ambitious, unrelenting Joycean qualities.

Joyce's friend, Frank Budgen, has argued that the 'Circe' episode 'is generally regarded as the *clou* to *Ulysses*, at any rate as the most original and striking of all the eighteen episodes'.[110] That's one way of putting it, but it is also a truly daunting read. Having just exited from 'Oxen of the Sun' – which is arguably the most difficult episode of *Ulysses*, up there with 'Proteus' in terms of the challenges it poses – 'Circe' plunges us into a full-length surrealistic play complete with copious stage directions and a mammoth cast of characters drawn from among the living and the dead. It does, like all of Joyce's work, have some fine descriptive writing: 'Snakes of river fog creep slowly. From drains, clefts, cesspools, middens arise on all sides stagnant fumes. A glow leaps in the south beyond the seaward reaches of the river.' I'm not sure why, but I love that last line.

Why does Joyce go to such lengths to surprise and challenge us? Why not stick with the mix of narrative and stream of consciousness that characterises the first ten or so episodes of the novel, or even continue with the exuberant style of the 'Cyclops' episode? The answer, I think, is literary ambition. His collection of short stories, *Dubliners*, showed a similar flair for innovation, but it is set securely within the broad tradition of prose fiction. In *A Portrait of the Artist as a Young Man*, Joyce showed that he could write a more or less conventional novel that pushes the boundaries yes, but remains nonetheless a manageable read. He easily could have continued in that vein and been a successful, avant-garde novelist, but he wanted to be a true groundbreaker, and so he wrote *Ulysses*. And as he worked his way through the novel, he continued to want to innovate. When he finished *Ulysses*, he kept on innovating, the result being *Finnegans Wake*. But let's not go there.

Ezra Pound enthused about 'Circe'. 'Magnificent,' he wrote, 'a new Inferno in full sail'.[111] Joyce himself was proud of what he achieved in 'Circe', and told a friend that 'I think it is the best thing I have ever written.'[112] I am not sure I can agree with Joyce's appraisal. For his best writing, I would choose the final pages of *A Portrait of the Artist as a Young Man*, the closing scene of his short story, 'The Dead' and the last episode of *Ulysses*, which takes place inside the labyrinthine mind of Molly Bloom (and which Joyce wrote after he had completed 'Circe').

'Circe' is the last of the twelve episodes during which we follow Leopold Bloom's wanderings around Dublin. The last three episodes of the novel will chronicle Bloom's return home to Molly (our Joycean Penelope) and unveil her coruscating review of their relationship (among many other things). 'Circe', which is where Bloom's connection with Stephen begins to pick up pace, is in some ways a summary of what has gone before it, for many characters from earlier episodes reappear here, often in a surrealistic guise. Ideas and phrases from earlier episodes crop up again in 'Circe'. From this new (and strange) angle of vision, we get some fresh insights into the lives of Bloom, Stephen and Molly.

In Homer, Odysseus and his crew come to the island of Aeaea, 'the realm of Circe, a most beautiful and most dangerous witch',[113] who turns men into beasts. Here, the role of Circe is taken by Dublin brothel-owner Bella Cohen, described as 'a massive whoremistress' with 'falcon eyes'. There are lots of beasts on the loose here.

In 'Circe', Bloom follows Stephen and his fellow carouser, Vincent Lynch, to Dublin's nighttown, where he has a series of both real and hallucinatory experiences, although it is sometimes difficult to spot where reality cedes ground to some form of hyperreality.

On his way to nighttown, Bloom gets separated from Stephen and Lynch, and is almost run over while crossing a street. This causes an ever-cautious Bloom to remember to insure himself against street accidents. He comes across two British soldiers, Privates Compton and Carr, the use of the latter's name being a little act of revenge on Joyce's part. Henry Carr was an employee of the British Consulate in Zurich during the First World War against whom Joyce took legal action because of a dispute about the production of a play in which both were involved. Britain's wartime representative in Switzerland, Sir Horace Rumbold, who was unsympathetic to Joyce, is name-checked here and in the 'Cyclops' episode as an executioner!

Bloom encounters Jacky and Tommy Caffrey, the two toddlers who were being looked after by Cissy Caffrey on the beach at Sandymount in the 'Nausicaa' episode. This doesn't make any sense, for how could two children be roaming around Dublin's red-light district after midnight? This tells us that we are not in a naturalistic environment, but immersed in some kind of wild fantasy.

Bloom meets his dead father, who chides him for wasting his money and abandoning his Jewish faith. His mother, Ellen, also makes a fleeting appearance, as does Molly, dressed in Turkish costume, though she is actually at home in Eccles Street. She refers to her husband as 'a poor old stick in the mud' and urges him to 'Go and see life. See the wide world.' Gerty MacDowell pops up to accuse Bloom of being a 'Dirty married man'. Mrs Breen, who we met in the 'Lestrygonians' episode, and who appeared again in 'Cyclops', where she was vainly trying to rein in her manic husband, catches Bloom red-handed 'in the haunts of sin'. He lamely maintains that he is there for the 'rescue of fallen women'. (William Ewart Gladstone used the same rationale for his habit of mounting rescue operations in London's Victorian 'haunts of sin' during his time as Prime Minister.) It is revealed that Bloom once had 'a soft corner' for Mrs Breen, who replies that Bloom was 'always a favourite with the ladies'.

Bloom's amorous pen pal, Martha Clifford (her real name is Peggy Griffin), enters the action in Bloom's evidently overexcited imagination, and calls him a 'heartless flirt'. Bloom insists that he is 'a respectable married man' without a stain on his character. Well, yes, to a point. He is accused of plagiarism by Philip Beaufoy, author of a story Bloom read that morning in *Titbits*, which prompted him to toy with the idea of concocting a similar yarn for publication and financial gain. The soap he had bought in Sweny's that morning is also part of this bizarre *dramatis personae*.

Meanwhile, Bloom finds himself on trial, accused by a succession of women of a range of sexual transgressions. Mary Driscoll, a servant girl, alleges that, while Molly was out shopping, he held her and she was 'discoloured in four places as a result'. Mrs Yelverton Barry joins the fray, alleging that Bloom offered to send her a copy of *The Girl with the Three Pairs of Stays* by French popular novelist Paul de Kock. It may be recalled from the 'Calypso' chapter that de Kock was one of Molly's preferred authors.

Next up in this surreal trial is a Mrs Bellingham, who testifies that Bloom had urged her 'to defile the marriage bed, to commit adultery at the earliest possible opportunity.' And last but not least, the Honourable Mrs Mervin Talboys ('*In amazon costume, hard hat, jackboots, cockspurred ...*') asserts that Bloom sent her 'an obscene photograph, such as are sold after dark on Paris boulevards' and urged her to give him 'a most vicious horsewhipping'. She describes him as 'a wellknown cuckold', which, as this is happening in Bloom's imagination, means he suspects that plenty of Dubliners are aware of his marital misfortunes. We are evidently in the realms here of Bloom's (and Joyce's) sexual obsessions and fantasies. Bloom is branded as 'a fiendish libertine from his earliest years' and is diagnosed by Buck Mulligan as 'bisexually abnormal' and showing symptoms of 'chronic exhibitionism'. The jury is made up of Dubliners we have already met, including the ubiquitous Simon Dedalus, so Bloom is evidently imagining himself being weighed up by his acquaintances, and probably fearing the worst from them. There is a hell of a lot going on in Bloom's psyche, which 'Circe' extravagantly draws to our attention.

Throughout this, Bloom is defended by J. J. O'Molloy, who describes his client as 'an innately bashful man ... the last man in the world to do anything ungentlemanly which injured modesty could object to'. There are hints of anti-Jewish prejudice working against Bloom, 'the hidden hand is again at its old game. When in doubt persecute Bloom.'

Abruptly, the fantasy shifts in a political direction, as Bloom is conjured up as Lord Mayor of Dublin and described as 'the world's greatest reformer'. John Howard Parnell sees him as 'Successor to my famous brother!' This imaginary politician promises to usher in 'the new Bloomusalem in the Nova Hibernia of the future'. Bloom's political manifesto is hilarious, and thoroughly Bloomite: 'the reform of municipal morals and the plain ten commandments. New worlds for old. Union of all, jew, moslem and gentile. Three acres and a cow for all children of nature.' It goes on, ending with 'Free money, free rent, free love and a free lay church in a free lay state.' It all sounds very 1960s to me, but I'm probably showing my age.

Bloom eventually re-joins Stephen and Lynch in the brothel belonging to Bella Cohen, who proceeds to give Bloom and Stephen a hard time. Bella takes on a male identity, Bello, and proceeds to dominate Bloom, who assumes female form. We have already had hints about Bloom's sexuality, as when he is described earlier in the episode as 'the new womanly man'. Bello threatens Bloom with all kinds of tortures – 'you will be laced with cruel force into vicelike corsets'. 'The Sins of the Past' (Bloom's past) manifest themselves '*In a medley of voices*' accusing Bloom of offering 'his nuptial partner to all strongmembered males'. Bello brings up Molly's infidelity: 'there's a man of brawn in possession there.... Wait for nine months, my lad!' Bloom has a hallucinatory encounter with Blazes Boylan, who tells Bloom that he has 'a little private business with your wife. You understand?' Bloom asks Boylan if he can 'witness the deed and take a snapshot?' Is there some sense in which Bloom welcomes the challenge posed for him by Molly's infidelity?

One of the strangest scenes in this strange episode comes when a nymph, whose image (referred to in the 'Calypso' episode) Bloom had framed and put above his bed at Eccles Street, emerges to complain about what she has seen and heard (words that 'are not in my dictionary') from her privileged vantage point.

When Bloom and Stephen look in a mirror they see an image of a beardless Shakespeare, whose appearance recalls the episode in the National Library where discussion centred around the father-son theme in *Hamlet*, a theme that is in the course of being played out between Bloom and Stephen.

Stephen becomes uncontrollably agitated when his dead mother appears. He smashes a chandelier and flees into the street, leaving Bloom to pay for the damage. We know from the book's opening episode that Stephen has a bad conscience about his mother's death, having refused her dying wish that he pray with her. Mulligan, appearing in a vision, jolts him by claiming that he was responsible for her death. Stephen replies 'Cancer did it, not I. Destiny.'

The episode ends with Bloom, the good Samaritan, saving Stephen from the ire of two British soldiers, one of whom knocks Stephen unconscious. Expressing his (and Joyce's) instinctive scepticism about patriotic zeal, Stephen says: 'Let my country die for me … Damn death. Long live life.' Yes. Yet another Joycean affirmation of life.

The last apparition is of Bloom's deceased son, Rudy, who died when he was just eleven days old. Rudy says nothing, while Bloom '*(wonderstruck, calls inaudibly)* Rudy!'

What we see played out in this episode are Bloom's (and very often Joyce's) fantasies. We know from explicit letters exchanged between Joyce and Nora that they may have had an unusually intense sex life, at least on paper. This aspect of *Ulysses* will be brought to its conclusion in the book's final episode. It was brave of Joyce to include such material, which he surely knew would land him in strife with censors and potential publishers. He wrote 'Circe' after the 'Nausicaa' episode had provoked a ban on his work in the USA. Some critics speculate that 'Circe' was a kind of rejoinder, sticking it to the censorious. The liaison between Bloom and Stephen, which has been seeded in Bella Cohen's house of ill repute on Tyrone Street, is set to grow, but not too dramatically, as *Ulysses* draws to a close.

EPISODE 16, 'EUMAEUS':
Skipper Murphy Sails Again

E CAN'T

change the country. Let us change the subject.
   – Stephen Dedalus to Leopold Bloom

'Country', 'Change'. Yes, from my first days of reading Irish history, I have been much taken by the flurry of political activity that changed Ireland in the opening decades of the twentieth century.[114] How could this sort of transformation have occurred with such apparent suddenness and conspicuous success? In his own way, James Joyce provides some of the answers to that question, and that is part of what has encouraged me to write about him.

While Joyce may have been sceptical about the shibboleths of the Irish nationalist tradition within which he was raised, by the time he got into his stride writing *Ulysses*, the Ireland he had left behind in 1904 really had, as W. B. Yeats memorably put it, 'changed utterly'. Indeed, Joyce's *Ulysses* years (1914–21) turned out to be highly charged ones for Ireland, marked by the 1916 Easter Rising; the 1918 election that saw Sinn Féin triumph; the establishment of the First Dáil in 1919; the War of Independence, 1919–21; and, as he was busy correcting proofs, the Anglo-Irish Treaty of 1921. I am reminded of the lines from Tom Stoppard's play, *Travesties*, 'What did you do in the Great War, Mr Joyce? I wrote *Ulysses*. What did you do?' That's what he was doing too when Ireland was being transformed by the actions of his own contemporaries.

Joyce had a gift for capturing the fibres of Irish life from his eyrie of 'exile and cunning'[115] in cities on the continental mainland. John J. Horgan, Joyce's contemporary, testifies to how well Joyce 'recaptures the tense atmosphere of those days' in the wake of the Parnell split. Horgan writes that the exchanges recorded in *A Portrait* 'with its bitter language reproduces only too well the scenes which then occurred in many Irish homes'.[116] I see *Ulysses* in a similar vein, exploring as it does the cusp between the last generation of Home Rulers and the game-changing separatists who came into their own in the second decade of the twentieth century while Joyce was busy writing.

If Joyce had any time to spare to think about such things as he laboured to complete his novel, he would have concluded that his countrymen and women had indeed successfully changed the subject and, thus, their country. In political terms, Joyce's Ireland was that of the pre-1916 Irish party anatomised in his story 'Ivy Day at the Committee Room', still pining for the dead 'king', Parnell. It was the Ireland of the Sheehys, mentioned in 'Wandering Rocks'; of his father's friends yearning for Irish Home Rule; of politicians like former Dublin Lord Mayor and MP Tim Harrington, referred to in 'Circe', who supplied the young writer with a letter of introduction when he left for Paris in 1902; and of that 'coming man', Arthur Griffith. There is little mention in *Ulysses* of the radical element that engineered the Easter Rising, of Patrick Pearse, whom Joyce knew, or of Thomas MacDonagh, whose work he must have known. They were not part of his, or his father's, Irish world in the way that MPs such as Nannetti and Field – two far less significant figures – were.

It's time for me to change the subject by turning to the 'Eumaeus' episode. Here's how it begins:

'Preparatory to anything else Mr. Bloom brushed off the bulk of the shavings and handed Stephen the hat and ashplant and bucked him up generally in orthodox Samaritan fashion, which he very badly needed.'

Readers will notice the change of style and tone from its predecessor. We have gone from the phantasmagoric style of 'Circe' to a matter-of-fact form of writing. Joyce told his friend Frank Budgen that, after the great technical difficulties 'Circe' had posed for him 'and for the reader something worse', in 'Eumaeus' the style is 'quite plain',[117] and that is true. Plain and ponderous. No serious reader will be put off by this episode, although the writing is more than a little prolix. Critic Maud Ellmann has observed about 'Eumaeus' and its successor, 'Ithaca', that: 'In place of the traditional economy of plot, where the supply of words is budgeted to the demands of action, Joyce introduces a throwaway aesthetic in which words outnumber deeds by at least 20:1.' She is not best pleased with 'Eumaeus', describing it as 'a crashing anti-climax' afflicted by 'narcolepsy' and 'drowned in a barrage of clichés'.[118] Ouch.

Allow me to demur and say that I rather like this episode, probably because it explores Irish history more intensively than any of its predecessors other than my personal favourite, 'Cyclops'. In 'Eumaeus', we get a more measured political analysis, sleepy even at times, contrasting with the frenetic outbursts that characterise 'Cyclops'. I confess that I also have a curious affection for the writing style Joyce employs here, languid and long-winded though it undoubtedly is. What we get here is one of the most complete accounts of Bloom's mentality, his political views, his taste in music and his religious outlook.

As in 'Cyclops', 'Eumaeus' has an unnamed narrator (who is privy to all of Bloom's thoughts), and there are those who consider that Bloom himself could actually be playing that role, as the narrator's lumbering attitudes and carefully modulated, if over-elaborate, language seem quite Bloom-like.[119] This narrator certainly contrasts with his counterpart in 'Cyclops', who is aggressively opinionated. Our narrator here appears to have no opinions at all, just a 'doubting Thomas' approach to everything.

In the *Odyssey*, the homecoming hero Odysseus, arriving back in Ithaca in disguise, spends time with his swineherd, Eumaeus. In this episode, there is much that is disguised or misleading, and the narrator regularly alludes to the uncertainties surrounding the information he imparts. Two of the characters who appear here, the owner of the cabman's shelter, Fitzharris, and the *soi-disant* sailor, W. B. Murphy, may not be who they are reputed, or pretend, to be. Bloom is trying to conjure up a father-son rapport with Stephen, who, for his part, when asked by Murphy if he knew Simon Dedalus (his father's name), says he has 'heard of him', and that he is 'all too Irish'. It turns out that the Simon Dedalus referred to in this instance is a circus performer, but that may also be a made-up yarn. Asked by Bloom why he had left the family home, Stephen cryptically replies, 'to seek misfortune'.

After the frenzied whirlpool that was 'Circe', we are now in calmer waters as we accompany an exhausted Bloom (this episode takes place after midnight) and Stephen after they leave nighttown. A 'disgustingly sober' Bloom, in paternalistic mode, offers a 'not yet perfectly sober' Stephen some sage advice, about 'the dangers of nighttown, women of ill fame and swell mobsmen'. He urges Stephen not to repose much trust 'in that boon companion of yours, who contributes the humorous element', Buck Mulligan.

As the two walk the streets of Dublin, they come across John Corley, who is down on his luck and in dire need of money. The sceptical narrator wonders about Corley's hard-luck story, and 'if the whole thing wasn't a complete fabrication from start to finish', another illustration of how nothing here can be taken at face value. Recognising Bloom and believing him to be an associate of Blazes Boylan, Corley asks Stephen if Bloom might intercede on his behalf to get him a job with Boylan as a 'billsticker'. Is this further oblique evidence that the Molly-Boylan nexus is a known fact around Dublin?

They end up in a cabman's shelter at Butt Bridge, populated by a 'decidedly miscellaneous collection of waifs and strays and other nondescript specimens of the genus *homo*', for a late-night coffee and a bun, or, as Joyce's narrator chooses to describe Bloom's purchase, 'a choice concoction labelled coffee' and 'a rather antediluvian specimen of a bun, or so it seemed'. This narrator is a master of the tentative remark.

The shelter is being run by someone thought to be Skin-the-Goat Fitzharris, a member of the Invincibles, an offshoot of the Fenians who equates with Homer's Eumaeus, although it is hard to see the correspondence. Eumaeus doesn't recognise Odysseus, while Bloom is not sure if it is really Fitzharris running the cabman's shelter. Given the intimate nature of early twentieth-century Dublin as demonstrated throughout *Ulysses*, it seems strange that there would have been any uncertainty surrounding someone as notorious as 'Skin-the-Goat'. Uncertainty is, however, the stock in trade of this part of the book.

This, incidentally, is the closest brush we get with separatist Irish nationalism, for even the fiery 'citizen' in 'Cyclops' was more of a cultural nationalist, advocating for an Irish Ireland, than an outright exponent of physical force in pursuit of political ends. Fitzharris was jailed for twenty years for being an accomplice in the assassination in May 1882 (just months after Joyce's birth) of the Irish Chief Secretary, Lord Frederick Cavendish, and his Deputy, T. H. Burke. Those murders were probably the biggest blow to the British administration in Ireland throughout the whole of the nineteenth century.[120]

In a piece he published about Fenianism in a Trieste newspaper in 1907, Joyce wrote that 'any concession by England to Ireland has been granted unwillingly, at bayonet point, as the saying goes'.[121] This indicates that, while decidedly a pacifist in outlook, he was familiar with the perspective of Ireland's Fenian tradition and its disdain for the gradualist approach of nineteenth-century Irish parliamentarians. Elsewhere, Joyce wrote that Parnell had 'set out on a march along the borders of insurrection',[122] implying that Parnell's political success had been aided by his deft invocation of the spectre of revolution. The narrator records Bloom telling Stephen about Fitzharris, but adds that 'he wouldn't vouch for the actual facts, which quite possibly there was not one vestige of truth in'.

The most colourful character in 'Eumaeus' is the aforementioned W. B. Murphy, a verbose sailor. When

I organised my first ever Bloomsday at the Consulate General in Edinburgh in June 1999, one of our readers was the Edinburgh-based Irish poet Hayden Murphy. On that occasion, Hayden read a few passages pertaining to 'Skipper' Murphy. At the time, this seemed like an obscure choice, for most of our readers had selected passages featuring Stephen Dedalus, Leopold Bloom or the voluble 'citizen'. I now realise that Murphy is actually a significant, if insubstantial and possibly fraudulent, character in the novel. Whereas Bloom is clearly the prime counterpart of Homer's Odysseus, here Murphy, a mariner with many questionable yarns to tell of his travels to faraway places, also represents Homer's hero, and the possibility that the whole Homeric shebang is a tall tale. Murphy has been seven years at sea compared with Odysseus's ten years away from Ithaca and Bloom's seventeen hours on the loose around Dublin. Joyce also spent seven years writing *Ulysses.*

Murphy has more than a touch of the fabulist about him. He claims not to have seen 'his own true wife' who lives in Queenstown (now Cobh) in Cork for seven years, a peculiarly lengthy separation even for an early twentieth-century 'old sea dog'. On his travels, he has seen a crocodile 'bite the fluke of an anchor', and 'maneaters in Peru that eats corpses and the livers of horses'. Joyce wrote to a friend that he was 'heaping all kinds of lies in to the mouth of that sailorman in "Eumaeus" which will make you laugh'.[123]

Inevitably, discussion turns to Irish politics. Skin-the-Goat echoes some of the political complaints heard from 'the citizen' and others earlier in the day. He sees Ireland as 'the richest country in the world bar none on the face of God's earth, far and away superior to England'. He taps into the idea, common among turn-of-the-century nationalists, that Ireland was overtaxed with 'all the riches drained out of it by England levying taxes on the poor that paid through the nose always'. There was 'a day of reckoning' in store 'for mighty England', and he predicted that 'the Germans and the Japs were going to have their little lookin'. The Boer War was, he insisted, 'the beginning of the end' for the British Empire, and Ireland would be England's Achilles' heel. Sailor Murphy retorts that the Irish were the pick of the British Army, and that the Irish Catholic peasant was 'the backbone of our empire'. In Skin-the-Goat's adamant opinion, 'no Irishman worthy of his salt' would serve the British state.

This prompts a discussion between Bloom and Stephen. Ever the moderate, Bloom is inclined 'to poohpooh' Skin-the-Goat's arguments as 'egregious balderdash'. Our English neighbours, he thinks, 'rather concealed their strength than the opposite'. He sees it as highly advisable 'to try to make the most of both countries, even though poles apart'. As we already know, Bloom resents 'violence or intolerance in any shape or form', and argues that 'A revolution must come on the due instalments plan.' Not many impatient revolutionaries would share this incremental view of the dynamics of history and politics. Stephen, in his self-absorbed fashion, muses that 'Ireland must be important because it belongs to me.' Understandably, this display of prim arrogance puzzles Bloom, but Stephen then comes up with a show stopper that ends this train of conversation: 'We can't change the country. Let us change the subject.' Stephen's ability to express himself with such precision while still sobering up is strangely inspiring. I don't know many, if any, who can match that feat.

We also get a sight of Bloom's more expansive political philosophy, his egalitarianism, desiring a society 'where you can live well ... if you work.' He wants to see all classes and creeds 'having a comfortable tidysized income, in no niggard fashion either, something in the neighbourhood of £300 per annum. That's the vital issue at stake and it's feasible and would be provocative of friendlier intercourse between man and man.... I call that patriotism.' Bloom (and Joyce) is ahead of his time as an advocate of a guaranteed minimum income, a concept now being seriously discussed in some countries.

No reference to Irish politics in Joyce's work would be complete without Charles Stewart Parnell making his presence felt, and that's what happens here too. One cabman recalls a Dublin Fusilier claiming to have seen Parnell in South Africa. It was alleged that Parnell's coffin was full of stones and that 'he changed his name to De Wet, the Boer general'. Bloom's response, conveyed via the narrator, is quintessentially prudent and guarded: 'Highly unlikely of course that there was even a shadow of truth in the stories and, even supposing, he thought a return highly inadvisable, all things considered', because times move on. They certainly do.

Mention of Parnell generates lively exchanges. Skin-the-Goat blames Katherine O'Shea for Parnell's travails. 'She put the first nail in his coffin.' To one of the customers she was a 'fine lump of a woman ... and plenty of her'. This reminds me of descriptions of Molly that are sprinkled throughout the novel, 'a good armful', etc. Bloom, who is sympathetic to Parnell and Katherine

O'Shea, describes their situation in terms uncannily like his own predicament, with Bloom as Captain O'Shea and Blazes Boylan as Parnell: 'it was simply a case of the husband not being up to scratch, with nothing in common between them beyond the name, and then a real man arriving on the scene, strong to the verge of weakness, falling victim to her siren charms and forgetting home ties'. He asks 'the eternal question of the life connubial.... Can real love, supposing there happens to be another chap in the case, exist between married folk?' Yes, it can, and does, although the intrusion of 'another chap' would surely complicate matters!

Bloom fishes a photo of Molly from his pocket to show Stephen. The narrator describes her as 'a large sized lady, with her fleshy charms on evidence in an open fashion'. Bloom presents her as 'Mrs Bloom my wife the *prima donna* Madam Marion Tweedy'. It's as if he's asking Stephen to audition Molly. Bloom almost ogles the photo of his wife. It 'did not do justice to her figure which came in for a lot of notice usually'. He wanted Stephen to 'drink in the beauty for himself'. Strange stuff this. Stephen considers Molly's photo to be 'handsome'. Bloom revels in Stephen's company, for he is 'educated, *distingué* and impulsive into the bargain'.

On their way back to Eccles Street, they talk about music, 'a form of art for which Bloom, as a pure amateur, possessed the greatest love'. He professes a preference for operas such as Mozart's *Don Giovanni* and von Flotow's *Martha*. Stephen displays his 'phenomenally beautiful tenor voice'. Joyce was a gifted singer who could perhaps have made a career for himself as a concert performer. Bloom fantasises about acting as Stephen's manager.

[246]

In a short study of James Joyce published in 1971, the critic John Gross wrote that: 'Reduced to its simplest terms, *Ulysses* is the story of a chance encounter between two men who have been wandering around Dublin all day, and its possible life-enhancing repercussions.' That makes 'Eumaeus' a key part of the book, for it is where Bloom and Stephen spend what you might call 'quality time' together for the first time. Sure, they have almost met in 'Aeolus', brushed past each other in 'Scylla and Charybdis', been in the same room in 'Oxen of the Sun' and interacted in the chaotic, hallucinatory 'Circe', but it is in this unprepossessing shelter near Butt Bridge that they finally bond. They do not actually become bosom buddies. In truth, they are on different wavelengths, but that's often the way it is even between family and friends. Bloom struggles to keep up with Stephen's elliptical observations, but the time they spend together clearly pleases Bloom. Stephen's opinion of his companion is more difficult to discern, as 'Eumaeus' gives us no access to Stephen's thoughts. Bloom's Odyssean wanderings will end in Stephen's company, as Odysseus and Telemachus, father and son, wend their weary way back to Bloom's Ithaca on Dublin's Eccles Street.

EPISODE 1 7, 'ITHACA':
Joyce's Universal Catechism

HAT

relation existed between their ages?

16 years before in 1888 when Bloom was of Stephen's present age Stephen was 6. 16 years after in 1920 when Stephen would be of Bloom's present age Bloom would be 54. In 1936 when Bloom would be 70 and Stephen 54 their ages initially in the ratio of 16 to 0 would be as 17½ to 13½, the proportion increasing and the disparity diminishing according as arbitrary future years were added, for if the proportion existing in 1883 had continued immutable, conceiving that to be possible, till then 1904 when Stephen was 22 Bloom would be 374 ...

What events might nullify these calculations?

The cessation of existence of both or either, the inauguration of a new era or calendar, the annihilation of the world and consequent extermination of the human species, inevitable but impredictable.'

– *Ulysses*, 'Ithaca'

What is the style in which this episode is written?

Always a good question when it comes to episodes of *Ulysses*, with their diverse, continually shifting styles. The current style is exemplified by the sample passage reproduced above. Mathematical, pseudo-scientific, philosophical in a homespun kind of way, more than a trifle pedantic perhaps. And, of course, it is written in the form of a question-and-answer session, as this chapter is too.

What has Pete Buttigieg to do with the 'Ithaca' episode of *Ulysses*?

Sometime in the opening months of the year 2020, while Mayor Pete Buttigieg was still a candidate in the primaries to choose a Democratic contender for that year's US presidential election, I watched him doing a TV interview from his home in South Bend, Indiana, and noticed that the bookshelf behind him displayed a number of copies of *Ulysses*. This intrigued me until I recalled that he had previously revealed Joyce's novel to be his all-time favourite. With a little research I discovered that the mayor's late father had been a Joyce scholar at the University of Notre Dame. I invited Mayor Pete (US Secretary for Transport since February 2021) to take part in our virtual Bloomsday celebration in June. He graciously agreed to do so, and duly sent us a video in which he commented: 'I've come to believe that good politics is about the everyday and so is much of the greatest literature in the English language, most notably *Ulysses*.' He contributed an excellent reading from the 'Ithaca' episode focused on Bloom's enchantment with water:

> What in water did Bloom, waterlover, drawer of water, watercarrier, returning to the range, admire? Its universality: its democratic equality and constancy to its nature in seeking its own level: its vastness in the ocean of Mercator's projection: its unplumbed profundity in the Sundam trench of the Pacific exceeding 8000 fathoms: the restlessness of its waves and surface particles visiting in turn all points of its seaboard: ...

and so forth (Bloom's water whimsy gushes on for two pages in my edition). My favourite bit describes water's 'metamorphoses as vapour, mist, cloud, rain, sleet, snow, hail'.

Catechism – why?

This is another unusual piece of writing. The entire episode, one of the longest in the novel, takes the form of what Joyce himself called 'a mathematical catechism' in which 'all events are resolved into their cosmic physical, psychical etc. equivalents'.[124] Critic Stuart Gilbert wrote about 'Ithaca' that 'the flesh of sentiment and trappings of style have been stripped till it is little more than a skeleton'.[125] Yet, there is a lot to this skeleton, even if much of it is buried under an avalanche of extended sentences delving encyclopaedically into a diverse set of topics. In truth, it can get a little tedious at times, but it is worth persevering with. Joyce told Frank Budgen that 'Ithaca' was his favourite episode, although this does not sit all that comfortably with his comment, also reported by Budgen, that 'it is the ugly duckling of the book'.[126]

There are those who question why Joyce chose to use this curious technique for the climax of his novel. Why not allow his readers direct access via an interior monologue to the thoughts of Bloom and Stephen as their father-son nexus reaches its apogee? What we get is an account of the exchanges between Bloom and Stephen and, after Stephen departs Eccles Street, an exploration of Bloom's nocturnal thoughts, mediated through an opaque prism lit by an over-elaborate, mock-scientific prose. There is also a lot of seemingly excessive detail, as when the flow of water from Bloom's kitchen tap is traced back to the reservoir at Roundwood, 'a cubic capacity of 2400 million gallons, percolating through a subterranean aqueduct of filter mains of single and double pipeage constructed at an initial plant cost of £5 per linear yard …' He goes on to map the route of the water and to record the name of the waterworks' engineer, Mr Spencer Harty, C. E., and of 'the law agent of the corporation, Mr Ignatius Rice, solicitor …' Too much information perhaps.

Why is this episode called Ithaca?

In Homer, Ithaca is Odysseus's home place, to which he returns at the end of his Odyssey to be reunited with his wife, Penelope, and his son, Telemachus. In Joyce's 'Ithaca', Bloom invites Stephen back to his home at Eccles Street, where he serves him a cup of cocoa and invites him to stay overnight, an offer Stephen declines. He is keen for Stephen to meet Molly, and suggests she give him singing lessons. They talk in the kitchen and then urinate together in the garden before Stephen takes his leave. Bloom then reviews his day's wanderings, calculates his expenditure and thinks about his daughter Milly before retiring to bed and conversing briefly with a sleepy Molly. He then falls asleep, leaving Molly to her thoughts, which will form the substance of the novel's closing chapter. Thus, we have the novel's three main characters together for the first time under the same roof. As far as we know, Molly has not left her house all day, although she has hosted an amorous visitor. Bloom and Stephen have been on the go since morning, rambling around Dublin, haunted in Bloom's case by his wife's infidelity and in Stephen's case by his family and his artistic ambitions.

What subjects are discussed by Bloom and Stephen?

After leaving the cabman's shelter on their way to Eccles Street, we are told that they discuss 'Music, literature, Ireland, Dublin, Paris, friendship, women, prostitution, diet, the influence of gaslight or the light of arc and glow-lamps on the growth of adjoining paraheliotropic trees …' and on and on it goes. The number of subjects mentioned seems like a hell of a lot of ground to cover on a late-night walk, and we are given little or no information about what was said on most of those subjects. We do learn, however, that both were 'sensitive to artistic impressions, musical in preference to plastic or pictorial', and that 'both preferred a continental to an insular manner of life'. In Stephen's case, that seems reasonable, as he had recently returned from Paris to see his dying mother, but Bloom is not well travelled, although, as we know from earlier episodes, he has a vivid imagination when it comes to distant lands.

Bloom and Stephen are described as having 'an inherited tenacity of heterodox resistance'. As a result, they 'professed their disbelief in many orthodox religious, national, social and ethical doctrines'. And 'both admitted the alternately stimulating and obtunding influence of heterosexual magnetism'. This is consistent with what we have learned of the two throughout the preceding sixteen episodes. Both are semi-outsiders in the city in which they live. Both have sexual hang-ups. Stephen's are those of youth, while Bloom's are associated with his disordered marriage.

There is no great hoopla about this ultimate coming together of two of the novel's main characters. It is not exactly a display of searing intimacy. Their exchanges are friendly but unemotional. That's who they are, and that's how they behave.

Displaying an extraordinary lack of tact, Stephen regales Bloom with an offensively anti-Semitic song about a Jewish girl who cuts off the head of a 'pretty little boy', Harry Hughes, but Bloom takes it all calmly in his stride.

What did Bloom forget?

When they reach Eccles Street, Bloom realises he has forgotten his latchkey. This irritates him, 'because he remembered that he had reminded himself twice not to forget'. Don't we all. Unwilling to wake Molly, he decides to enter through the basement kitchen. While Joyce was completing this episode, he wrote to his aunt, Josephine Murray, to ask if a normal person could climb over the railings at No. 7 Eccles Street and drop down to the ground without hurting himself.[127] Such was Joyce's obsession with exactitude as he laboured over the final stretch of his seven-year writing marathon.

What does Bloom do when he enters his home?

He lights a fire in his kitchen, or rather kindles the 'best Abram coal ... thereby releasing the potential energy contained in the fuel by allowing its carbon and hydrogen elements to enter into free union with the oxygen of the air.' Later, we are invited to inspect

[256]

Bloom's bookshelf, with its impressively eclectic ensemble, including *Thom's Dublin Post Office Directory, 1886*, which Joyce made use of when writing *Ulysses*, and his desk drawers, containing, among many other things, a copy of his father's suicide note and financial documentation revealing that he is moderately well off through his savings.

What do we learn about Stephen's personal hygiene?

That he is a hydrophobe, who had his last bath nine months before, whereas, by contrast, a fastidious Bloom had bathed that very day. Stephen dislikes 'aqueous substances of glass and crystal', and distrusts 'aquacities of thought and language'. Bloom considers offering his young friend some advice about hygiene, but holds back because of 'the incompatibility of aquacity with the erratic originality of genius.'

How do Bloom and Stephen differ in their attitude to literature?

Quite a bit. For Bloom, it is a source of 'instruction rather than amusement'. He had, he said, more than once referred to the works of Shakespeare 'for the solution of difficult problems in imaginary or real life', although he had only derived 'imperfect conviction from the text'. For his part, Stephen sees in literature 'the eternal affirmation of the spirit of man', but that is a bit too airy-fairy for Bloom's taste, as he possesses a scientific temperament in contrast to Stephen's artistic one.

What do we get to see in Bloom's kitchen dresser?

Joyce goes into considerable detail about its contents – crockery, olives, tea, cocoa, 'white invalid port' and a jar of cream from the Irish Model Dairy. Included is an empty pot of Plumtree's potted meat, which we have come across in Davy Byrne's 'moral pub'.

Had Bloom and Stephen met before 16 June 1904?

Yes, on two occasions. First, at the home of Matthew Dillon in 1887, when Stephen was five years old; and second, five years later, in the coffee room of Breslin's Hotel. And there is a third link between them in the shape of Mrs Dante Riordan. Readers of *A Portrait of the Artist as a Young Man* will recall the Christmas dinner scene in which Mrs Riordan engages in a flaming row with Stephen's father about Charles Stewart Parnell, in whose fall from grace she revels, while Simon Dedalus defends Parnell to the hilt. Mrs Riordan was a friend of the Dedalus family, and had also been a neighbour of the Blooms for a couple of years in the City Arms Hotel, where Leopold had paid great attention to her in the hope of being written into her will.

What do we find out about Bloom's political outlook?

Today, he would be called a progressive who 'desired to amend many social conditions, the product of inequality and avarice and international animosity'.

Do you have a favourite passage in this episode?

Yes, and it's a short one, a rarity in this very wordy part of the novel. It occurs when the two go into Bloom's garden and find 'The heaventree of stars hung with humid nightblue fruit.'

What evidence of Blazes Boylan's afternoon visit to Molly does Bloom uncover?

He notices 'two lacerated scarlet betting tickets' connected with that day's Ascot Gold Cup. We know from an earlier episode that Boylan had placed a bet on the race on behalf of a lady friend, which means that he had lost money. This ought to have pleased Bloom, who has no interest in betting. Some pieces of furniture have been moved, and we also get sight of a musical score for 'Love's Old Sweet Song', which Molly had rehearsed with Boylan (the promoter of her upcoming concert tour) that afternoon. When Bloom goes to his bed, he detects on the 'new clean bedlinen … the imprint of a human form, male, not his' but Boylan's.

What transpires between Leopold and Molly when they are reunited?

She asks him about his day, of which he offers her a polite but incomplete account, omitting the embarrassing bits, such as his infatuation with Gerty MacDowell and his visit to nighttown. We will learn in the closing episode that Molly is not fooled. She searches his pockets for evidence of wrongdoing on his part, even though she professes not to care what he does during the day (within limits, of course). Bloom avoids questioning her because he knows what she's been up to.

What do we learn about Bloom's response to Molly's infidelity?

We can hardly fail to be struck by the equanimity with which Bloom deals with Molly's behaviour. He is neither angry, vengeful nor resentful, but takes the whole affair in his stride, expressing a philosophical acceptance of his fate as a cuckold. He lists Molly's putative lovers (most probably not lovers in any full sense, more admirers), ending with 'Hugh E. (Blazes) Boylan', 'a bounder ... a billsticker ... a bester' and 'a boaster'. He envies Boylan's sexual energy and is jealous of his attractiveness to Molly. He then goes on to concede that Boylan's transgression was a 'natural act' that has happened umpteen times throughout human history. In the grand scheme of things, it was not 'as calamitous as a cataclysmic annihilation of the planet in consequence of a collision with a dark sun'. It was 'less reprehensible than theft, highway robbery, cruelty to children and animals ...' and so the list of crimes more serious than adultery continues at some length. Whereas in Homer, Odysseus and Telemachus, on their return to Ithaca, slay Penelope's suitors, Bloom, who eschews violence, dismisses the option of assassination or duel by combat as 'two wrongs did not make one right'. Instead, he routs Molly's suitors by highlighting the cosmic irrelevance of their antics, pointing to 'the apathy of the stars'.

There cannot be many men, in literature or in life, who would respond to infidelity and adultery in this calm, collected manner. Our Leopold is quite an extraordinary, even unique, Everyman.

As we take our leave of Leopold Bloom after an acquaintance lasting many hundreds of pages, how can his character be summarised?

Impossible, of course, to capture fully such a complex character in a single paragraph, but here are a few words that may help sum him up, for the most part: belligerent (very occasionally, as when provoked by 'the citizen'), cautious, considerate (in his efforts to sort out deceased Paddy Dignam's life assurance, and in visiting the Dignam family), earnest, embattled (by the hostility of many of his fellow Dubliners), fatherless (as a result of his father's suicide), furtive (for example, about his clandestine correspondence with Martha Clifford), long-winded, pacifistic, passive, paternal (in his concern for Stephen), patriotic (he defines his nation as 'Ireland ... I was born here. Ireland'), 'plabbery' (according to Molly, and she would know; this made-up word could also be applied to Molly herself), politically moderate, preoccupied (with his wife and her behaviour), profound (from time to time, and of the common or garden variety), prudent, religiously sceptical, scientific (some would say pseudo, but he does his best), sober, sonless (since the death of Rudy in infancy), tolerant and wary. I could go on, but you get the idea.

How does it end?

With a 'Where?' and a big full stop, designed I think, to indicate that our marathon journey in the company of Leopold Bloom has come to an end.

What's next?

As this long Dublin day ends, we turn to the formidable Molly Bloom. We have met her briefly in 'Calypso', Episode 4, where we caught a glimpse of her feistiness and the manner in which she is fussed over by her Poldy. Since then, we have viewed her through the prism of her husband's thoughts and the fleeting, largely ungenerous assessments of her on the part of some of the book's minor characters. Now is our chance to become acquainted with her in a major way. What a knowing person she will turn out to be, and what a lot of knowledge she has to impart. Enter Mrs Marion (Molly) Bloom, née Tweedy, who will perform the final aria of this epic, comic, mock-heroic opera called *Ulysses*.

EPISODE 18, 'PENELOPE':
Lots and Lots of Yesses – and One Full Stop!

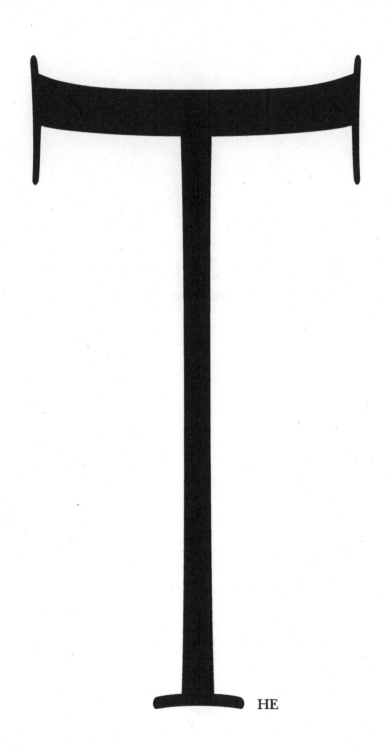

HE

women are always egging on to that putting it on thick when hes there they know by his sly eye blinking a bit putting on the indifferent when they come out with something the kind he is what spoils him I don't wonder in the least because he was very handsome at that time trying to look like Lord Byron I said I liked him though he was too beautiful for a man and he was a little before we got engaged ...

– Molly Bloom in 'Penelope'

It's all there in this sample passage from the 'Penelope' episode. The torrent of thoughts and impressions, the total absence of punctuation, the cocksure posture. There's more to it than that of course, for we see how Molly knows her man and his weaknesses all too well ('his sly eye' around other women) and how, despite all that has come between them (the death of their son, a curtailed sexual life and Boylan, of course), she still has positive memories of Bloom. Her remembrance that 'he was too beautiful for a man' echoes an earlier description of Bloom as a 'womanly man'. Questions about the nature of Bloom's sexuality represent one of the many undercurrents that flow through *Ulysses*. This is Bloom's comeback episode. Not only has he come back home to the bed he shares with Molly, but he is also the main occupant, albeit not always in flattering terms, of her dreamlike thoughts. He can't stop thinking of her throughout the day, while she can't bring herself to banish him from her night-time musings (or amusements, perhaps I should call them, for Molly is amusing, among other things).

The 'Penelope' episode belongs from start to finish to Molly. One source has described our belated entry into the mind of Molly as a 'plunge into a flowing river', with 'refreshing, life-giving waters' and the power to renew us.[128] While her husband, Leopold – or Poldy, as she calls him – is the paramount presence throughout the novel, there is no episode where he is so completely dominant as Molly is here. Everything in these pages happens within her fertile, fractious mind.

One telling influence on this part of the novel may well be Nora Barnacle Joyce, the woman James Joyce first stepped out with on 16 June 1904, an otherwise ordinary Dublin day he decided to immortalise in his novel. Frank Budgen, a close friend of Joyce during his time in Zurich and Trieste, wrote approvingly of Nora:

> Mrs Joyce was a stately presence, but what was most impressive on acquaintance was her absolute independence. Her judgements of men and things were swift and forthright and proceeded from a scale of values entirely personal, unimitated, unmodified … 'What do you think, Mr. Budgen, of a book with a big, fat, horrible married woman as the heroine?'[129]

The Paris-based publisher of *Ulysses*, Sylvia Beach, described Nora as 'charming, with her reddish curly hair and eyelashes, her eyes with a twinkle in them, her voice with its Irish inflections, and a certain dignity that is so Irish also'.[130] For Mary Colum, Nora 'was not only beautiful but vivacious and humorous. Though she had but little education, she had natural aptitudes, among them a love and understanding of music.'[131]

Nora has been the subject of a full-length biography by Brenda Maddox, and more recently a novel by Nuala O'Connor. Her biographer paints an alluring portrait of her: 'She was ordinary. Nobody who loves Joyce will underestimate what that conveys. She was amusing, passionate, courageous, spontaneous and articulate; she talked and talked. Joyce listened and listened, and put her voice into all his major female characters.'[132] Joyce wrote about her that 'Wherever thou art shall be Erin to me'.[133] She was clearly an impressive presence in Joyce's life, but was Nora the inspiration for Molly Bloom? In part, I think, yes. It is difficult to imagine that Joyce would have created a character like Molly without reference to the woman he had lived with for all of seventeen years by the time he wrote 'Penelope'. In all of Joyce's work, his characters are composed of elements from real life seasoned by his literary imagination. Whatever Molly's provenance may be, Joyce's creation is certainly one of the most intriguing characters in all of literature, and he wrote about her in an unmatched virtuoso style.

And what can be said about Molly? Frank Budgen, with whom Joyce discussed *Ulysses* extensively, and who thus knew the novel intimately, has written that: 'There can be but few women in literature that do not look sickly in their virtues and vices alongside Molly Bloom. She has neither vice nor virtue. She is neither mysterious vamp nor sentimental angel.'[134] For the early Joyce scholar Stuart Gilbert, 'the force of this long, unpunctuated meditation, in which a drowsy woman's vagrant thoughts are transferred in all their naked candour of self-revelation on to the written record, lies precisely in its universality'.[135] That all seems about right to me. Molly is an intriguing, mysterious character who confronts life with an extraordinary, but credible candour.

In planning Bloomsday events around the world, one of the essential tasks that always had to be addressed was 'finding a Molly'. I remember in Malaysia having to persuade a member of the Irish community there to take on the task of playing Molly. She did it with aplomb, turning up in a nightdress to deliver those spectacular words towards the end of the monologue. In Berlin, a friend, Dulcie Smart, a Germany-based, New Zealand-born actor, played an impressive Molly in German and English at a Bloomsday function held at the historic Mendelssohn House. During my time in London, I was able to call on British actor Anna Friel, and on the wonderful Angeline Ball, star of *The Commitments* (1991) and *Bloom* (2004), in which she played Molly. In 2019, Irish actor Lisa Dwan delivered a terrific rendition of those famous passages at our Washington residence. And in 2021, Christina Sevilla, US trade negotiator by day and talented thespian outside of office hours, sparkled in the role of Molly.

Here's how Joyce launches us into this closing episode:

Yes because he never did a thing like that before as ask to get his breakfast in bed with a couple of eggs since the *City Arms* hotel when he used to be pretending to be laid up with a sick voice doing his highness to make himself interesting to that old faggot Mrs Riordan that he thought he had a great leg of and she never left us a farthing all for masses for herself and her soul greatest miser ever was actually ...

This is not the first time we have come across Molly. She appears in Episode 4, 'Calypso', where her husband serves her breakfast in bed before setting off on his wanderings around Dublin. She surfaces again in the 'Wandering Rocks' episode, when her arm is seen thrust out of her bedroom window as she throws down a coin to a beggar passing her house. In the 'Circe' episode, she appears in one of Bloom's hallucinations, and we see her briefly in 'Ithaca', where she and Bloom have a brief exchange before he falls asleep after kissing the 'plump mellow yellow smellow melons of her rump'. The rest of the novel is replete with references to her, as Bloom obsesses about her infidelity and other characters make sometimes uncomplimentary remarks about her. Dublin solicitor Henry Menton describes her in her younger days as 'a good armful' who 'had plenty of game in her', but Molly appears to have brushed off his advances. Menton wonders how she got stuck with Bloom. Elsewhere she is described as 'a fat phenomenon' with 'a back on her like a ball alley'. Given what we learn about Molly in 'Penelope', she would surely have given as good as she got in the insults department. She certainly takes a dim view of men and what she views as their foibles and sexual hang-ups.

One Joyce scholar has described 'Penelope' as 'the most inspired, the greatest of Joyce's achievements'.[136] I must agree with that assessment. The last few pages of *Ulysses* are up there with the closing passage of his short story 'The Dead' as examples of Joyce's writing at its very best:

> yes he said I was a flower of the mountain yes so
> we are flowers all a womans body yes that was one

true thing he said in his life and the sun shines
for you today yes that was why I liked him because
I saw he understood or felt what a woman is and
I knew I could always get round him and I gave
him all the pleasure I could ...

Molly's sumptuous monologue continues in this vein for another page and more until its famous last words 'yes I said yes I will Yes'.

The absence of any punctuation marks throughout 'Penelope' may put off some readers, but I do not see this as a real barrier to getting to grips with its wondrous brio. In the above passage, it's not that difficult to supply the missing full stops, apostrophes and commas, and to figure out that the word 'yes' marks the start of each sentence. This is definitely the book's 'Yes' episode, for that word bookends its pages and pops up a lot throughout. Joyce saw 'yes' as a female word.[137]

Joyce was pleased with what he had achieved with 'Penelope'. He wrote that: 'The last word (human, all too human) is left to Penelope. This is the indispensable countersign to Bloom's passport to eternity.'[138] He realised that he was pushing the boat out with the explicitness of this closing episode: 'Though probably more obscene than any preceding episode it seems to me to be perfectly sane full amoral fertilisable untrustworthy engaging shrewd limited prudent indifferent *Weib. Ich bin der Fleisch der stets bejaht*'[139] (translation: 'Woman. I am the flesh that always affirms', although Joyce gets his German grammar wrong).

Here we get Molly's side of the story. She is forthright, raunchy at times, irreverent and thoroughly independent-minded, her own woman, someone who refuses to conform, who views the world around her through her own searing lens. She wonders 'why cant you kiss a man without going and marrying him first'. We hear her break wind, accompany her to the commode and she lets us know that her period has begun. She is down on killjoys like Mrs Riordan: 'let us have a bit of fun first God help the world if all the women were her sort down on bathingsuits and lownecks'. She is not exactly constant or consistent. At one point, she argues that 'itd be much better for the world to be governed by the women in it', but just a page later she has changed her tune about her sex, and says that it is 'no wonder they treat us the way they do we are a dreadful lot of bitches'. Puzzle that!

She is ambivalent about her husband. On the one hand, she likes the fact that 'he is polite to old women like that and waiters and beggars too', but is suspicious of his dalliances with other women, who she thinks may be trying to wheedle money out of him, because there's 'no fool like an old fool'. We might recall that Bloom is not yet forty. She complains that he can never explain things simply, and is irked by his odd habits, such as sleeping with his head at the bottom of the bed and his feet in her face! He is so complex and convoluted that she thinks he should be 'in the budget'. Yet she resents the way some of his fellow Dubliners criticise him behind his back (as we know they do).

Molly recalls her first encounters with Bloom. They 'had the standup row over politics'. Molly has little time for Bloom's moderately nationalist leanings, and takes a dim view of what she calls 'them Sinner Fein' (the original Sinn Féin, an advocate of a dual monarchy for Ireland along Austro-Hungarian lines, was founded in 1905), and of their leader, Arthur Griffith. Bloom sees him as a coming man, but Molly disagrees: 'he doesnt look it thats all I can say'. She is also dismissive of Bloom's 'blather about home rule and the land league'. Molly's leanings are clearly pro-British in a city where opposition to Ireland's political union with Britain ran deep.

Although, like Bloom, she accepts that things had never been the same between them since the death of their son Rudy, Molly blames Bloom for the difficulties in their marriage, due to his patchy employment record and failure to keep her in the manner to which she would like to be accustomed. There is never enough money for her to have a proper wardrobe, and she takes the view that 'you cant get on in this world without style'. She even attributes responsibility for her own behaviour to Bloom: 'its all his own fault if I am an adulteress ... O much about it if thats all the harm ever we did in this vale of tears God knows its not much ...' Thus Molly's self-justification mirrors Bloom's attitude in the 'Ithaca' episode, where he reflects on the cosmic insignificance of his wife's infidelity.

As for her paramour, Blazes Boylan, Molly is clearly attracted by his physicality and sexual energy, but doesn't like his excessive familiarity and his having the temerity to slap her behind – 'Im not a horse or an ass am I'. We get a taste of Molly's singular approach to life when she remarks that 'its all very well a husband but you cant fool a lover'. Yet she plans to continue her liaison with Boylan during her concert tour in Belfast, when Bloom will be safely in Ennis for the anniversary of his father's suicide there. She is drawn to Boylan in part because he has money and she believes she can charm expensive gifts out of him. Ultimately, however, she derides Boylan as 'barefaced' and 'vulgar', with 'no manners' and 'no refinement', which is not unlike Bloom's own assessment of his rival for Molly's affections. She comments that (unlike Bloom and Stephen), Boylan is 'an ignoramus that doesnt know poetry from a cabbage'! Interesting that it should all come down to the poetic gift.

Her religious outlook is also eccentric. She has no time for 'atheists or whatever they call themselves', nor for religious scepticism like her husband's, who says 'you have no soul inside only grey matter because he doesent know what it is to have one' – but she doesn't like the roundabout way in which Father Corrigan presses her in the confessional about the scope of her erotic experiences – 'O Lord couldnt he say bottom right out and have done with it'. She also fantasises about having an affair with a priest or a bishop.

Molly offers us an ambiguous account of her various lovers. Two in particular seem to mean most to her – Mulvey, a naval officer she met while growing up in Gibraltar, and Gardner, an officer in the East Lancashire Regiment, 'a lovely fellow in khaki', who died of enteric fever during the Boer War. Molly holds this against the Boers, 'killing any finelooking man were there with their fever'.

Towards the end of her monologue, she develops a preoccupation with Stephen Dedalus, who had just left Eccles Street, having declined Bloom's offer that he stay the night. Molly wishes he had stayed, as she ruminates about serving Stephen breakfast in bed and wonders if she is too old for him. In the two preceding episodes, Bloom seemed eager to have Stephen get to know Molly.

As her monologue roars to its climax, it's her husband who presses his way into Molly's dream thoughts: 'the sun shines for you he said the day we were lying among the rhododendrons on Howth head in the grey tweed suit and his straw hat the day I got him to propose to me'. Even then, enigmatically, she remembers things Bloom didn't know of 'Mulvey and Mr Stanhope and Hester and father and old captain Groves'. As she rhapsodises about saying Yes to Bloom sixteen years before on Howth Head, she alludes to 'how he kissed me under the Moorish wall'. This must be a reference to Mulvey, as I doubt there is a Moorish wall on Dublin's hill of Howth.

Although the novel ends with a remembrance of her first sexual encounter with Bloom ('and I thought well as well him as another'), given what we have learned about Molly from her monologue, I would not wager too much on the further course of the Blooms' marriage. 'I suppose Ill have to put up with it' is how she sizes up her situation, so this is clearly no marriage of true minds, and there are plenty of impediments in play. We know that Bloom has asked to have his breakfast in bed, which means that 17 June 1904 will have a different start for the Blooms of Eccles Street, but beyond that we can only imagine. What we do know though is that, in *Ulysses*, Molly's last word before sleep is directed at Poldy – and it's a yes with a capital y. Yes. That has to mean something, and it does. Leopold – Joyce's own Odysseus, or Ulysses if you will – registers a modest domestic triumph, though it is a far cry from Homeric heroism. That's the modern world for you!

A Parting Glass:

Last Words on Ulysses

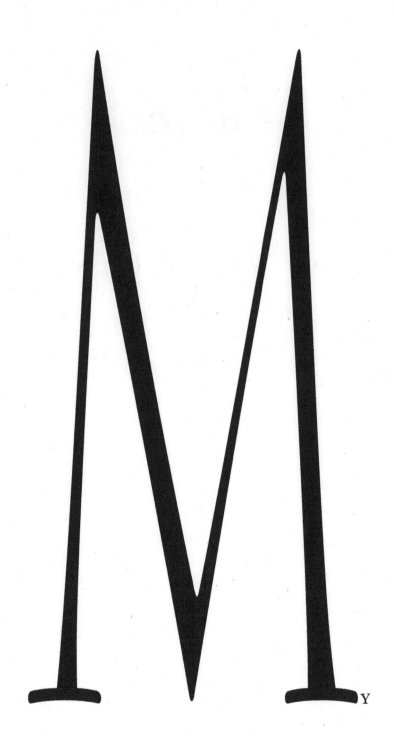

Y

intention was to write a chapter of the moral history of my country.

                                 – James Joyce

I began this project in May 2018 as a *Ulysses* blog that I posted on the website of the Embassy of Ireland in Washington DC. This book is based on that blog. The aim was to be helpful to readers attempting to come to grips with the twentieth century's most famous novel. My analysis has evolved substantially since those early days, and the preceding chapters that dealt with individual episodes of *Ulysses* are significantly different from what I originally included in my blog. In the years that followed that initial effort, I have spent an inordinate amount of my leisure time poring over the book's eighteen episodes and reading extensively about James Joyce and his famous novel.

In all, I have probably read the entire novel three or four times since 2018, but let me admit to you that I still have not gotten to the bottom of it. I fully expect to discover new things, many of them, when next I read *Ulysses*, something I intend to continue doing for pleasure and enlightenment. Joyce's creation is a bit of a bottomless well, whose hidden depths require assiduous plumbing. It's not only me who feels that way, for, as one expert source has put it, 'there is always more to *Ulysses* than meets the eye of any one observer during any particular reading'.[140] Yet the question persists, how do I rationalise my decision to invest so much time in ploughing through this gargantuan novel, and on what basis do I urge others to mount a similar venture? Here is my parting glass, my closing statement on *Ulysses*.

'MORAL HISTORY'

James Joyce could never be accused of lacking literary ambition, and when he talked about contributing to the 'moral history' of Ireland, this boast has to be taken seriously – but what did he mean by it, and was he successful? It seems to me that Joyce thought he could correct Ireland's course by conducting an arms-length examination and putting it boldly into print.

Joyce came of age at the tail end of the nineteenth century, at the close of what had been a disastrous hundred years for Ireland, marked by the catastrophe of the Great Famine, economic stagnation, mass emigration, and the failure of successive generations of Irish nationalists to undo the union with Britain that had been formed in 1800.

The snuffing out of the promise of Home Rule with the defeat in 1893 of Gladstone's second effort to deliver that form of self-government dashed the hopes of the generation to which Joyce's father belonged, and the malaise that engulfed them thereafter is, it seems to me, persuasively conjured up in *Ulysses*. The entry in the *Dictionary of Irish Biography*[141] on the life of John Stanislaus Joyce (1849–1931) bolsters my point by arguing that 'The fall of John Joyce coincided with the political fall and death of C.S. Parnell, whom John Joyce (and his son) vigorously supported. John took little interest in active politics after this, even after the Irish Party reunited' in 1900.

In an exercise in counterfactual history, it would be possible to imagine John Joyce being a significant figure in a Home Rule Ireland had it come into being in the 1890s. In that version of history, one could contemplate his talented son, James, settling down in Dublin as part of the Irish Catholic elite coming into its own in the twentieth century, with an auxiliary role in the running of the British Empire. In *Ulysses*, Simon Dedalus, based on John Joyce, with his mordant turn of phrase and a corrosive irresponsibility regarding the care of his family, exudes the disappointments and frustrations that must have been felt by those who believed in Parnell when he fell from grace so unexpectedly and shockingly in 1890.

There were those, of course, W. B. Yeats included, who saw in the post-Parnell era an opportunity to do something different, in Yeats's case to create for Ireland a national literature in the English language. This was to be a contribution to the creation of a new Ireland, fit for purpose in a new century. James Joyce, who perhaps had more of a hands-on understanding of the Ireland of his youth, did not like what he saw emerging, and boldly resolved to cut himself loose from his homeland. As he once wrote about the Ireland he left in 1904, 'It is well past time for Ireland to have done once and for all with failure.'[142] His intensive, masterful interrogation of the country he left behind is what we have before us in *Ulysses*. One source has described it as 'his gift to Ireland and the fulfilment of his old promise to forge abroad, in the smithy of his soul, the uncreated conscience of his race'.[143] No other writer managed, or even attempted, such a lavishly forensic portrait of Ireland, and that is why, especially for Irish people, reading *Ulysses* is an invaluable venture. For me, as an Irish historian and a lifelong advocate for Ireland and its literature, the fascination I find in *Ulysses* is in its exploration of a country on the verge, with an old order slowly dying and a new one still in the realms of its conception.

Joyce's work had little demonstrable impact on Ireland during the early decades of independence, when *Ulysses*, though never banned, was probably little read. If Bloom represents Joyce's own vision for Ireland, as I believe he in many ways does, his progressive attitudes, pluralist approach and international orientation did not make much headway during those years. At that time, perhaps unavoidably, the Irish Free State was preoccupied with the internal dynamics of nation-building at a difficult time in world history, even if their contributions to the evolution of the British Empire and the League of Nations demonstrated that successive Irish governments in the 1920s and 1930s were not devoid of international ambitions, but those were viewed largely through the prism of constitutional imperatives. As time wore on, however, increasing respect for Joyce has gone hand in hand with a gradual opening up of Irish society, to the point where the Museum of Literature Ireland (MoLI) is devoted primarily to his legacy. Although I can't be sure that the advances Ireland has made in recent decades represent a chapter in the 'moral history' of my country as Joyce envisioned it, I see it as entirely appropriate to celebrate the publication of *Ulysses* alongside the birth of Irish independence. Those two events were, after all, near contemporaries in that epoch-making year, 1922, which also saw the publication of T. S. Eliot's great modernist poem, *The Waste Land*.

AN ADVENTURE IN LANGUAGE

While the searching portrait that *Ulysses* offers of early twentieth-century Dublin is in itself a compelling incentive for reading it, and not just for Irish people (after all, you don't need to be English to enjoy Dickens), that quality alone would not have secured its canonical status internationally. There is also the adventure in language to be considered.

Those who have taken this journey with me will now know that reading *Ulysses* is a daunting undertaking. It is a test of patience and concentration, and it is not an easy or convenient read. With its frequent shifts of writing style and the mix of narrative, dialogue and interior monologue, Joyce routinely stretches and discommodes his readers. His preference appears to be to surprise and bewilder us. The almost three-hundred-page sweep between the beginning of 'Oxen of the Sun' and the end of 'Circe' is a bracing experience. The novel's highlight comes, at least in my estimation, at the very end, with Molly's gripping monologue.

Is the joy of Joyce's prose a sufficient compensation for the labour involved? My answer is yes, but I would say that, wouldn't I? There is, I believe, sufficient weight and luminosity to Joyce's prose to make it a valuable venture for serious readers.

Let's take one example, a short passage that Joyce claimed to have laboured over for a full day, although there is some doubt about that: 'A warm human plumpness settled down on his brain. His brain yielded. Perfume of embraces all him assailed. With hungered flesh obscurely, he mutely craved to adore.'

Those richly-endowed sentences reproduce Leopold Bloom's thoughts just after he has been looking at the window display at Brown Thomas, a shop that has survived the test of time on Dublin's Grafton Street. Bloom sees a display of petticoats and silk stockings, and thinks about buying Molly something even though his mind is troubled by his knowledge of her infidelity. We know about Bloom's troubled mind, because Joyce throws in a couple of short verbal darts as Bloom reminds himself of his predicament: 'Useless to go back. Had to be. Tell me all.' Thus in the space of less than a page Joyce reveals Bloom's yearnings for 'warm human plumpness', the existence of his 'hungered flesh' and its mute cravings, and the stoic acceptance of his lot. Then Joyce snaps his character out of this reverie with some sharply contrasting, bodily reactions. 'Duke Street. Here we are. Must eat. The Burton. Feel better then.'

This is also where we learn that Molly's birthday falls on 8 September (by coincidence, the same as my wife, Greta's). Despite everything, Bloom can't get rid of his memories of Molly: 'Perfumed bodies, warm, full. All kissed, yielded: in deep summer fields, tangled pressed grass, in trickling hallways of tenements, along sofas, creaking beds.' That's quite a feat of writing, and *Ulysses* is richly adorned with such gems. If W. B. Yeats was right that 'words alone are certain good', then that's what I call good use of words.

ENCYCLOPAEDIC *Ulysses*

The extraordinary Edna O'Brien, someone I got to know and greatly admired during my time in London, has written that '*Ulysses* is the quintessence of everything he had seen, heard and overheard, consecration and desecration, at once serious and comical, hermetic and skittish, full of consequence and inconsequence, sounds and silences ...'[144] I fully agree. It is a cornucopia of Joyce's experiences prior to his departure from Dublin. He put into his book all he knew, all he heard and all he had learned.

Ulysses is an encyclopaedic novel. In one of his letters, Joyce admitted that it had 'enormous bulk and more than enormous complexity'.[145] I was reminded of this recently, when I recalled the provenance of Bloom's pen name for his correspondence with Martha Clifford. Henry Flower was not just a name casually plucked from mid-air because of its word association with Bloom. I have written about the real Henry Flower, a member of the Dublin Metropolitan Police who was implicated in the murder of Bridget Gannon, a domestic servant whose body was fished out of the Dodder River in August 1900 by a group of policemen that included Flower. In what became known as the Dodder mystery, Bridget Gannon's body was twice exhumed, but Constable Flower was eventually acquitted on account of a lack of proof that he had been responsible for her death. The presiding judge was sharply critical of Flower, and concluded that the victim had fallen into the river as a result of Flower 'taking liberties or larking with her'. The judge condemned him for having 'with inconceivable baseness allowed her to perish'. Joyce, who had a keen eye for juicy criminal cases, evidently remembered Flower's name and put him into *Ulysses*, perhaps with the implication that Bloom had chosen the name on account of his, in Molly's estimation, unseemly interest in their domestic staff.[146] To make the connection more interesting, Henry Flower was defended by the lawyer/politician Tim Harrington, who was a friend of the Joyce family and is mentioned in *Ulysses.*

[283]

Even a passing reference in *Ulysses* can uncover multitudes. In my chapter on 'Wandering Rocks', I wrote about Fr Conmee's conversation with Mrs Sheehy, and how mention of her takes us right back into the world of the Irish Party, the milieu of Joyce's father, as it awaited the Promised Land of Home Rule. By the time *Ulysses* was being written, Home Rule had, like all of those favoured but beaten horses in the 1904 Ascot Gold Cup, run its course and become a political also-ran, a throwaway.

My point is that *Ulysses* is a novel in which there are piles and piles of consequential and inconsequential details, and it is often extremely difficult to distinguish between the two. While this is not quite necessary for an understanding of *Ulysses*, it can be fun to pursue the various hares that Joyce releases. For those with an interest in such hare-chasing, I can recommend Vivien Igoe's book, *The Real People of Joyce's Ulysses*, which pursues every biographical hare here, there and everywhere.

THE OPPOSITE OF HATE

Over the years, as I returned to *Ulysses*, I have found different avenues of approach. My Champs-Élysées when I engage with Joyce's work has generally been early twentieth-century Irish history. When I was in Germany, I came to believe that the novel has a wider reference beyond its rootedness in the Irish experience. At Bloomsday events I organised in Berlin, I always read the lines in which Bloom defines his nation as 'Ireland ... I was born here. Ireland'. My comment on this, thinking of Germany's twentieth-century nightmare, was that the history of Europe could have been very different had Bloom's notion of nationality been widely accepted. Understandably, that point reso-nated with my German audiences. Thus, the target of Joyce's novel was not just the paralysing narrowness he detected in his father's Ireland, but manifestations of intolerance wherever they were to be found, and there was plenty of that about as Joyce knuckled down to write with a world war raging around him.

This all leads me to revere the passage from *Ulysses* in which Bloom sets out his credo.

> — And I belong to a race too, says Bloom, that is hated and persecuted ...
> — But it's no use, says he. Force, hatred, his-tory, all that. That's not life for men and women, insult and hatred. And everybody knows that it's the very opposite of that that is really life.
> —What? says Alf.
> —Love, says Bloom. I mean the opposite of hatred.

Enough said. I'll leave it at that, except to add that the response from 'the citizen' shows what Bloom was up against. 'A new apostle to the gentiles ... Beggar my neighbour is his motto ... He's a nice pattern of a Romeo and Juliet.'

LAST WORDS – YES, REALLY

For all of its complexities and verbal pyrotechnics, *Ulysses* is ultimately a character-driven novel. Yes, it has Dublin at its heart. As Joyce's friend, the critic Mary Colum, once wrote: 'Nobody has ever written of the life of a city, so identified himself with that city and its history, as Joyce has with Dublin. The fact that he left it early and became a Berlitz teacher in Trieste, far from diminishing his impressions, clarified them, far from clouding his memory, made it more exact.'[147]

That sounds right to me. A fascination with Dublin fuelled Joyce's imagination, gave him a setting for his novel that he found inviting, and provided him with the myriad of minor characters that spice up its pages – 'the citizen', Simon Dedalus, Myles Crawford, Mrs Breen, Skin-the-Goat Fitzharris, Davy Byrne, Buck Mulligan, Blazes Boylan, Fr Conmee and so on. The beating heart of *Ulysses* is human, not urban.

It is a novel essentially about three characters: the Blooms and Stephen Dedalus. Although he occupies far more of the novel's pages than Molly, Stephen is the lesser of the three. In truth, he's a bit of a caricature of a highly intelligent but quite callow youth. He says superbly pretentious things like: 'A man of genius makes no mistakes. His errors are volitional and are the portals of discovery.'

Stephen is a strange mixture of pretentiousness and profundity. It is hard to disagree with Bloom's fears for him, that he is wasting his talents through a dissolute lifestyle, drinking and carousing instead of applying himself and using his talents properly. He clearly has ability, in that he has already been published, but he is no James Joyce. Despite his literary promise, Stephen doesn't get invited to the soiree at novelist George Moore's home, and he is not to be included in a collection of poetry by younger Irish writers that Æ is editing. His poetry, from what we have seen of it, is not that accomplished, and he probably needs to get away from Ireland again, to clear his head and get down to the serious business of being a writer. He could try Trieste perhaps!

Leopold Bloom is Joyce's masterwork, but Molly is his most interesting creation. Gerald Goldberg, who I remember as a Jewish Lord Mayor of Cork during the 1960s, once wrote about Bloom that he was 'not a perfect man', but that he had 'sympathy for the sick, the lame, the blind, the old, the widow, the orphan …' He was 'a little, little man, neither Jewish nor non-Jewish, Irish nor non-Irish, but a loyal, lovable, kindly human …'[148] To me, Bloom is simply Irish, and with a Jewish heritage.

That's the thing about Bloom. He's an exceptional figure on account of his essential ordinariness. He has absolutely no traditional Odyssean qualities. With the exception of his contretemps with 'the citizen', when Bloom cuts loose, he doesn't generally assert himself. He accepts his lot as a cuckold, an unsuccessful advertisement salesman and a dreamer of unfulfilled dreams. As the critic Denis Donoghue has written, 'Bloom accepts the conditions of his life and wants only to succeed in forgetting their most painful embodiments'. He makes 'the middling best' of his unheroic life.[149] Bloom was clearly able to cut a dash as a younger man, and Molly believed in his Byronic potential. Now, he is seen as 'old Bloom', evidently aged before his time, a cautious, fastidious, excessively ponderous individual. But he endures and, by doing so, records a minor triumph when he returns to his Ithaca, unchanged and unfulfilled but also undaunted.

For me, Molly is the pick of the bunch. She is lively, opinionated, even funny in parts: 'God send him sense and me more money'. She is in two minds about most things, and especially on the subject of her husband, Poldy, who frustrates her, but for whom she retains a grudging respect. She's even protective of him: 'theyre not going to get my husband again into their clutches if I can help it'. In her confused way, as she falls asleep, it is Bloom who is her 'Yes' man. Her take on life is inimitable, and she literally has the last word.

When I was discussing the 'Telemachus' episode, I quoted Yeats's assessment of *Ulysses*: 'It is a work perhaps of genius.' I said that, for me, the word 'perhaps' could be replaced by 'essentially'. It is essentially a work of genius. I say that because there is a lot of genius running through its pages, the grand conception of the novel, its execution, Joyce's command of character and ingenious use of language. I readily concede, however, that not everything Joyce attempts there is gilded with stardust. It falls down in places. There are times when Joyce goes on too long, parts of *Ulysses* that would have benefited from a good editor, who would admittedly have had to be a strongman to get around Joyce's adamantine insistence on artistic independence, some kind of editorial 'Turko the Terrible'. 'Circe' does not need to consume 150 pages, while 'Ithaca' could have profited from a bit of shortening, for its catechism format and linguistic excesses threaten to drown out its content. 'Oxen of the Sun' is excessively showy and devilishly opaque. I do not go along fully with Joyce's argument that he needed to shuffle his writing methods in order properly to render the life of the mind, and the world enveloping it, on that mock epic Dublin day.

My hesitations about *Ulysses* are of a kind that would no doubt be viewed by Stephen, and by Joyce, as essential 'portals of discovery' on the road to *Finnegans Wake*, but, again, I'm not going there. On a holiday visit to the Greek island of Santorini in 2017, I wandered into a wonderful bookshop, Atlantis Books, which is built into the area's volcanic rock. Because of where I was, I bought a book on Homer, which concluded that what was valuable and essential about him was 'the ability to regard all aspects of life with clarity, equanimity and sympathy, with a loving heart and an unclouded eye'.[150] That's our Leopold Bloom to a tee, the man that 'Homer' Joyce made sing, plaintively and with an all too human voice.

ACKNOWLEDGEMENTS

Even more than is customarily the case, this book, and its imperfections, are all my own responsibility, in that, unlike many other writers about James Joyce and his work, I am not part of an academic community devoted to the subject. I have not spoken at or attended scholarly conferences at which ideas about Joyce's work can be tested in front of an expert audience. While I have published pieces about Joyce in Malaysia, Thailand, Germany, Britain and the United States, those were aimed at a general readership. I have not dipped my pen into the crowded world of Joycean scholarship by writing for the *James Joyce Quarterly,* the holy grail for Joyce savants. My work may well suffer from that vacuum in my bio, but I hope that it will also offer insights derived from my own experience of living with *Ulysses* over the years as part of my personal literary landscape.

This book was written in the main during the protracted lockdown brought about by the coronavirus pandemic. It had of course been gestating for quite a number of years, and thus a lot of people undoubtedly influenced my thinking, for the most part unknowingly. I refer to numerous individuals, colleagues in the Department of Foreign Affairs and others, with whom I have over the years discussed Ireland, our history and our literature. None had any involvement with this book, which means that, as always, all errors of fact and interpretation are mine and mine alone.

I owe the biggest debt of gratitude to my wife, Greta, who has read every line of this book many times over. She was especially assiduous in the days before I submitted the manuscript, working with me into the small hours of an arduous weekend of writing, correcting and proofreading. Thank you, Greta. My granddaughters, Alice and Jessica Goodall, watched over me while I was editing the book at their home in Scotland, and made bookmarks to help me identify key passages from *Ulysses*.

My great friend, Joe Hassett, Washington lawyer and literary scholar, read a number of my chapters and provided sage advice and helpful suggestions, for which I was deeply grateful. A couple of years back, Joyce scholar Cóilín Parsons of Georgetown University invited me to address his *Ulysses* class, where I developed some of my ideas about Joyce's novel. I appreciated his expert advice on navigating the maze of Joyce scholarship.

Thank you also to the many of my followers on social media who conveyed their appreciation of the *Ulysses* blog on which this book is loosely based. Colleagues at the Embassy in Washington, Norma Ces, Ragnar Almqvist, Lillian Gisselquist and Emily Speelman, helped with the proofreading and posting of my *Ulysses* blogs, and in organising Bloomsday celebrations, including a virtual one in June 2020. Our dear friend, Sharon Lynch, read and commented on one of my chapters.

I owe a debt of thanks to Edwin Higel and the team at New Island Books for seeing the potential of this book and helping me bring it to fruition. I was happy to work with Neil

Burkey as my editor and with Stephen Reid who did the copy editing. My thanks go also to Ray Ryan of Cambridge University Press, a friend who offered advice on the publishing industry.

I wish to thank Sandra Collins and Katherine McSharry at the National Library of Ireland, James Maynard at the University of Buffalo and Kelsey Bates and her staff at the fabulous Rosenbach Museum and Library for their assistance with the illustrations. Thanks also to Derrick Dreyer, former Director of the Rosenbach for inviting me to read from *Ulysses* at the annual Bloomsday celebrations in Philadelphia which, on account of the impressive attendance they attracted, convinced me that *Ulysses* is, despite, or perhaps because of, its manifold complexities, a compelling achievement with a surprisingly wide appeal. *Ulysses* is worthy, certainly, of this book of mine to mark the centenary of its publication.

BIBLIOGRAPHY

Works by James Joyce

Ellmann, R. (ed.) (1975), *Selected Letters of James Joyce*, New York: Viking Press

Joyce, J. (2000) *A Portrait of the Artist as a Young Man*, London, Penguin Modern Classics

Ibid. (1961), *Ulysses*, New York: Vintage Books

Ibid. (1986), *Ulysses*, London: The Bodley Head

Joyce, J., Levin, H. (1963), *The Essential James Joyce*, London: Penguin Books

Joyce, J. (1992), *Dubliners*, London: Penguin Classics

Ibid. (1992), *Ulysses: Annotated Student Edition*, London: Penguin Classics

Joyce, J, Barry, K. (ed.) (2000), *Occasional, Critical, and Political Writing*, Oxford: Oxford World's Classics

Joyce, J. (2018), *The Day of the Rabblement*, Dublin: MoLI Editions

O'Connell, J. (ed.) (2017), *Best-Loved Joyce*, Dublin: The O'Brien Press

Biographical

Bowker, G. (2012), *James Joyce: A New Biography*, New York: Farrar, Straus and Giroux

Budgen, F. (1960), *James Joyce and the Making of Ulysses*, Bloomington: Indiana University Press

Colum, M. (1947), *Life and the Dream*, London: Macmillan

Colum, M. and P. (1958), *Our Friend James Joyce*, New York: Doubleday

Costello, P. (1992), *James Joyce: The Years of Growth 1882–1915*, London: Kyle Cathie

Curran, C. P. (1970), *Under the Receding Wave*, Dublin: Gill and MacMillan

Ellmann, R. (1959), *James Joyce*, London: Oxford University Press

Flynn, C. (2019), *James Joyce and the Matter of Paris*, Cambridge: Cambridge University Press

Gogarty, O. St J. (1968), *As I was Going Down Sackville Street*, London: Sphere Books

Gorman, H. (1948), *James Joyce*, New York: Rinehart & Company

Igoe, V. (2016), *The Real People of Joyce's Ulysses: A Biographical Guide*, Dublin: University College Dublin Press

Hardiman, A. (2017), *Joyce in Court: James Joyce and the Law*, London: Head of Zeus

Hassett, J. M. (2016), *The Ulysses Trials: Beauty and Truth Meet the Law*, Dublin: The Lilliput Press

Jackson, J. W. and Costello, P. (1997), *John Stanislaus Joyce: The Voluminous Life and Genius of James Joyce's Father*, London: Fourth Estate

Joyce, S. (1958), *My Brother's Keeper: James Joyce's Early Years*, New York: The Viking Press

Maddox, B. (1989), *Nora: A Biography of Nora Joyce*, London: Minerva

Manganiello, D. (1980), *Joyce's Politics*, London: Routledge and Kegan Paul

McCourt, J. (2001), *The Years of Bloom: James Joyce in Trieste, 1904–1920*, Dublin: The Lilliput Press

Murphy, W. M. (1978), *Prodigal Father: The Life of John Butler Yeats (1839–1922)*, London: Cornell University Press

O'Brien, E. (2000), *James Joyce*, London: Phoenix

O'Connor, N. (2021), *Nora*, Dublin: New Island Books

O'Connor, U. (2000), *Oliver St John Gogarty*, Dublin: The O'Brien Press

Pierce, D. (1992), *James Joyce's Ireland*, London: Yale University Press

Studies: An Irish Quarterly Review (Summer 2004), 'Celebrating James Joyce'

Tóibín, C. (2018), *Mad, Bad, Dangerous to Know: The Fathers of Wilde, Yeats and Joyce*, London: Viking

Historical

Abels, J. (1966), *The Parnell Tragedy*, London: The Bodley Head

Akenson, D. (1994), *Conor: A Biography of Conor Cruise O'Brien, Volume 1*, Montreal: McGill-Queen's University Press

Bartlett, T. (ed.) (2018), *The Cambridge History of Ireland Volume IV 1880 to the Present*, Cambridge: Cambridge University Press

Bew, J. (2012), *Castlereagh: A Life*, Oxford: Oxford University Press

Biagini, E. and Mulhall, D. (eds) (2016), *The Shaping of Modern Ireland: A Centenary Assessment*, Dublin: Irish Academic Press

Birmingham, K. (2014), *The Most Dangerous Book: The Battle of James Joyce's Ulysses*, London: Head of Zeus

Connolly, S. J. (1998), *The Oxford Companion to Irish History*, Oxford: Oxford University Press

Ferriter, D. (2004), *The Transformation of Ireland 1900–2000*, London: Profile Books

Fitch, N. R., *Sylvia Beach and the Lost Generation: A History of Literary Paris in the Twenties & Thirties*, New York: W. W. Norton

Garvin, T. (1987), *Nationalist Revolutionaries in Ireland 1858–1928*, Oxford: Clarendon Press

Griffith, A. (2003), *The Resurrection of Hungary*, 3rd edn, Dublin: University College Dublin Press

Horgan, J. J. (1948), *Parnell to Pearse: Some Recollections and Reflections*, Dublin: Browne & Nolan

Kavanagh, J. (2021), *The Irish Assassins: Conspiracy, Revenge, and the Phoenix Park Murders that Stunned Victorian England*, New York: Atlantic Monthly Press

Keogh, D. (1998), *Jews in Twentieth-Century Ireland*, Cork: Cork University Press

Lee, J. (1973), *The Modernisation of Irish Society*, Dublin: Gill & Macmillan

Leerssen, J. (ed.) (2021) *Parnell and his Times*, Cambridge: Cambridge University Press

Lyons, F. S. L. (1973), *Ireland since the Famine*, London: Collins/Fontana

Maume, P. (1999), *The Long Gestation: Irish Nationalist Life 1891–1918*, Dublin: Gill and Macmillan

Mulhall, D. (1999), *A New Day Dawning: A Portrait of Ireland in 1900*, Cork: The Collins Press

Mulhall, D. (1999), 'Ireland at the Turn of the Century', *History Ireland*, vol. 7, no. 4, pp. 32–6

Mulhall, D. (2004), 'The Age of Ulysses', *History Ireland*, vol. 12, no. 2

O'Brien, C.C. (1998), *Memoir: My Life and Themes*, Dublin: Poolbeg Press

O'Dowd, N. (2018) *Lincoln and the Irish: The Untold Story of How the Irish Helped Lincoln Save the Union*, New York: Skyhorse Publishing

O'Neill, M. (1991), *From Parnell to de Valera: A Biography of Jennie Wyse Power, 1858–1941*, Dublin: Blackwater Press

Orel, H. (1976), *Irish History and Culture: Aspects of a People's Heritage*, Lawrence: University of Kansas Press

Stewart, A. T. Q. (2001), *The Shape of Irish History*, Belfast: The Blackstaff Press

Vaughan, W. E. (ed.) (1989), *A New History of Ireland VI: Ireland under the Union II 1870–1921*, Oxford: Oxford University Press

Literary Criticism

Allen, N. (2021), *Ireland, Literature and the Coast: Seatangled,* Oxford: Oxford University Press

Bidwell, B. and Heffer, L. (1981), *The Joycean Way: A Topographic Guide to Dubliners and a Portrait of the Artist as a Young Man,* Dublin: Wolfhound Press

Blamires, H. (1988), *The New Bloomsday Book*, London: Routledge

Boyle, N. (1991), *Goethe: The Poet and the Age, Vol I, The Poetry of Desire*, Oxford: Oxford University Press

Cleary, J. (2021), *Modernism, Empire, World Literature,* Cambridge: Cambridge University Press

Delaney, F. (1981), *James Joyce's Odyssey: A Guide to the Dublin of Ulysses*, London: Hodder and Stoughton

Donoghue, D. (2011), *Irish Essays*, Cambridge: University of Cambridge Press

Donoghue, D. (1986), *We Irish*, Berkeley: University of California Press

Ellmann, R. (1974), *Ulysses on the Liffey*, London: Faber and Faber

Fargnoli, A. N. and Gillespie, M. P. (1996), *James Joyce A–Z: The Essential Reference to His Life and Writings*, Oxford: Oxford University Press

Gibbons, L. (2015), *Joyce's Ghosts: Ireland, Modernism, and Memory*, Chicago: The University of Chicago Press

Gilbert, S. (1955), *James Joyce's Ulysses: A Study*, New York: Vintage Books/Random House

Gross, J. (1971), *Joyce*, London: Fontana

Hart, C. and Hayman, D. (eds) (1974), *James Joyce's Ulysses: Critical Essays*, Berkeley: University of California

Howes, M. E. (2020), *Irish Literature in Transition, 1880-1940*, Cambridge: Cambridge University Press

Hutton, C. (2003), 'Joyce and the Institutions of Revivalism, *Irish University Review: A Journal of Irish Studies*, vol. 33, no. 1

Kearney, R. and Hederman, M.P. (eds.) (1982) *The Crane Bag: James Joyce and the Arts in Ireland, Vol. 6, No. 1*, Greystones: The Crane Bag

Kenner, H. (1987), *Ulysses: Revised Edition*, Baltimore: The Johns Hopkins' University Press

Kiberd, D. (1996), *Inventing Ireland: The Literature of the Modern Nation*, London: Vintage

Kiberd, D. (2009), *Ulysses and Us: The Art of Everyday Living*, London: Faber and Faber

Killeen, T. (2014), *Ulysses Unbound*, Dublin: Wordwell

Latham, S. (ed.) (1963-Present) *James Joyce Quarterly*, Tulsa: University of Tulsa

Latham, S. (ed.) (2014), *The Cambridge Companion to Ulysses*, Cambridge: Cambridge University Press

Levin, H. (1960), *James Joyce: A Critical Introduction*, 2nd edn, London: Faber and Faber

McCarthy, J. and Rose, D. (1988), *Joyce's Dublin: A Walking Guide to Ulysses*, New York: St Martin's Press

McCourt, J. (ed.) (2019), *James Joyce in Context*, Cambridge: Cambridge University Press

Mulhall, D. (2019), 'All the Living and the Dead', London: *The London Magazine*, December/January

Mulhall, D. (2016), *A Portrait of the Artist and his Young Country*, London: *The London Magazine*, October/November

Mulhall, D. (2011), *Irish Literature and the Making of Modern Ireland*, Marburger: Philipps-Universtät

Nicolson, A. (2014), *The Mighty Dead: Why Homer Matters*, London: William Collins

Nicholson, R. (2019), *The Ulysses Guide: Tours Through Joyce's Dublin*, Dublin: New Island Books

Pelaschiar, L. (ed.) (2015), *Joyce/Shakespeare*, New York: Syracuse University Press

Raleigh, J. H. (1977), *The Chronicle of Leopold and Molly Bloom: Ulysses as Narrative*, Berkeley: University of California Press

Read, F. (ed.) (1970), *Pound/Joyce: The Letters of Ezra Pound to James Joyce with Pound's Essays on Joyce*, New York: New Directions

Tindall, W. Y. (1959), *A Reader's Guide to James Joyce*, London: Thames and Hudson

Welch, R. A. (2014), *The Cold of May Day Monday: An Approach to Irish Literary History*, Oxford: Oxford University Press

Wilson, E. (1961), *Axel's Castle: A Study in the Imaginative Literature of 1870–1930*, London: Fontana

Homeric/Mythological

Hamilton, E. (1940), *Mythology*, New York: Mentor

Lemprière's Classical Dictionary (1987), 3rd edn, London: Routledge and Kegan Paul

The Odyssey of Homer (1967), New York: Harper and Row

Homer, *The Odyssey (1999),* London: Penguin Books

NOTES

1   Levin, H. (1960), *James Joyce: A Critical Introduction*, 2nd edn, London: Faber and Faber, p. 20.

2   McCourt, J. (2001), *The Years of Bloom: James Joyce in Trieste, 1904–1920,* Dublin: The Lilliput Press, p. 3.

3   Bowker, G. (2012), *James Joyce: A New Biography*, New York: Farrar, Straus and Giroux, p. 281.

4   Cleeve, B. (1966), *Dictionary of Irish Writers: First Series,* Cork: Mercier Press, p. 65.

5   Comerford, R. V. (1989), 'The Land and the Politics of Distress, 1877–82' in Vaughan, W. E. (ed.), *A New History of Ireland, VI*, pp. 49–50.

6   Bowker, *James Joyce*, p. 303.

7   Ackroyd, P. (1984), *T. S. Eliot: A Life*, New York: Simon and Schuster, p. 119.

8   Hardiman, A. (2017), Joyce in Court: *James Joyce and the Law*, London: Head of Zeus, p. 273. See also, Hassett, J. M. (2016), *The Ulysses Trials: Beauty and Truth Meet the Law*, Dublin: The Lilliput Press, pp. 125–65.

9   Joyce, (1961), *Ulysses*, p. xii.

10   Hardiman, *Joyce in Court*, p. 279.

11   Ellmann, R. (1959), *James Joyce*, London: Oxford University Press, p. 545.

12 Gogarty, O. St J. (1968), *As I was Going Down Sackville Street*, London: Sphere Books, p. 294.

13 O'Connor, U. (2000), *Oliver St John Gogarty*, Dublin: The O'Brien Press, p. 60.

14 Yeats, W. B. (ed.) (1936), *The Oxford Book of Modern Verse, 1892–1935*, Oxford: Oxford University Press, p. xv.

15 Igoe, V. (2016), *The Real People of Joyce's Ulysses: A Biographical Guide*, Dublin: University College Dublin Press, pp. 132–3.

16 *The Odyssey of Homer* (1967), New York: Harper and Row, p. 27.

17 Wilson, E. (1961), *Axel's Castle: A Study in the Imaginative Literature of* 1870–1930, London: Fontana, p. 167.

18 Wade, A. (1954), *The Letters of W. B. Yeats*, London: Rupert Hart-Davis, p. 679.

19 Ibid., p. 545.

20 Ellmann, *James Joyce*, p. 62.

21 Goldberg, J. '"Ireland is the only country …": Joyce and the Jewish Dimension', *The Crane Bag*, vol. 6, no. 1, 1982, p. 5.

22 Manganiello, D. (1980), *Joyce's Politics*, London: Routledge and Kegan Paul, pp. 52–6.

23 Epstein, E. L., 'Nestor' in Hart, C. and Hayman, D. (eds) (1974), *James Joyce's Ulysses: Critical Essays*, Berkeley: University of California, pp.17–18.

24 Kiberd, D. (2009), *Ulysses and Us: The Art of Everyday Living*, London: Faber and Faber, p. 56.

25 *Lemprière's Classical Dictionary* (1987), 3rd edn, London: Routledge and Kegan Paul, p. 405.

26   Joyce, S. (1958), *My Brother's Keeper: James Joyce's Early Years*, New York: The Viking Press, p. 41.

27   Joyce, J., Barry, K. (ed.) (2000), *Occasional, Critical, and Political Writing*, Oxford: Oxford World's Classics, pp. 206–8.

28   Bew, J. (2012), *Castlereagh: A Life*, Oxford: Oxford University Press, p. 101.

29   Keogh, D. (1998), *Jews in Twentieth-Century Ireland*, Cork: Cork University Press, pp. 9–10.

30   Ellmann, *James Joyce*, p. 535.

31   Hassett, *The Ulysses Trials,* p. 200.

32   *The Odyssey of Homer*, p. 75.

33   *Lemprière's Classical Dictionary*, 3rd edn, p. 523.

34   Morse, J. M., 'Proteus' in Hart and Hayman, *James Joyce's Ulysses: critical essays*, p. 33.

35   Flynn, C. (2019), *James Joyce and the Matter of Paris*, Cambridge: Cambridge University Press, p. 75.

36   O'Rourke, F., 'Philosophy' in McCourt, J. (ed.) (2019), *James Joyce in Context*, Cambridge: Cambridge University Press, p. 320.

37   Budgen, F. (1960), *James Joyce and the Making of Ulysses*, Bloomington: Indiana University Press pp. 47–8.

38   Read, F. (ed.) (1970), *Pound/Joyce: The Letters of Ezra Pound to James Joyce with Pound's Essays on Joyce,* New York: New Directions, p.199.

39   Ellmann, R. (1974), *Ulysses on the Liffey*, London: Faber and Faber, p. 33.

40   Ellmann, *James Joyce*, p. 457.

41   Budgen, *James Joyce and the Making of Ulysses*, p. 19.

42 There was no such butcher's shop in Dublin in 1904. In this case, Joyce used the name of one of his pupils in Trieste, Moses Dlugacz (1884–1943), who worked for the Cunard Line there and may have taught Joyce some Hebrew. See Igoe, *The Real People of Joyce's Ulysses*, p. 85.

43 Wicht, W., 'Bleibtreustrasse, 34, Berlin W. 15.' (U4.199) 'Once Again', *James Joyce Quarterly*, 40.4 (Summer 2003), pp. 797–811.

44 Kiberd, *Ulysses and Us*, p. 97.

45 Welch, R. A. (2014), *The Cold of May Day Monday: An Approach to Irish Literary History*, Oxford: Oxford University Press, p. 152.

46 Nicholson, R. (2019), T*he Ulysses Guide: Tours Through Joyce's Dublin*, Dublin: New Island Books, p. 59.

47 Ibid., p. 11.

48 Ellmann, *James Joyce*, p. 538.

49 Jackson, J. W. and Costello, P. (1997), *John Stanislaus Joyce: The Voluminous Life and Genius of James Joyce's Father*, London: Fourth Estate, p. xiii.

50 Ibid., p. 378.

51 Tóibín, C. (2018), *Mad, Bad, Dangerous to Know: The Fathers of Wilde, Yeats and Joyce*, London: Viking, p. 135.

52 Abels, J. (1966), *The Parnell Tragedy*, London: The Bodley Head, p. 331.

53 Leerssen, J. (ed.) (2021) *Parnell and his Times*, Cambridge, Cambridge University Press, p. 4.

54 *The Odyssey of Homer*, pp. 152–3.

55 Latham, S. (2014), *The Cambridge Companion to*

Ulysses, Cambridge: Cambridge University Press, p. 65 and p. 113.

56   Igoe, *The Real People of Joyce's Ulysses,* pp. 67–8.

57   For an account of Æ's contribution as an editor and political thinker, see Mulhall, D., 'George Russell, D. P. Moran and Tom Kettle' in Biagini, E. and Mulhall, D. (eds) (2016), *The Shaping of Modern Ireland: A Centenary Assessment*, Dublin: Irish Academic Press, pp. 124–38.

58   Ellman, *James Joyce*, p. 520.

59   Murphy, W. M. (1978), *Prodigal Father: The Life of John Butler Yeats (1839–1922)*, London: Cornell University Press, pp. 520–1.

60   For an account of 'The American Trials of *Ulysses*, 1919–1933', see Hardiman, *Joyce in Court*, pp. 253–82 and Hassett, *The Ulysses Trials*.

61   Igoe, *The Real People of Joyce's Ulysses*, p. 44.

62   Bowker, *James Joyce*, p. 305.

63   Gorman, H. (1948), *James Joyce*, New York: Rinehart & Company, p. 168.

64   O'Neill, M. (1991), *From Parnell to de Valera: A Biography of Jennie Wyse Power, 1858–1941*, Dublin: Blackwater Press, pp. 82–3.

65   Pelaschiar, L. (ed.) (2015), *Joyce/Shakespeare*, New York: Syracuse University Press, contains ten essays analysing the 'overwhelming affair' that is 'Shakespeare's presence in Joyce'.

66   Ellmann, *Ulysses on the Liffey*, p. 81.

67   For example, McCourt, *The Years of Bloom*.

68   McCourt, J., 'Joyce's Shakespeare: a view from Trieste' in *Pelaschiar* (2015), p. 73.

69   *New York Times Book Review* (11 April 2021), p. 14.

70   Budgen, *James Joyce and the Making of Ulysses*, p. 107.

71   Joyce, J., Barry, K. (ed.), 'The Soul of Ireland', *James Joyce: Occasional, Critical, and Political Writing*, pp. 74–6.

72   Boyle, N. (1991) *Goethe: The Poet and the Age, Vol I, The Poetry of Desire*, Oxford: Oxford University Press, p. 404.

73   Budgen, *James Joyce and the Making of Ulysses*, p. 118.

74   Blamires, H. (1988), *The New Bloomsday Book*, London: Routledge, p. 87.

75   Nicholson, *The Ulysses Guide*, pp. 180–1, contains a map that traces the Earl of Dudley's journey from the Phoenix Park to the RDS Grounds in Ballsbridge.

76   O'Brien, C.C. (1998) *Memoir: My Life and Themes*, Dublin: Poolbeg Press, p. 8.

77   I have written about Kettle in 'The Easter Rising, and a tale of two friends torn apart by war', *The Guardian*, 14 March 2016.

78   Akenson, D. (1994), *Conor: A Biography of Conor Cruise O'Brien, Volume 1*, Montreal: McGill-Queen's University Press, pp. 11–15.

79   See Mulhall, D. (1999), *A New Day Dawning: A Portrait of Ireland in 1900*, Cork: The Collins Press, especially pp. 87–121, for an account of the politics of turn-of-the-century Ireland.

80   Birmingham, K. (2014), *The Most Dangerous Book: The Battle of James Joyce's Ulysses*, London: Head of Zeus, pp. 131–2.

81   Ellmann, *James Joyce*, p. 473.

82   Kenner, H. (1987), *Ulysses: Revised Edition*, Baltimore: The Johns Hopkins' University Press, p. 51.

83   Read (ed.), *Pound/Joyce: The Letters of Ezra Pound to James Joyce*, p. 157.

84   Ellmann, R. (ed.) (1975), *Selected Letters of James Joyce*, New York: Viking Press, p. 240.

85   Ellmann, *James Joyce*, p. 475.

86   O'Dowd, N. (2018), *Lincoln and the Irish: The Untold Story of How the Irish Helped Lincoln Save the Union*, New York: Skyhorse Publishing, p. 13.

87   Ellmann (ed.), *Selected Letters of James Joyce*, p. 239.

88   Lyons, F. S. L. (1973), *Ireland since the Famine*, London: Collins/Fontana, p. 227.

89   Usually spelt 'Cúchulainn', the hero of the Irish mythological epic, *Táin Bó Cúailnge*.

90   Igoe, *The Real People of Joyce's Ulysses*, pp. 218–19.

91   Connolly, S. J. (1998), *The Oxford Companion to Irish History*, Oxford: Oxford University Press, p. 373.

92   Manganiello, *Joyce's Politics*, p. 119.

93   Ibid., p. 149.

94   For the European dimension to *Ulysses*, see my essay, 'What would James Joyce have thought of Brexit', *New America*, 25 July 2019, which was written in response to a question to me from a student at Georgetown University. My conclusion was 'James Joyce would not have fancied Brexit, which has its roots in the kind of nationalistic urges that were never to his liking'.

95   Kiberd, *Ulysses and Us*, p. 193.

96   O'Brien, E. (2000), *James Joyce*, London: Phoenix, p. 114.

97   Hassett, *The Ulysses Trials*, p. 177.

98   Blamires, *The New Bloomsday Book*, p. 128.

99   Delaney, F. (1981), *James Joyce's Odyssey: A Guide to the Dublin of Ulysses*, London: Hodder and Stoughton, pp. 135–6.

100 Killeen, T. (2014), *Ulysses Unbound*, Dublin: Wordwell, p. 166.

101 Ellmann (ed.), *Selected Letters of James Joyce*, p. 249.

102 Killeen, *Ulysses Unbound*, pp. 163–6.

103 Igoe, *The Real People of Joyce's Ulysses*, p. 252.

104 Ellmann (ed.), *Selected Letters of James Joyce*, pp. 251–2.

105 Colum, M. and P. (1958), *Our Friend James Joyce*, New York: Doubleday, p. 14.

106 Ellmann, *Ulysses on the Liffey*, p. 140.

107 Kenner, H., 'Circe' in Hart and Hayman, *James Joyce's Ulysses*, p. 351.

108 Kiberd, *Ulysses and Us*, p. 226.

109 From Harold Bloom, *The Bright Book of Life*, quoted in Wendy Smith, 'Harold Bloom's rereading list scintillates but fails to satisfy', *Washington Post*, 27 December 2020, p. E4.

110 Budgen, *James Joyce and the Making of Ulysses*, p. 244

111 Ellmann, *James Joyce*, p. 523.

112 Ibid., p. 511.

113 Hamilton, E. (1940), *Mythology*, New York: Mentor, p. 211.

114 This was the subject of my MA thesis, and of two previous publications of mine. "'The indomitable Irishry': Writers and Politics in Ireland, 1890– 1939", M.A. Thesis: University College Cork, 1978; Mulhall, *A New Day Dawning: A Portrait of Ireland in 1900*; Biagini and Mulhall (eds), *The Shaping of Modern Ireland.*

115 A Portrait of the Artist as a Young Man in Joyce, J. (1963), *The Essential James Joyce*, London: Penguin Books, p. 247.

116 John J. Horgan, *Parnell to Pearse: Some Recollections and Reflections*, Dublin: University College Dublin Press, p. 55.

117 Ellmann (ed.), *Selected Letters of James Joyce*, p. 266.

118 Ellmann, M., 'Endings' in Latham (ed.), *The Cambridge Companion to Ulysses*, p. 96 and p. 99.

119 Killeen, *Ulysses Unbound*, pp. 204–5.

120 See Kavanagh, J. (2021), *The Irish Assassins: Conspiracy, Revenge, and the Phoenix Park Murders that Stunned Victorian England*, New York: Atlantic Monthly Press.

121 Joyce, *Occasional, Critical, and Political Writing*, p. 138.

122 Ibid., p. 195.

123 Ellmann (ed.), *Selected Letters of James Joyce*, p. 279.

124 *Ibid.*, p. 278.

125 Gilbert, S. (1955), *James Joyce's Ulysses: A Study*, New York: Vintage Books/Random House, p. 369.

126 Budgen, *James Joyce and the Making of Ulysses*, p. 258.

127 Ellmann (ed.), *Selected Letters of James Joyce*, p. 286.

128 Blamires, *The New Bloomsday Book,* p. 225.

129 Budgen, *James Joyce and the Making of Ulysses,* pp. 36–7.

130 Fitch, N. R., *Sylvia Beach and the Lost Generation: A History of Literary Paris in the Twenties & Thirties,* New York: W. W. Norton, pp. 62–3.

131 Colum, M. and P., *Our Friend James Joyce,* p. 11.

132 Maddox, B. (1989), *Nora: A Biography of Nora Joyce,* London: Minerva, pp. 4–5.

133 O'Connor, N. (2021), *Nora,* Dublin: New Island Books, Epigraph.

134 Budgen, *James Joyce and the Making of Ulysses,* p. 266.

135 Gilbert, *James Joyce's Ulysses,* p. 385.

136 Killeen, *Ulysses Unbound,* p. 237.

137 Ellmann (ed.), *Selected Letters of James Joyce,* p. 285

138 Ibid., p. 278.

139 Ibid., p. 285. Joyce's German is faulty here. It should read '*Ich bin das Fleisch das stets bejaht*'.

140 Hart, C. & Hayman, D. 'Preface' in Hart and Hayman, *James Joyce's Ulysses,* p. ix.

141 There is open access to the *Dictionary of Irish Biography* at www.dib.ie.

142 James Joyce quoted in Orel, H. 'The Two Attitudes of James Joyce' in Orel, H. (1976), *Irish History and Culture: Aspects of a People's Heritage,* Lawrence: University of Kansas Press, p. 325.

143 Kenner, H. *Ulysses,* p. 1.

144 O'Brien, *James Joyce,* pp. 93–4.

145 Tindall, W. Y. (1959), *A Reader's Guide to James Joyce,* London: Thames and Hudson, p. 123

146 Mulhall, *A New Day Dawning,* pp. 31–4.

147 Colum, M. (1947), *Life and the Dream*, London: Macmillan, p. 381.

148 Goldberg, '"Ireland is the only country ..." p. 5.

149 Donoghue, D. (1986), *We Irish*, Berkeley: University of California Press, p. 93.

150 Nicolson, A. (2014), *The Mighty Dead: Why Homer Matters*, London: William Collins, p. 249.

IMAGE CREDITS

1. Phillips, Philip (1900-1994). 7 Eccles St. Dublin, Ireland, 1950. Gift of Sayre P. Sheldon and Lady Richard Davies. The Rosenbach, Philadelphia (2006.0004.0099)

2. Phillips, Philip (1900-1994). Martello Tower, Sandycove, 1950. Gift of Sayre P. Sheldon and Lady Richard Davies. The Rosenbach, Philadelphia (2006.0004.0143)

3. Joyce, James (1882-1941) *Ulysses:* autograph manuscript, title page. Zurich, [September-October 1917]. The Rosenbach, Philadelphia (EL4 .J89ul 922 MS)

4. Joyce, James (1882-1941) *Ulysses:* autograph manuscript, Telemachus episode, page 1. Zurich, [September-October 1917]. The Rosenbach, Philadelphia (EL4 .J89ul 922 MS)

5. Joyce, James (1882-1941) *Ulysses:* autograph manuscript, Cyclops episode, page 45. Zurich,

[August-September 1919]. The Rosenbach, Philadelphia (EL4 .J89ul 922 MS)

6. Ray, Man, photographer. [James Joyce]. Inscribed by Joyce to Maurice Darantière, 11 April 1922. The Rosenbach, Philadelphia (EMs 1293/8)

7. Portrait of George Russell (1867-1935) by Fisher, Alfred Hugh, 1867-1945. Image Courtesy of the National Library of Ireland.

8. Men and women walking by tram stop at Trinity College, Dublin. Clarke Photographic Collection, Courtesy of the National Library of Ireland.

9. Portrait of Charles Stewart Parnell, Clonbrock Photographic Collection, Courtesy of the National Library of Ireland.

10. Formal portrait of Nora Joyce, standing, wearing white dress and gloves, Zurich, no date. Photographer unknown. The Poetry Collection of the University Libraries, University at Buffalo, The State University of New York.

11. James Joyce and Sylvia Beach outside Shakespeare and Company, 1921. Photographer unknown. The Poetry Collection of the University Libraries, University at Buffalo, The State University of New York.